DEADLY DRIVER

A THRILLER BY

J.K. KELLY

This book is a work of fiction. Any references to historical events, real people, or real places are used fictitiously. Other names, characters, places, and events are products of the author's imagination, and any resemblance to actual events or places or persons living or dead is entirely coincidental.

Library of Congress Control Number: 2021902581

Philadelphia, PA USA

ISBN: 978-0-9994099-8-5 paperback

ISBN: 978-0-9994099-9-2 eBook

This novel is dedicated to my father
for encouraging me to continue writing
even long after he was gone

and

To Dani

CHAPTER ONE

THE SOUND FROM the car's racing engine screamed past the start finish line and the excited public address announcer, first in Russian then in English, let the packed crowd know they'd just witnessed history. "And there it is, Bryce Winters demolishes another track record to claim his fifth pole of the season!" Hours later, in a much different environment, Winters would shatter something else.

"Perhaps one of his victims has exacted revenge?" the raspy-voiced detective said as he exhaled cigarette smoke into the face of a hotel security agent. Having just recently been acquitted on a technicality of dozens of drug trafficking and weapons charges the now deceased Russian multi-millionaire had been celebrating his release in high style. In the blink of an eye it had been lights out for the bastard.

"It would seem there was an explosive device of some sort in the man's team cap," the medical examiner commented as his team placed the body on a stretcher. The autopsy would be a formality to confirm the cause of death. "Anyone know what he was doing wearing a cap at a formal gathering like this?"

"It's the race crowd. Team hats were everywhere," someone offered. "So the victim's hat detonated, while he sat in the bathroom, blowing his lid off?" the detective had asked through a smoker's cough, making sure he understood exactly what had happened.

"Boom," the Medical Examiner said, gesturing with both hands to demonstrate an explosion.

Sochi may have hosted the Winter Olympics back in 2014, but the cold-weather athletes and the massive trademark flame were now long gone. The sound of record-setting runs on the ski slopes overlooking the city on the Black Sea had been replaced by something just as sleek but noticeably faster and with a much more intriguing sound. The global traveling circus that is Formula One racing had returned to Sochi. The cocktail party held for the drivers and wealthy VIPs was in full swing on the hotel's veranda, overlooking a massive swimming pool, surrounded by palm trees and overlooking the sea. While the technological advancements over the years had made this type of racing safer, death was always a possibility on the track. Almost no one had expected it here, in the midst of a party.

CHAPTER TWO

FORMULA ONE DRIVER Bryce Winters, a world champion, was one of the star attractions at the gathering and he'd taken the elevator down from his suite on the top floor of the Radisson Blu hotel just past eight o'clock. With his confidence and enthusiasm at full throttle he made the rounds of the party, shaking hands, posing for photos, hugging, kissing, joking. The intensity of the day, pushing the edge during the three qualifying sessions and being "on" for the countless interviews he'd given had exhausted him but he could turn the charm back on and work a room like no other. He pretended to throw a punch at boxing's heavyweight champion from Britain who had come to meet the American racer. A beautiful Russian fashion model, her flowing blonde locks coming to rest on the shoulders of a blood red dress was craving his attention and tried her best to lure him in with her piercing blue eyes.

By nine o'clock Bryce was hoping for a good night's sleep to prepare for tomorrow's race. There'd be two hours of exhilarating acceleration, punishing G-forces of the high-speed left and right hand turns, eighteen in all again and again for 53 laps, racing with rivals at over 200 miles per hour. But first, of all things, he needed to attend to something in the men's room. He'd spotted his prey and the stalk had begun. Minutes later, his business behind him, he came upon two familiar faces. Jack Madigan, an engineer on the race team, was leaning against a wall, beer in hand, talking with an attractive blonde Bryce would normally have been drawn to, an American, Joan Myers. Bryce acknowledged his friend with a smile but frowned at Myers and walked past them without saying a word. It was late and he was done.

In the elevator headed back up to his suite, he thought of his home far away in his country's Mountain West. He longed for it. Park City, Utah has something for just about everyone who enjoys the outdoors, particularly if you are a patriotic American. The area Bryce chose to live in was spectacular and full of mountains, moose, elk and mule deer. It was the home of the Sundance Film Festival and was a ski-lovers playground for the rich and famous. A good number of retired Navy SEALS and Army Rangers called the Park City area home, and it was also the site of the Olympic Winter Games in 2002, where many other Americans had earned medals of their own. Athletes intending to represent their countries in ski and snowboarding competitions continued to train at the Olympic Park. When he was in town, Bryce often went there to offer encouragement and, more times than he could remember, to offer financial help where needed. The area was flush with patriots and proud Americans of all sorts. Representing his country, as the lone American competing in the global arena that was Formula One, he felt proud and swore to always do his best. He wished someday that the walls of his trophy room there might bear an award from the government for his clandestine service, but he knew that would never come to pass. CIA operations were top-secret and known to only a handful of people: his handler Myers, his accomplice Madigan, and just a few more back in Langley, Virginia.

The next morning, after a short ride in a van with the team publicist and Bryce's personal aide to the paddock area of the race circuit, he took time to pose for photos with the early birds, the race fans that showed up at sunrise to get the best spot on the fence line to see their heroes up close. He spent a few extra minutes with a young Russian family that had dressed their three children up like little racers in Bryce's team colors. They didn't speak English but their gestures and smiles between them were universal and easily understood. When the woman pointed with concern to Bryce's battered knuckles as he signed an event program for them he smiled as if they were okay.

"Punched a hotel wall in frustration last night," he uttered knowing she wouldn't understand. He spent the morning joking with the dozen or so team members doing a last-minute inspection of his Mercedes-powered canary yellow and fire engine red Formula One car. News of the murder spread through the paddock at the track almost as fast as the cars racing in a preliminary event leading up to the F1 race. Bryce shook his head in amazement, stunned to hear that such a thing could have happened. When he encountered Jack Madigan, they simply fist-bumped, smiled, and went about their racing business.

The two had first connected back in North Carolina when Bryce was racing NASCAR stock cars. They had hit it off from the start, almost as if they were long lost brothers. Just like Bryce, Jack's heart was in racing and he worked weekends as part of an "over the wall gang" - the pit crew. The two had been on a winning team that seemed destined to claim the NASCAR championship. That was, until a 210-mph crash at Talladega in Alabama broke Bryce's left leg and ended his run for that title. Frustrated, the team owner lost interest in the North American market and decided it was time to perform in the ultimate arena where over 400 million passionate fans around the world watched every race on TV – Formula One. Bryce was game and encouraged Madigan to come along.

After doing interviews with various media, Bryce posed for photos with at least ten gorgeous Russian women and another dozen of the country's wealthiest men – their clients, dates or husbands. He finally retreated to his private quarters on the second level of one of the team's two hospitality trailers in Sochi. For races in Europe, the team had built a state-of-the-art soundproof VIP suite complete with bathroom, shower, bed, flat screen TV, surround-sound system, a fully stocked kitchenette with small dining table, two black leather captain's chairs, a desk and matching loveseat. While everything outside of the suite was covered in the vibrant red and yellow of their team owner and sponsors' brands, the wall panels and décor of this interior space were much more subdued in subtle yellow and contrasting black lines. Bryce poured his fifth coffee of the morning, turned down the volume on the television and thought about one of the Russian beauties he'd just met. *Must be something in the water here.* But soon a hard knock at the door interrupted his fantasy.

Two homicide detectives from the Sochi police department stood with one of F1's plainclothes security force. They had questions and wanted answers *now*, not later.

"Mr. Winters," one of the men said as he held a silver badge up for Bryce to inspect. "There was a homicide at your hotel last night. May we come in?" It took Bryce a second to smile and welcome them inside. At a nod from Bryce, the escort moved off. Bryce held the door open and asked if either of the two wanted coffee or water. This was happening in Russia, a place where opponents of the country's president were known to be poisoned or disappear without a trace. If a homicide detective wanted to talk, it was smarter to agree than make an international incident out of it.

Bryce sat back down and gestured to the black leather chairs facing his spot on the loveseat. He was repulsed by the cigarette smoke on their clothing but chose not to comment. The expression on his face let his guests know he wasn't pleased.

The first detective sat while the second man closed the door behind him then stood guard, leaning against the door jam without saying a word. The lead detective introduced himself as he accepted a bottled water Bryce handed over.

"Nikolai Volkoff," the detective said as he adjusted his suit coat and placed his phone on his knee and hit the record button.

"Bryce Winters," the American responded. "What can I do for you?"

Bryce listened as Volkoff described what had occurred in a men's toilet just off the large banquet hall of the host hotel.

"We have closed circuit video recordings of the deceased, Gregori Ivanova, entering the toilet. Forty-three seconds later you followed him into the room.

"Really? I wouldn't say I followed him. I didn't know the man." Bryce watched as Volkoff broke eye contact with him and looked to the man guarding the door. The man unzipped a leather attaché he'd been carrying and removed an iPad, handing it to Volkoff before returning to his spot at the door.

Volkoff stood up and sat down close to Bryce. "Please watch this video." As the black-and-white recording, taken by a camera outside the men's room in the hallway, began—the victim was seen entering the men's toilet.

"Notice the hat he is wearing. It is the same color as your race team's sponsor, and that company name appears above the bill."

Bryce nodded. "German company. They have holdings here in your country, I believe. They make everything from wine and weapons to military drones and jet airplanes."

The video continued, nothing of note happening until Bryce came into view. Without any cameras inside the room itself, there was nothing more to watch other than one man leaving the room, then a second man. Thirty-one seconds after that – nearly three minutes after he had entered the room—Bryce was seen leaving it. Twenty-six seconds later, an attendant was seen entering the room and shortly thereafter, the same man rushed into the hallway outside the men's toilet waving frantically for help.

"So how can I help you?" Bryce asked as he sat back into the plush sofa.

"You told us when we arrived that you did not know the victim," Volkoff said as he leaned in toward Bryce.

"So far so good," Bryce responded.

"How do you explain this then?" Volkoff asked. He placed the iPad in front of Bryce again. There on the screen were two images; on the left, a black-and-white image of the hat the victim had worn entering the toilet. To the right of it was an image of a yellow and red ball cap, the top of it torn away, but the bill showing something that wasn't there when the man had entered the room. It was Bryce's autograph.

"Explain," Volkoff demanded.

Bryce smiled."Sure." He got up, grabbed a bottle of orange Powerade Zero from the cabinet, retook his spot, and told them his story. He said he had noticed the big fella with the ball cap at the opposite end of the urinals. He'd found it strange that someone at such a high-class event was wearing the hat but thought the guy might be a guest of the sponsor.

Bryce recounted that the man had been speaking in Russian to someone on his phone. There had been two other men there as Bryce remembered it. One was washing his hands and the other was coming out of one of the stalls.

"Sounded like a cocaine blast if you ask me, but who knows. Maybe he just had a runny nose." Bryce opened the sports drink and chugged half of it down.

"When the big guy saw me standing there, he ended his call, zipped up, and came charging towards me like he was going to give me a damn bear hug. And I was still pissing!"

The man at the door began to laugh, but Volkoff's glare stopped him.

"So, I put my right hand out and asked him to wait. I finished and washed my hands while this guy's pulling his phone back out of his pocket and asking for a selfie, right there in the damn john." Bryce explained that he posed for the photo and told the stranger that since he was wearing his sponsor's hat he'd autograph it, if he wanted. And he did. Then the man grabbed Bryce's hand and shook it. "But as he did, his expression changed. The guy thanked me, wished me good luck in the race, and then ran into a stall. Strange move. I don't usually have that effect on people."

"Yes. Strange." The detective frowned.

"Maybe he had to poo. Anyway, I washed my hands, *again*, and then left the men's room." Bryce watched Volkoff take it all in.

"Did you overhear any of the conversation he had on his phone?" the detective asked. Bryce shook his head no. "Did you see him talk to anyone else in the room, or did anyone else approach him while you were there?"

"No sorry."

"Did you hear if the victim locked the stall door?" the detective asked.

"Nope, I didn't. I just left the room, reunited with some friends, and then headed up to my suite and called for room service."

Volkoff shook his head as if he didn't understand. "Room service with all the food and drink at the party?"

"*Da*," Bryce said. "Yesterday morning at a press breakfast, I watched the locals eat cucumbers and sardines and boiled potatoes for breakfast. Then I saw black fish, caviar, all sorts of pickled who knows what, at the buffet last night. No thanks. I love the fans and love racing here, but I went upstairs and ordered a cheeseburger and fries and that hit the spot."

Volkoff looked to his partner and smiled. "I prefer American food, too," he said. "Just don't tell anyone I said so." He laughed.

Bryce looked at the digital clock on the wall and then apologized but told the detectives that he desperately needed to relax before the race. "Unless there's anything else, I'd appreciate it if you would leave me to it."

"Of course," Volkoff said, but then looked up sheepishly at Bryce. "A selfie - if you don't mind?"

Over the next few minutes Bryce obliged their request. He posed for their photos and then pulled two ball caps out of a cabinet, took a Sharpie from his pocket, and signed both bills. His autographs were always big, bold, and easy to read.

"You carry those with you all the time?" Volkoff asked, gesturing to the Sharpie seemingly amused.

"Always. You can't imagine what some people ask me to sign. Boobs, babies, whatever."

Volkoff stared at Bryce and tilted his head. "Boobs?" he asked.

Bryce smiled and held his arms out, his palms cupped toward his own chest. Volkoff laughed then turned to leave. He stopped shy of the door and spent a moment looking at the three photos mounted on the wall.

"I have always wondered what driving a race car would be like," Volkoff said as he maintained his focus on the pictures.

"It's amazing. You know amusement rides like roller coasters and such yes?" he asked. Volkoff turned and nodded.

"Well imagine you're on the fastest roller coaster ride ever but *you* get to control the speed. You can go as fast as you want but too fast and you'll fly off the tracks. Not fast enough and the car behind you might knock you out of the way. You throw the ride to the left and to the right, your head feels like it weighs ninety pounds because of the G-forces, and then you fly down a straightaway and at the very last second you hit the brakes to slow the car. Hit them too late or too hard and you're off the track. Then you accelerate again, faster than ever, again and again and again. And remember, it's hot – very hot – and you're stuffed into a very snug helmet and fire resistant suit, gloves, and shoes." Volkoff smiled.

"And if *you* come up on a car that is going too slow?"

"Well you can out brake them into a turn, pass on a straightaway if your car is fast enough, or back in the states when I raced NASCAR you just gave them a little push to bump them out of the way. But you're doing all this at maybe three to four times faster speed than people drive on the highways. It's a thrill ride like no other. Remember too that this goes on for ninety minutes except for the pit stops and they happen in the blink of an eye – perhaps two and a half seconds."

"You operate in an exciting but dangerous world Mr. Winters. Thank you for your cooperation and best wishes for a safe race."

"It would seem that I do detective. Spasibo – thank you," Bryce offered as he walked back to the sofa but turned to ask one last question. "I forgot to ask." He looked from one detective to the other. "Do bad guys get bumped off this way here a lot? Blowing the top of a guy's head off seems a bit grand."

Volkoff nodded and stepped back into the room. The smell of cigarettes and big, yellowed teeth coming too close for comfort. Bryce took a step back and covered for himself by reaching for his energy drink.

"How did you know the extent of the victim's injury?" he asked as he focused on Bryce's eyes.

"Heard it on the news this morning and a lot of people were talking about it in the garage when I got here." He watched as Volkoff stared at the hat he'd just been given. The detective turned it upside down and inspected the inside of it then looked back at Bryce, perhaps looking for a reaction it seemed but Bryce gave none.

"The deceased was the leader of many warring factions here in Russia – the mob, you would call them. There is more money in Moscow than there is in your Beverly Hills. Whoever did this was making a declaration of sorts, we believe. I expect much more blood will flow in the coming weeks."

Bryce watched and let out a sigh of relief as the detectives finally let themselves out. He sat back down, closed his eyes and replayed what had actually happened the night before.

While Ivanova was focused on texting the selfies he had just taken with the race driver Bryce signed the man's hat and then attached a round, flat disc – the size of an American nickel – to the inside of the hat and handed it back to him. As Bryce left the toilet he remembered seeing Madigan and Myers standing twenty feet from him, engrossed in conversation, waiting for him. As he passed them, Bryce squeezed a second Sharpie in his pants pocket—a detonator. The mini-explosive device he'd planted moments earlier brought to an abrupt halt the life of a real piece of shit - a man who had been targeted by the CIA for assassination.

Madigan was the only outsider who knew of Bryce's clandestine behavior and often helped facilitate it. He was a computer consultant for the race team but also excelled at designing things like mini-bombs for baseball caps, eavesdropping equipment, and hacking computers. The CIA had wanted something dramatic to stir up trouble in the Russian underworld and it was Madigan's design that helped pull it off. He'd also been an Army Ranger who spent a short time after he left the service working as a contractor of another sort, something he rarely talked about. If they had helped to start a civil war among very dangerous people there, as long as it could benefit or protect their own country's interests, that was something Madigan and Bryce could live with.

As Bryce lay on the sofa, trying to clear his mind and prepare for the race to come he began to dose off but he'd run out of time. Another knock at the door and it was time to go race. Hours later, after a disappointing second-place finish at Sochi, he and two other drivers would fly to Abu Dhabi on a private jet furnished by the sponsor of the season finale to be held there.

With the race six weeks out, local media and VIPs clamored for time with the driving stars. The drivers would be paid handsomely for their time helping to promote the race and their sponsors – as long as the jet ride and accommodations were free of charge. He could count on one hand the number of times he'd be doing appearances like this. With the finish line in sight, he was happy to oblige. The racing life had given him more than he could ever have dreamed. Bryce had plans on winning this championship and retiring after he took the crown. But he kept that a secret. The CIA had planned to use him as long as he raced around the globe and securing the title and hanging up his helmet would get the CIA off his back for good.

After two days of non-stop interviews, photo ops, dinners, and turns behind the wheel of the track's pace cars, giving white-knuckled celebrity and VIP guests the fastest rides of their lives, Bryce and the other race drivers went their separate ways. They'd all meet again soon. He boarded an A380 full-length double decker jumbo jet for the long flight east over India to Thailand, a quick stopover in Bangkok, and the final leg to Japan. Somewhere over China, as he enjoyed the luxurious comforts of his private, First Class mini-cabin, Bryce thought back to what seemed a lifetime ago, when he lived in an RV, was starting to win races, and had his first encounter with a monster.

CHAPTER THREE

Lebanon Valley is a nationally known motorsports facility located southeast of Albany in New York. There's a quarter-mile drag strip at one end of the property and a dirt oval track at the other. Bryce had cut his teeth on ACT stocks and NASCAR's open-wheel modified cars racing on asphalt ovals in New England. From time to time he tried to secure a dirt-car ride. Racers want to race. Pursuing their passion on different tracks, types of race cars, and competitors can afford a novice driver with big ambitions the opportunity to learn a lot and make a name for themselves.

There were a handful of drivers like international legend Mario Andretti, and from more recent times retired NASCAR champions Tony Stewart and Jeff Gordon, who seemed to find victory lanes in America no matter what they drove or the type of surface they raced on. Having the right horse under you always helped most drivers. But a few drivers brought something special to the table that allowed or propelled their success.

Bryce's reputation and career trajectory had started on

a pace that could have put his name in the history books right alongside Andretti's. That fateful night at the Valley, after making his way to the front to take the lead, the engine in Bryce's ride failed and ended his night prematurely. Frustrated, he abruptly parked the car behind the team's hauler in the dusty infield pits.

With lap after lap of action continuing on the track, Bryce must have been the only person not glued to it. Instead, he headed for a personal pit stop, distracted and furious at being forced to drop out. He entered what at first had appeared to be a vacant men's room, the sound of the thirty race cars still flying around the track making it impossible to hear anything else. It took a moment before he realized that something strange was going on and it was very, very wrong.

There, in a stall, he saw the back of a big man, perhaps 6'3 and 250 pounds, in a dirty white t-shirt, denim coveralls, and work boots. He seemed to be struggling with someone. Then Bryce realized the animal was trying to force himself on a woman. All Bryce could see of her were her long legs, flips flops hanging off her feet as she screamed and tried to fight the man off. He jumped into action.

Bryce grabbed at the man's coveralls and tried to pull him off the girl. Enraged at the interruption, the attacker turned and smashed Bryce hard across the side of his head with his elbow knocking him to the ground. Dazed, trying to clear his head, Bryce saw the man return his focus to the victim as she tried to slip past him and run from the stall.

The noise of the cars continued to drown out the woman's cries for help. Bryce staggered to his feet and tried to get in between the monster and his prey. He felt the man's breath on him as he saw the look on the girls' face. She was petrified, fighting for her life. The man grabbed Bryce by the throat, squeezed it hard, and threw him back out of the stall.

Suddenly, Bryce felt a hand pushing his shoulder.

"Wake up, Mr. Winters. Mr. Winters, wake up." Confused and still half asleep, he sat up straight, pulled the warm gold-colored blanket off, and stared up at the flight attendant.

"Are we landing?" he asked as he turned to the window and opened the shade. It was still dark, and there were no city lights below.

"No, Mr. Winters, we won't land in Tokyo for another three hours. I heard you from the galley. It sounded like you were having a bad dream so I came in to check on you. I hope you are not angry with me," she said tentatively.

First Class cabins on airlines like Singapore, Emirates, and a few others are state of the art. Some highfliers will pay over $20,000 for a spot up with the elite. Bryce had never considered himself as one of them though, the elite. He was just a guy from back in New England who was good, really good, at driving race cars. He preferred blue jeans and beer instead of champagne – unless it was being served in victory lane. He'd never lost the sense of where he came from or who he was. But if one of the fruits of his labor was an abundance of legroom and better pillows and blankets he was in. Often the accommodations include a leather captains' chair with a small desk and flat-screen TV, full-length bed with plush pillows and silk sheets, all housed in a private cubicle with walls from floor to near ceiling and a sliding door. VIPs were assured privacy so they can sit, sleep, and dine, without anyone taking a photo or gawking at them when their guard is down. On many of these airlines a walk-in shower is available and, in some cases, a full walk-up bar for socializing. For Bryce, if he were going to spend as many as eighteen hours in the air, *this* was the only way to go.

His head clearing and with a coffee and some sweets ordered, Bryce moved from the bed to the captain's chair, brought the blanket along to cover his legs, and got to work on the iPad that displayed a variety of menu options, operated the lights, temperature, and entertainment system in his private cabin. Once his drink arrived and the attendant slid the door closed behind her, he sat back and peered out the window and up at the stars. He didn't need to fall back into a nightmare to go back to that dirt track though; he could see it unfold in his mind as vividly as the night it happened.

He remembered getting up from the floor and, desperate to find a way to stop the man, stepping into the next stall. He grabbed the white porcelain lid off the toilet tank, and then clobbered the big guy, hitting him in the back of the head with the lid as hard as he could. The man dropped first to his knees and then doubled back over them toward Bryce, his fractured skull staring up at Bryce, blood seeping from the man's ears, nose, and mouth.

Bryce reached in and pulled the hysterical woman toward him and out of the stall. But once clear of the bleeding lump on the floor, she let go of his hand and ran. He watched her bolt out the door. Adrenaline continued to surge through him. But now that he'd won that fight he needed to calm himself and think.

He remembered his uncle's words the first time they'd gone hunting together. Bryce, then just fourteen, had lined up a big healthy buck in his rifle sights. That animal would feed the Winters households for weeks if he just made this first kill. He was so excited the rifle was shaking in his hands, just a little, but enough to make the shot miss at that range.

"Breathe," he could hear Pete whisper. "Breathe." Just as he had on that mountain, Bryce took a deep breath and then another. He could feel his mind calm and refocus, his heart slowing, with each relaxing breath. It was the same exercise he'd done dozens of times in the race car when he was flustered - just breathe.

At any moment either a security guard or race fans could charge through the restroom door. The girl might even have called the police. *THINK!* He placed the porcelain lid back in its place, grabbed a handful of toilet paper and wiped his fingerprints from it. He needed to get out of there. If he encountered anyone as he left the room, he could say he was running after the girl to see if she was okay. He took another deep breath, and then another, and walked slowly out of the john. When no one approached him, he snaked his way between car haulers in and out of the track's infield lighting. He stopped and casually ordered a plate of Lebanon Valley's famous baked beans and sausage and a hot dog. Eating as he walked, he eventually reached his crew.

Inside the hauler's lounge, he trashed the empty paper plate and then took his time changing out of his fire resistant driving suit and into his black golf shirt, blue jeans, and hiking boots. He was surprised that he hadn't been discovered but was even more surprised that he felt as calm as he actually was. He'd just killed a man. He wasn't proud he'd killed the guy—not at all. He felt gratified at having saved the woman from being raped, at the very least. But, he was scared. If he got caught and couldn't beat the rap, his racing career would be over. And *that* was not going to happen. It was all he had, and he was good at it - really good. By the time the noise and dirt blown up by the race cars died down outside the hauler, he had made a decision. He headed across the highway to the parking area where the track allowed RV's to pre-game and bed down after the event.

The next morning, Bryce woke early. He flipped on the generator, turned on the heat, and started a pot of coffee before jumping back into his sleeping bag until things warmed up. He watched reports on TV of the attempted rape and murder at the track on the local news as he stared at the coffeemaker, wondering if there was some way of making it brew even faster. He needed coffee, bad. The newscaster reported that while State Police would be investigating, the victim was in a state of shock and unable to provide much information. She didn't remember any of what had happened. The attacker, long known to law enforcement for his violent criminal record as long as he was tall, wasn't a threat to anyone anymore. Bryce got the sense there wouldn't be much enthusiasm wasted on the investigation and crossed his fingers as he stepped outside. Fall was coming and there was crispness to the cool morning air.

The truck camper he spent the night in, actually most race nights in, was mounted on the bed of his white Dodge dually pickup and both were covered with a fine brown dust that had carried across from the track. The truck was relatively new, he'd bought it used, but the camper—his father's—had seen much better days. It had saved him a fortune as he traveled the racing road, and he just couldn't let it go. There were too many memories - some good and some not.

Bryce smiled as the captain announced they'd be landing shortly in Tokyo. As the lights in the cabin went to full bright, he requested another coffee on the iPad and got ready for the land of the rising sun. As soon as they landed and were taxiing toward the gate at Narita International, he turned on his cell and saw a simple text from Madigan. 008

It was a joke between them but it meant only one thing. The CIA had given them another assignment.

CHAPTER FOUR

Working in a sub-basement 4 x 4' cubicle at CIA Headquarters in Virginia was the polar opposite of the high-life Formula One driving champion Bryce Winters was living. But when an introverted analyst named Jon discovered something he felt like he'd just scored a victory of his own. The CIA had noticed the bodies pile up overseas, but it wasn't until Jon noticed what they had in common – they were all tied to auto racing events. As soon as "The Company" knew where to focus they eventually zeroed in on Bryce and his shadow – Madigan.

Late one night on a yacht Bryce had rented as a party boat for friends and sponsors at the Yas Marina Circuit in Abu Dhabi, two non descript young men wearing white golf shirts and tan khakis and an attractive blonde woman in her mid-30's and a red blouse with tight white capris discreetly presented their credentials and followed him to a suite below deck and read him the riot act. They showed Bryce what they had on him, CCTV of him and Jack dumping a body here, a body there. They explained that they intended to prosecute, or perhaps share the info with other interested parties. Bryce and his partner in crime begrudgingly accepted their deal. The woman, Joan Myers, would become his handler.

He had been immediately drawn to her and she, the professional that she was, read him like a book. If Bryce did have an Achilles, she could be one. He insisted on her codename though. She'd be Nitro because she was a knockout. Nitro being short for Nitromethane, a chemical used as a fuel primarily in drag racing because it packs a very powerful punch. So much so that in 1995 domestic terrorists used the material to destroy the federal building in Oklahoma City. He thought the name was very fitting. Myers *was* dangerous and like the potent chemical, both had a sweet scent.

CHAPTER FIVE

THE SUZUKA CIRCUIT in Japan is located almost directly between Tokyo and Hiroshima to the south. Bryce had been to Japan many times and had already visited the site of the first Atomic Bomb attack. He'd stood by the mound where the cremated remains of tens of thousands of Japanese men, women, and children were interred. He'd seen the watch on display in the museum, its arms frozen in time at 8:15 when the blast had occurred. He'd been to the spot where the silhouette of a person was burned into concrete by the brightness of the nuclear explosion.

He'd never served in the military but wore another type of uniform, a fire-resistant one, also displaying a forward facing American flag on its right shoulder sleeve. He had killed for his country, for the CIA, but not like this. The scale of this attack, which left 80,000 dead, still amazed him. Technology had stopped the madness of World War II in the pacific, but soon it would be time to focus on technology of another kind – all that made a Formula One race car become a guided missile on wheels.

His jet lag was long gone and Bryce had elected to

take a walking tour of downtown Tokyo before boarding one of the island country's 190 mph bullet trains and heading to Suzuka. He took the steps to the top of the orange tower, Tokyo Tower. It resembles the Eiffel in Paris in design but is actually much taller. Bryce's brisk, long walk and the steps up the 333-meter structure satisfied his cardio requirements for the day, but the high he was feeling was disrupted by a call from Madigan.

"I got your 008 so what's up?"

"Oh that? I was just screwing with you. Welcome you to Japan."

"Prick. Now I owe you one," he said with a laugh. "See you at the hotel tonight and you're buying." Once the call ended, Bryce went back to enjoying the view only to be interrupted again. A young couple, from France he assumed from their accents, asked if he would take a photo of them. Afterward they made small talk but got into a bit of a tiff over who was right.

"Eiffel taller," the proud Frenchman insisted.

"This one taller, by 13 meters my friend," he responded. To Bryce's surprise the Frenchmen grew indignant, insisting he was right.

"You Americans think you know everything," he said. And then Bryce made matters worse, intentionally.

Bryce suggested the man take his photo and then smiled, his anonymity maintained by blue-mirror sunglasses and a faded blue Olympic Park ball cap from Park City, the middle finger of his right hand presenting a salute to the now indignant tourist. The petite woman pushed her much larger mate away, insisting he stop this now. Bryce laughed openly.

Even when they are cursing their language sounds sexy, he thought.

Checking his watch, he found it was time for him to go, too. Back down the 1100' to ground level and then a quick ride to the five-star Aman Hotel to retrieve his bags and head off to Suzuka. When he finished packing, he stared out the window of his suite at Mount Fuji, the snow-covered mountain that rose to 12,000' over the city. He had always been fascinated by the many cultures he got to experience, and usually appreciate, while traveling around the world and Japan was one he particularly enjoyed, for the people and their history. He loved the Tom Cruise film, *The Last Samurai,* and had always been attracted to the exquisite look of the women of that country. Their silky, black hair and almond shaped eyes always got his attention wherever he was. They were much different than the blonde-haired, blue-eyed Vermont beauty he'd lost years before, the only woman he'd ever loved and thought he ever would. *Who knows,* he'd often thought in the quiet moments when loneliness would creep in. *Maybe someday I could fall for someone who wouldn't, who couldn't, remind me of her.*

The short ride to the train station, and a one-hour trip on the bullet train took him 185 miles south to what would be his home on the road for the next few days. The train tracks were banked through the bends and curves so the cars would not fly off the tracks when traveling at such high speeds. He smiled as he thought of the banking at Daytona and so many other race tracks back in the States. *This is cool,* he'd always thought. If it hadn't been for a man named Werner, Bryce knew he probably would never have seen Tokyo or the rest of the world for that matter. On the ride, he thought fondly of his friend – his backer - and how they first met.

He remembered how chilly it had been in his RV that morning back in Upstate New York. All the other drivers and crewmembers had left the track late the night before, immediately after the race concluded, and headed for home. Without any plans or races to pursue until the next weekend he decided to take the short ride down to Albany and park his rig at the Amtrak train station. Parking in New York City cost a fortune and parking an RV there near impossible. It was cheaper for Bryce to buy a round-trip ticket and ride the train down to Penn Station to take in the town. Knowing the entertainment buffet the city had to offer, he stuffed his backpack with what he'd need just in case he decided to stay the night. *So much for saving money*, he thought with a smile. Little did he know how much this journey would change everything.

The Big Apple, the City that Never Sleeps, has more than something for everybody, offering sensory overload to anyone unaccustomed to big city life.

As Bryce rode the escalator from the train station up to ground level, he walked half a block, south toward Ground Zero, and turned to look back at the massive structure that sat above Penn Station - Madison Square Garden. He thought back to a time so many years before that for his birthday his uncle Pete brought him there to attend a hockey game between the New York Rangers and his team, the group once nicknamed the Broad

Street Bullies – the Philadelphia Flyers. Bryce smiled as he remembered the great time he'd had. The Flyers had won. But then he remembered the disappointment that his father hadn't been able to walk onto the train back in Burlington. Small spaces, other than his precious truck camper, would send the man into a tailspin. He and his uncle had continued on, determined not to miss out on the special day.

Bryce shook off the recollection, looked up at the fall sky and took a breath of the city air – warm now at mid-day but full of the concoction of aromas that make any big city have that *special* scent. Checking his watch, Bryce set a goal. He intended to walk straight down to Ground Zero, pay his respects there, and then continue through Wall Street and take the ferry over to the Statue of Liberty. At a brisk pace, he figured he could make it there- at least to the wharf – in 90 minutes. Normally he'd have preferred to spend his time hiking somewhere in New England or Eastern Canada, but although the terrain on 7th Avenue and then Broadway was flat as a nickel there would be something to see on every block, on every street corner. And that made it a fair exchange.

After a somber visit to Ground Zero where he ran his hands across the names of so many of the lost on 9/11, he paused to look straight up into the sky at the top of Freedom Tower, the 1776' tall structure that was part of the city's and the country's rebuild after the terrorist attacks. Bryce smiled. He looked at the massive thrust into the sky as a middle finger to anyone who wished to screw with America. From there he headed toward Wall Street but then changed his mind. As he took his first step in that direction, he thought of the financial crisis the bastards there had caused and his emotions turned to anger. He thought of the night before, the big guy trying to harm the much smaller woman.

Not one of those Wall Street traders, CEO's and power players of the financial district lost their fortunes or went to jail. *Bastards.* Shaking the dark thoughts from his mind he suddenly realized that he hadn't eaten. He grabbed a hot dog and water from a street vendor working out of a tiny silver trailer parked on the sidewalk, then headed for the ferry to Lady Liberty.

The boat ride was short and the views spectacular, but the crowds were a bit much. He grew frustrated with the tourists who stopped dead wherever they decided and took selfies, endless selfies. He circled the statue but on hearing of the two- hour wait for access to the stairs he really wanted to climb – apparently someone who should have known better was in need of medical attention somewhere up there and had shut things down. That was it.

She's not going anywhere – I'll come back, he thought. He watched the monument grow smaller and smaller as the ferry took him back to the base of the thin, vertical strip of land known as Manhattan. It was growing dark and a chill had wandered in through the streets that ran between the endless tall buildings and skyscrapers. He opted for a cab with the intention of heading back to Penn Station and then the train ride back to his truck parked in Albany.

Just as the taxi approached his destination on 34th Street he got an idea. "Change of plans, buddy," he said, "take me to the theater district."

Bryce knew there would be restaurants on 44th Street, all of which were accustomed to turning tables so diners could get to the theater in time for curtain call. A lesson learned as part of yet another birthday trip his uncle had taken him on. He hopped out of the cab and looked up and down the street. He was standing right in front of Sardis and when he read the sign his memory kicked in. The restaurant was known for good food and drink, but it was most recognized by the hundreds of caricatures of movie stars hung on nearly every vertical space.

Bryce recalled television shows and movies that had used the restaurant for a scene. He decided it was time to see it in person, maybe dinner and a beer before heading home. Once inside, he saw they had NFL football on in the bar and grabbed a seat. He chowed down on a burger, fries, and a few beers while watching the Giants lose to the Eagles. He struck up a conversation with the bartender. It was there and then that Bryce's world changed forever.

"The what?" he asked the bartender again.

"Madison Avenue Sports Car and Chowder Society," the man repeated through his heavy Brooklyn accent. "Like I said, it's a bunch of car lovers and they meet here upstairs once a month."

"When do they meet next?" Bryce asked.

The bartender turned and checked his calendar. "Since you're a race car driver you're in luck," he continued. "They meet here tomorrow at noon. Maybe you can come back and meet some people, shake some hands, ask for sponsorship if you are any good behind the wheel like you say you are. Who knows - someday, you might have *your* face on one of these walls!"

CHAPTER SIX

The Marriott Marquis hotel is situated on Times Square and surrounded by the sights and sounds that make the area a must-see for anyone able to make it to New York. Just a short walk from Sardis, Bryce managed to use his charm and good looks to get a single room for the night as cheaply as possible. He settled for the windowless room on the third level for $99, breakfast not included, and spent the rest of his night watching Sunday night football and then a motorsports show on ESPN that summarized the weekend's action.

He steered clear of the mini-bar. Although the Beck's beer, Pringles chips, and massive Toblerone chocolate bar looked like a party. All-in, they'd add $20 easily to his bill. Instead, he called it a night and looked forward to seeing what the people at the Chowder Society were all about.

Up early the next morning, he prepared for what was in store, figuring out for the first time ever how to use the iron to freshen the shirt he'd stuffed in his backpack. Once at Sardis, he went up the steps and began walking around the banquet meeting room where three dozen or so men and women of all shapes and sizes dressed from casual in jeans and polo shirts to stylish dresses and tailored suits, were catching up over cocktails. A guest speaker would be introduced and lunch served soon.

Suddenly, someone decided to rain on his parade.

"Sir," said the maître d' as he tapped Bryce on the right shoulder. "Sir," he continued, "this is a private function for members only. You'll have to leave."

Bryce overheard someone tell the maître d' that he reminded them of a young, handsome actor Paul Newman – brilliant blue eyes and all.

"Follow me downstairs, please," the maître d' insisted, "or we'll have the two policemen having coffee at the bar help find your way out the door." The man was just doing his job, so Bryce relented.

"If you are here to make connections in the movie business you are in the wrong place," the man told him as they reached the landing. "That group is into fast cars and auto racing so you are trying to crash the wrong party."

"You didn't know Paul Newman was a racer, too?" Bryce offered, but it was too late.

⁂

Bryce took a seat at the massive mahogany bar, two stools over from New York's finest, and made small talk with the bartender until the police left. He considered making another run for the stairs but thought it best to call it a day and perhaps head back to Penn Station for the ride north and home. In a booth behind him, though, it was clear someone had intentions of an entirely different kind.

"You can't ask me that," the young woman sitting on

the red leather booth bench on the street side of the bar said sternly. Bryce listened but noticed the mirror behind some of the liquor bottles that gave him a good look at what was going on.

"Just go away with me for the weekend," the man sitting across from her pleaded. He was tall, balding, perhaps late fifties, gray suit and blue tie. But what stood out most to Bryce was the man's arm stretched across the table; his hand was clutching hers. Nice Rolex, Bryce thought, but then focused on the girl and her body language.

She was perhaps early twenties and from her accent she was clearly not a New Yorker. *London maybe*? She wore a white, V-neck long-sleeve blouse and black slacks from what he could see. She was a natural beauty with little makeup and Bryce wondered if she was an actress, as attractive as she was, with that accent, sitting there in the theater district. She reminded him of Whitney Houston, early twenties, but a British version. Bryce watched as she yanked her hand away from the man. He reached for it again, this time leaning forward. His expression quickly changed to a menacing one.

That was all Bryce needed. He spun the barstool and spoke up. "Unless you two are rehearsing for a play," he began, "I suggest you sit back a bit there, buddy."

The man ignored Bryce and maintained his focus on the girl.

"Hey, shit head," Bryce said only this time louder. That got the man's attention. "Good, I didn't see a hearing aide."

The man looked around and then focused on Bryce. "Mind your own business." He turned back to the girl again.

Bryce looked to her and saw the fear in her eyes. Speaking directly to her, he made his intentions very clear. "Now I'm going to suggest you get up and come sit over here for a minute. This won't take long."

The maître d' had been around long enough to know where that was headed and managed to wave the two officers back inside just in time to witness it all.

She followed his suggestion. The man she'd been sitting with slid out of the bench seat, stood up, and took a swing at her man in shining armor. A second later, she was staring at the creep lying on the floor in front of her. He was unconscious, his nose shattered by the fast and hard defensive blow Bryce landed. Others in the restaurant chose to ignore the incident and continue eating while a few came closer to watch. Soon after, while one cop checked the man on the floor, the other congratulated Bryce for coming to the woman's defense.

"You ex-military?" the officer asked. "That was a trained move."

"My uncle was a Marine and showed me a thing or two."

"Max Werner," a man said introducing himself as he stepped in and extended his hand toward Bryce. "You are a lucky man," he continued in a thick German accent. "If it wasn't for the maître d' and the security cameras above," he said as he looked to the corner above them, "it could have been your word against his. Then it would have taken all day to sort this thing out. Well done."

Bryce shook Werner's hand but still showed concern for the young Brit who had finished giving the patrolmen her statement. She thanked Bryce again, and then followed the police out to a waiting cruiser for the ride to the station where she would be pressing assault charges.

"Come, let me buy you a drink," Max said, guiding Bryce to a barstool.

The two sat, and the German listened as Bryce retold the incident for what seemed like the twentieth time. Once Max asked him what had brought him to New York, what followed is what movies are made of. Bryce laid it all out for him; a race car driver in the city for a few days of sightseeing heard there were well-moneyed people who shared a passion for cars and racing gathering upstairs and he wanted to introduce himself to anyone who would listen.

"Most of the people in the group are here for networking, but many are just rich car collectors. One of them has one of Michael Schumacher's first F1 cars gathering dust in an old garage somewhere near here."

"And you, Mr. Werner, what brings you here?" he asked.

"Max – make it Max," he insisted. Werner was about the same height and weight as Bryce, but the similarity ended there. Werner said he was in his early forties and Bryce had fought hard to hide his surprise. To him, the man looked to be in his sixties.

"I've seen that face before, Bryce," he told him with a laugh. "Too much stress from running a big business, too many ex-wives, and a family history that not only makes me look much older than I am but will probably kill me long before someone my age should go."

Bryce thought for a moment. He wasn't sure if he should feel sorry for the man or what, but he went for the tension breaker.

"Any kids? Want to adopt one?" It worked and they both laughed as they finished their beers.

Then Max waved for another round. He went on to say that he had no children, none that he knew of at least, and that adoption wasn't an option even if Bryce was already potty trained. He volunteered that his family owned a large number of diverse businesses around the world, but home base was Munich. Annual sales the previous fiscal had exceeded their goal of 11.5 billion euros.

"You're definitely paying for these beers!" Bryce joked.

At Max's urging, Bryce summarized the chronology of his racing exploits to date.

Growing up in rural Vermont, Bryce had stumbled across racing at an early age. It wasn't the conventional types like NASCAR's oval track racing that he'd seen on television – this type came roaring out of the woods. He heard it first and then saw a blue flash go by as he and his best friend were hiking above Colchester, near Burlington. He'd come across a championship-winning Subaru campaigned by Vermont SportsCar and he loved it. He took the Team O'Neil rally school course, trading work around the shop for seat time, and soaked in every minute of it.

But he had two concerns. He wanted to race with other racers, side-by-side, and he had no interest in just racing a clock. Once he did get a ride in a competitive regional car he crashed hard and a pointed piece of wood – a branch from a tree—had come through the windshield like a spear. It missed his helmet by inches.

He'd always heard a racer's biggest fear was fire and he'd just experienced most drivers' second biggest fear - something coming into the car. That was enough for him. He'd learned things there in the woods that day. He wanted to be a race car driver. He knew he was good, really good, behind the wheel. And wanted to do it on the oval tracks, not through the forest.

"Anyone can go around and around, boy," Werner told him. "Strippers have been doing that with poles for centuries. How hard can it be?"

Bryce took offense at the remark and Werner must have seen it. "Don't get me wrong. I know it's not something just anyone can do. What I meant to say is making lefts and rights in open-wheeled cars and traffic has to be more of a challenge, and I would think more fulfilling."

Bryce took his words in. He'd been prepared to challenge Werner to take some laps at Thunder Road in Vermont or Stafford in Connecticut. Heck, the guy had enough money to buy not just the cars but the tracks, too. But he opted not to. *This guy could be the ticket to the big show*, Bryce thought. *Go along for the ride.*

"Besides, if you want to go NASCAR racing you can count on what—twenty million people watching the Daytona 500 on TV? Formula One – open wheeled cars on circuits – grabs over a four hundred million people from a global audience. That's bigger than the entire population of your country. Think of the potential. Think of the money!"

Bryce considered the cost of racing NASCAR versus Formula One, but that didn't concern him. His plan was to become a driver for hire. In addition to winning races and championships, it was the sponsorship money and lucrative driving contracts he'd be looking for if he ever got the shot.

"Is your company involved in racing?" Bryce asked. "What brought you here today?"

Werner shook his head no. Then he related how he'd been invited to the luncheon, it turned out, by someone who was trying to get Werner to buy his company.

"Must be tiresome, people always asking for money, always trying to get into your pants," Bryce suggested.

Werner shook his head yes and laughed.

"Well, don't worry, I'm not going to. I just appreciate the drinks," Bryce said as he downed his second beer and began to reach for his backpack.

"No need to rush," Werner suggested. "We're not finished here. No, I'm not in racing – not yet. Someday, when all the stars align, I want to win the German GP and the Formula One World Championship," he said. "But only when all the pieces fit together like a fine Swiss watch."

Werner ordered another round and excused himself to make a call and returned ten minutes later. He was smiling and Bryce had to ask why.

"I checked you out, Bryce Winters," he began, "you're a pretty good driver. A lot of race wins and a few track championships in New England. Congratulations. Now tell me," he asked, "do you know where Lime Rock Park is? And can you be there in the morning?"

CHAPTER SEVEN

A week later, the Bombardier private jet landed at Burlington International Airport at just past three o'clock on Friday afternoon. There might have been room for 18 on board but there was only one passenger and he'd been on the phone nearly the entire time since the plane left Munich seven hours prior.

Bryce had been told to pack for a week and be waiting at the Heritage Aviation hangar for a fast turnaround. He parked his Dodge pickup and checked in a half hour early. The same uncle who had taught him how to fight also taught him to be early.

Bryce watched as a U.S. Customs official boarded the plane to check flight docs and the passports of the cockpit crew, flight attendant, and the plane's owner, Max Werner. Then he watched as a half-dozen ground workers, acting much like a racing pit crew, serviced the plane. Fuel and catering in, trash and waste out. Once they had finished, a woman wearing jeans and a red sweater walked down the steps and waved for him to come aboard. Five hours later, after having only shaken hands with his host and dining on what had to be the best filet mignon he'd ever had, Bryce fell asleep somewhere during the second film he watched since they took off. Saving Private Ryan was his first choice followed by The Hunt for Red October. The pilot's landing was so soft and quiet that Bryce awoke only at the polite prodding Werner gave his shoulder.

"Let's get moving. There are some people I want you to meet."

Soon they were in a chauffeured Mercedes and headed for a cocktail party taking place in the suites overlooking the track at Laguna Seca Raceway in Monterey, California. The Indy Car series was in town and the rolling vistas, elevation changes, tight turns, and the famous downhill "corkscrew" made the event one that fans, racers, media, and industry types all looked forward to.

Max apologized that he hadn't been able to visit with his guest more but wasted no time in getting down to business. "My contacts at the Skip Barber School told me you were a natural," Max began. "They said you listened to their instructions, were fearless once you got used to the car and the track, and said you had a great deal of potential. Equally as important, at least in my mind, is that you listened and learned. That will save me time and money."

Bryce nodded with a curious smile while taking in the positive feedback. He took a moment to think about how fast things had moved over the last week. He'd killed a man at the Valley, saved one woman and then intervened to help another, met this billionaire who'd taken a liking to him, and now he'd been on his first private jet ride and first trip to California.

"I'm really appreciative of all of this," Bryce began, "I

really do Max. But where's this all headed? I have an idea but I'm also a realist, so...."

Max interrupted him. "Bryce, sit back and enjoy the day. I'm going to introduce you to some big shots, some Hollywood types, and then over dinner I'll tell you what I am thinking. Okay?"

Bryce nodded his head 'yes' and then turned his attention to the scenery that led up to the track. After meeting a handful of CEO's, two A-list movie stars who had a passion for motorsports, and a few media types, Max and Bryce were back in the Mercedes and headed for dinner at a restaurant on Fisherman's Wharf on the Monterey Bay. There, over dinner, Max explained things in very simple terms.

"Bryce, you have everything but one to become a superstar in auto racing," he began. "Looks, talent, balls, brains, a decent amount of track experience, and after watching how you behaved in New York and on the jet and tonight at the cocktail party I think you are the complete package. All you need is one more thing. Money. And that's where I come in."

Bryce felt a bit embarrassed at the high praise he'd just received. Growing up in the woods of Vermont, praise was something saved for the Lord. At least, as far as a set of identical twin brothers, his uncle and his father, were concerned. Bryce knew it was the way they were raised. His grandfather was a rural minister and had named them Peter and Paul on arrival. Luckily, at least in Bryce's mind, once the fire and brimstone minister died life up there in the hills, including the naming of what would have been the sole grandchild, relaxed quite a bit.

"So, if you are interested in working with me, and you'd be crazy not to be, here's what I propose."

Over the next thirty minutes, having waved off the servers after their first round of drinks had been delivered, Max outlined his plan, step by step.

First, Bryce would spend the next week there at Laguna Seca working with Skip Barber's West Coast team to get some seat time in a different car every day; each one offering much more horsepower and challenges than the previous. Then, the following week, if Bryce were given the green light to proceed, he'd fly to Las Vegas Motor Speedway where he'd spend two days in a NASCAR stock car under the tutelage of a retired crew chief who specialized in developing young drivers.

"It's October. If all continues to go as planned, you'll attempt to qualify for the Daytona 500 in February. I've already sent a $1,000,000 deposit to GNR in Charlotte. That team has won off-road, the 500, a series title, and also fielded a road-race team that has won the endurance races at Daytona and Sebring. We'll run the entire season, you will win the Rookie of the Year title and some races, I expect."

Bryce was flabbergasted, and his expression must have shown it. Max laughed and waved for the server to come take their orders for dinner.

"My intention is to put the very best cars under you and the best team around you - the best of everything. All you need to do in return is continue to learn, to develop – to give me your best – and to win."

The men sat quietly for a moment. At last, Max broke the tense silence. "We only have two questions to answer at this point, Bryce. Which of my companies will be the primary sponsor on the team and—" Max stopped and looked at Bryce.

"If the second one is if I'm in—then hell, yes, Max. Where do I sign?"

Max waved for a bottle of champagne, which seemed to have been standing by on ice, as if he'd known what Bryce's answer would be. He gestured for Bryce to follow him outside to the terrace where Max shook the bottle and then popped the cork out into the bay. They took turns drinking from the $400 bottle of bubbly. When they re-entered the restaurant, Bryce noticed the racing faces that had been watching the celebration. Most were curious; some offered congratulations even though they weren't sure for what. At least one – an angel with the face of a cover girl and the red hair of a super hero—smiled in the way only an interested woman can.

Once back at the table, Bryce thanked Max again and again and then excused himself and headed for the men's room. As he stood there staring into the mirror over the sink, he couldn't believe this was all happening. He turned on the faucet to wash his hands and found himself thinking back to that night at the dirt track, the dead guy lying on the bathroom floor.

A man walked out of one of the stalls, and Bryce jumped. *If anyone ever finds out about the Valley this will end faster than it began.* He tried to calm himself as he rinsed off his hands. Breathe.

As soon as he stepped out of the men's room, Bryce ran straight into the red head. Whether she'd followed him there, interested in a phone number, an introduction, or a ride inside one of the stalls, Bryce would never find out. The woman's date had followed her, and the expression he saw on the man's face showed he was a threat, and not just to this encounter. Bryce thought about all he had ahead of him and this was Tony Bishop – a rising star on the Indy Car circuit. It was an awkward moment, Bryce standing there with a woman who'd just been caught by her jealous boyfriend. Before words could be exchanged, Bishop's PR woman appeared, seemingly out of nowhere, and introduced herself to Bryce while stepping between the two drivers.

Bishop turned and left the restaurant. His date may have been on his arm but her interests were clearly elsewhere.

"Steer clear of Tony, at least for the rest of the weekend," the woman suggested. "He's got a temper. And he's politically connected with the officials and many of the sponsors. This racing world can be a bit incestuous, if you catch my drift."

Bryce smiled. "Thanks for the advice, but I'm going NASCAR racing next year. Maybe the next time we meet will be out on the track. Then it'll be just us."

The following week at Laguna Seca, Bryce spent an average of five hours each day out on the track, progressing from one fast ride to a faster one. By Friday morning he was asking, "What else you got?"

Satisfied with what he'd seen and heard, before he flew back to Germany, Werner executed a contract with Bryce and set him up as an employee with a company credit card, a $2,000 per week salary, health insurance, and a rental car. He also arranged for a private charter flight from Monterey to Vegas, for the following Monday's indoctrination and evaluation with a stock car racing legend.

Lefty Lozano, the owner of a vicious left hook, had been an up-and-coming boxer years before he became involved in big-league auto racing. Having worked at his father's Dallas garage during the day, he'd trained for fights at night and then traveled across Texas and the Southwest to race with his buddies on weekends. They were doing so well on the track, and he was doing so well in the ring, that at some point a decision had to be made – racing or the ring. Soon, a detached retina and a doctor's warning of pending blindness forced Lozano to hang up his gloves and go back to wrenching full time.

As NASCAR racing grew in popularity and became a national sport, rather than one based solely in the Southeast, the best of the best found work in the top stock car racing platform on the planet. Lozano helped many rookie drivers and owners to victory lane faster than most others. Many, if not all, of the racing fraternity thought Lozano's nickname came from oval track racers' propensity to turn left, unaware of his boxing prowess. Now retired, he kept busy at the speedway in Vegas, evaluating talent as a favor for a racing friend or charging $10,000 per day if he touched a wrench.

After the first day of Bryce's practice, Lozano called Max Werner and jokingly told him, "If you haven't signed this kid yet, don't – I'll sign him myself. He's a natural."

That night, Bryce thanked Lozano for all the help he had given him that day by taking him out for a surf-and-turf dinner at the Mirage on the strip. But the two were delayed when they came across a young woman holding a baby, stopped on the shoulder of the interstate with a flat tire.

As Bryce pulled his rent car up behind her vehicle and flipped on his flashers, he looked at Lozano and smiled. "Bet we can pit stop that ride in two minutes tops—what do you say?"

Lozano just smiled. In no time, the two men had the woman's trunk open, spare out, car jacked up, tires swapped, car dropped, trunk closed, and thanks exchanged. They were headed back to their car when a Nevada Highway Patrol vehicle, roof-mounted light bar lit blue and red, pulled up behind their rental.

The trooper was out of the car, clapping his hands with approval. "I was headed in the other direction when I saw you two pulling up and by the time I was able to hang a ubie you boys were done. It was less than three minutes," he said. He shook their hands and thanked them for taking care of the woman and her child.

Later that night, as Bryce watched Lozano savor the last forkful of his New York style cheesecake, he was surprised by the question the Texan offered.

"So, tell me, Bryce, what's wrong with you?" he asked.

Bryce's expression forced Lozano to ask it a different way.

"What I meant to ask is this – you're good looking, can drive the wheels off a race car, you handle yourself really well around people and you seem to be a genuinely nice guy. Once you get going the media's going to call you a phenom, a prodigy, and you'll turn into a star. So, what's your Achilles – what's your weakness? If there was one thing you could change about yourself, what would it be?" He paused. "What don't we know about you?"

Bryce sat back and considered the volley of questions hurled his way. "Hmmm," Bryce began but just as he started to answer, the waiter brought the check. "Your timing couldn't have been better," Bryce told the man.

With the check paid, the two headed back to the parking garage.

"Lefty," Bryce began as he drove back to the track, "maybe we haven't found it out yet. Maybe if I do become successful I'll screw up dealing with fame and fortune and all the stuff that comes along with it. But I hope not. Guess time will tell."

The food and drink took its toll on Lozano and that left Bryce alone with his thoughts. He hadn't mentioned trees through windshields or Christy. Maybe he would some other time.

CHAPTER EIGHT

THE FORMULA ONE race at Suzuka in Japan had been a wet one. A distant monsoon had worked up the sea and sky and drenched the entire weekend. Nevertheless, the event started on time. While the pace was slower, the competition was as intense as ever.

Bryce had grown up driving the slippery and slick roads throughout mountainous Vermont and New Hampshire. He had a natural feel for racing in the rain. Tony Bishop, Bryce's closest competitor in championship points, struggled the entire weekend and finished fifth to Bryce's win, his first in Japan. Despite the weather, a win would normally make a driver's day. But his meeting with Max Werner the night before at the hotel had nearly destroyed him.

They'd had dinner in Werner's suite and remained at the dining room table after it was cleared. With coffee served and the staff excused, Werner cut right to the chase. "Here's the situation," he began.

Bryce clenched his teeth. He knew Max well enough

to know something was going to be said that Bryce would prefer not to hear.

"As you can imagine, after a certain number of years most racing sponsorships level off. The return on investment, the ROI as we say, subsides. And that's when companies leave to invest their marketing money elsewhere. That is the case with Werner Industries."

"We're still racing the rest of this year?" Bryce asked, feeling even more concerned.

"Of course. I want to take the Werner brand to a second F1 championship."

"So, after Abu Dhabi are you selling the team or what? Max, what are you trying to say?"

Werner got up from the table and retrieved a folder from his briefcase in the next room. When he dropped it on the table in front of Bryce, it landed – at least to Bryce's ears – with an ominous thud.

Werner retook his seat and continued. "The good news is I am not selling the team. The other good news is that we have a folder full of companies, big companies, wanting to use F1 to grow their brand awareness and develop sales around the world."

Bryce began to tap his fingers on the table impatiently. Waiting for the real news.

"I can sign a one-hundred-million-dollar deal tomorrow morning if I want. And two associate deals worth another one hundred million. But here's the most important part - what you've been waiting to hear. In order to sign on the dotted line, they want you, Bryce Winters. They want *you* to drive *their* brand name on *my* cars in F1 for the next three years."

The air rushed out of Bryce's lungs as if he'd been gut punched. He stared incredulously at the man and then, distracted for a second, noticed the picture frame on the end table. A photo of Werner's young daughter, little Mila, his pride and joy. He immediately returned his attention to her father.

"You know I want to retire at the end of the year, providing we win the championship. No American has done this more than once. I want to beat Andretti's single F1 title and then go back to Park City and like you helped me. You know that's the plan."

Bryce sat back in his chair, tilting it onto its back legs as he stared up at the ceiling. He hadn't taken note of anything about the room until now. The artwork reminded him where he was, colorful sketches of Mt. Fuji mounted on the wall behind Werner, a Samurai to the left, a geisha to the right. While he enjoyed and appreciated the country he hadn't planned on coming back to Suzuka ever again. Werner had no idea of the position he'd just put his driver in. If he continued to drive F1 then the CIA would continue to hold a noose over his head and force him to do their dirty work. If he drove for three more seasons that would be three more years of taking risks, risks that could put him in a foreign prison or a morgue. The CIA was already holding him hostage and he hated it.

He slowly brought the chair back to the ground, stared at Max, and then smiled. "And you're going to tell me that without these sponsorships signed up you'll close the team and it'll be my fault that over four hundred people will be out of a job."

"Precisely!" Max shouted and then began to laugh.

"*Probably* is the more appropriate word. I would probably just sell the team and leave it at that."

The two sat quietly for a time sipping their drinks and then Bryce got up to leave. "Time for some sleep. When do you need an answer, Max?"

"The morning after Mexico. If we do this, they want to hold a press conference in Austin and display the new colors for next year's cars."

That would give Bryce a week to decide.

"You know this is going to cost you – a lot – if I do this," he said in a firm tone.

"No doubt. But why focus on just two championships when you might have five?"

Bryce walked around the table and as Max stood up he shook his hand and held it as he thanked him for everything he had ever done for him in his racing career. The two men stood silently, each lost in their own thoughts, and then Bryce left. Twenty-four hours later, Bryce was buckling into his window seat aboard a United Airlines 747 flight destined for Los Angeles. He'd flown this route before and particularly enjoyed the first-class cabin that occupied the area behind the cockpit. There was space for only a dozen travelers who climbed up the circular stairway into this cabin giving it the feel of a private area that promised peace and quiet and impeccable service.

If all went well, he'd spend the next nine hours sound asleep and then catch a small charter jet from LAX to Park City. He'd have a few days off before his scheduled meeting with his handler - Nitro. They hadn't spoken since his last assignment in Sochi and he'd been fine with that. But she had some news she'd rather deliver in person and he wasn't looking forward to her visit.

For the woman who took the seat beside his though, sleep was the last thing she had in mind. She was a nervous flier and needed to talk. Bryce let out a sigh of frustration as he rolled to his right to respond to the person's greeting. When he saw her face, with its exquisite Asian features, it was game over.

"I am so sorry to bother you," she'd said. "I fly all over the world. I have for years, but this still scares me - the takeoff that is. Once we're up, I'm fine. Crazy huh?"

Bryce smiled. "I'm the same way at the start of a race. Butterflies, I guess. But once we get going, I'm better, too." He introduced himself to her and she nodded in return.

"I recognized you in the lounge. My father was at the race this weekend. He goes every year."

He smiled again. Soon the jet lumbered down the long runway, and just as the pilot pulled back on the controls that lifted the massive jet up into the night air, she placed her hand on Bryce's and then grasped it. There were a few slight bumps as the plane rose to over 10,000 feet then the woman relaxed and drew back but the conversation continued. For the next nine hours they behaved like long-lost friends. They had so much in common and were so interested in the other's passions.

She talked about her degree in International Law from UCLA and some of the cases she'd been involved in around the world. Over the course of the flight she continued to impress. She had competed in Japan's version of the American Ninja Warrior athletic competition on TV, and he admired her form when he watched her get up to retrieve something from the overhead. Model looks, athletic body, great mind, and fascinating conversation made Bryce wish they'd been on a longer flight, perhaps the eighteen-hour marathon from New York to Hong Kong. He didn't want this journey to end.

When they did finally take a break to eat a meal, blackened salmon for them both, he laughed to himself when she selected the film *The Interview* on the in-flight entertainment. James Franco and Seth Rogan had made the movie years before about two men, a journalist and his TV producer, who travel to North Korea to conduct an interview and take out the supreme leader on behalf of the CIA. There were scenes where the woman snorted, she was laughing so hard, disturbing the snoring mess of a man sitting across from them. Bryce knew the movie but had never considered until that moment that he might someday find himself in a similar situation. As they landed, Bryce was disappointed their little party had come to an end.

"I'm off to Utah for a few days off and then Mexico City for the race. How about you?" he asked.

"A meeting in LA and then a flight to Washington tonight and then Brussels," she told him. He couldn't take his tired eyes off her and he sensed the same from her. "You know, I never asked," he began. "Are you in a relationship?"

Her expression turned serious but then changed to a sly smile. "No. My work and travel make that impossible. It's very hard to find anyone who understands the demands or has a similar lifestyle."

Bryce smiled again. He handed her his card even as she was taking one of hers from her bag.

"Kyoto Watanabe," he read and laughed. "Well, at least if we get married your initials won't have to change."

She laughed, "Neither will yours!"

He followed her down the circular stairs and through the long jet bridge until they got to the gate area and headed for U.S. Customs entry. They continued together through the expedited Global Entry zone and then stopped to say their goodbyes.

She turned, a look of embarrassment on her face. "I hate to ask but," she said, "my father would kill me if I didn't take a photo with you. May I?"

Bryce nodded and smiled as they stood close for the shot. "You owe me now. Dinner somewhere, sometime."

She nodded and waved as she headed off.

Their first date was over and each headed in very different directions. He liked this woman, really liked her, and as he walked to the shuttle to the charter terminal he smiled as he continued to think about her. It had been a very long time since someone had engaged him in such a way. He'd let his guard down for the first time since he watched as a casket was lowered into the ground back in Vermont. Headed up into the little Bombardier Learjet 75, one that seemed small enough to fit inside the 747 he'd just left, Bryce wondered if he would ever see Kyoto again.

Seven years had passed since the night Lozano asked Bryce those questions and the prodigy, as Lefty had called him, had taken off as expected. An Indy 500 winner's trophy sat resting in the great room of his mountain home, positioned alongside his Daytona 500 trophy and the multitude of race winner hardware he'd acquired. On the opposite wall, the Formula One Championship trophy and the many awards from the race wins Bryce had scored, securing the titles that complimented them.

Some people collected guns, wine, or fine art. Bryce collected race wins, titles, and the goods that came with them. But he wanted one more, in particular, and was convinced this might just be the year it happened. Then he looked to the aluminum crutches he was forced to rely on after a massive crash during that race at Talladega.

He'd been involved in what they call, "The Big One." At some point in every NASCAR race at Talladega, all hell breaks loose on the track and the ensuing debacle takes out a dozen or more cars. He'd had the crutches mounted and hung over the doorway as a reminder that as he put it, "Assume nothing." He thought back for a moment to the flight he'd taken from Tokyo to LA and smiled but then he found himself in the company of another woman and he couldn't wait to get rid of her.

CHAPTER NINE

Nitro, Joan Myers, looked incredible sitting there on a high stool at the island in the kitchen full of stainless-steel appliances he rarely used. Her long blonde hair pulled back, tight jeans, red-and-black flannel shirt with buttons left open to reveal the cleavage she often used to distract or entice people into doing what she wanted. But that had never worked on Bryce. She was part of an organization that had forced him into something, and he resented her for it although he did his best to hide the animosity. She was one trophy he wasn't interested in. She had a great personality, though, and Bryce got a kick out of the occasional sexual banter and jokes between Madigan and her.

Let them joke while I bide my time.

She was there to debrief on the hit in Sochi and prepare for their meeting with her new boss from Langley. They'd talk over dinner, over delivery pizza that was running late. She was only the messenger, she'd insisted as she performed her role, not the person blackmailing Bryce into a corner. What she and the CIA never considered of Bryce though was that cornered predators were the most dangerous.

"The Russian had children," Bryce said, tired of waiting and deciding to vent his frustration. "I told you before, I'll do what you ask me to as long as there are no kids involved."

"That was our mistake, Bryce, and I'm very sorry for it. Our intel was wrong – this time," she told him. He stared at her and shook his head while she tried to explain. "But you have to realize, he was a dead man walking. His children were going to be without a father whether you took him out or someone else did. Think of it this way, if it makes you feel any better. If someone else had done the deed, the hitter might have just blown the bastard's house up with his kids in it."

"Is that supposed to make me feel better – really?" he fumed. "My father wasn't around much, but that doesn't mean I'd have been better off without him at all. Damn it – I said nobody with kids!"

The bell at the front gate rang, providing a needed break in the escalating tension in the room. After he tipped the delivery girl and sent her on her way, he served up the food and neither of them spoke again. He grabbed the remote and scrolled through the movies until he found what he was looking for. *Three Days of the Condor*, the film starring Robert Redford and Faye Dunaway about a CIA code breaker who walks into his workplace and finds all of his coworkers have been murdered.

He looked to her for approval. Her mouth full of pizza, she shrugged her shoulders, her eyes saying why not? They watched the film for two hours without saying a word. Once it had ended she asked him if she could stay the night, try to mend what she had broken.

"The house is so quiet, you must be lonely here all by yourself," she called out as he went to use the bathroom. When he reentered the kitchen he had her coat in his hand, helped her on with it, and then walked her to her car. There were five bedrooms in his beautiful home, but she wasn't invited to stay, never.

Bryce walked back to the massive silver F1 championship trophy and stared at it. He'd done just about everything he'd wanted to do in motorsport except become regarded as the best from America. In order to do that, to surpass his hero Andretti, he'd have to win a second F1 title. *It can be done,* he told himself. Werner was up for it. He had funded Bryce's career and reaped dividends that kept his board of directors and shareholders very happy.

That said, with only a handful of F1 races left on the schedule, Bryce needed to concoct a plan to get what he wanted – not just more race wins and another title – but his freedom. He wanted to rid himself of the CIA. He had grown tired of the leverage they had over him. Instead of enjoying a rare night in his king bed he spent it staring through the skylights at the blanket of stars above and developed an action plan that just might work. Then he began to consider his contract with Werner that expired at the end of the year. He would never have gotten to where he was today without Max, but it *had* been a mutually beneficial relationship. He hoped his friend would remember that.

The Baja peninsula is a narrow strip of land that juts into the Pacific Ocean along its west coast and the Gulf of California along its eastern side. San Diego sits just across its northern border with the United States, and it runs south to Cabo San Lucas, the party town known for tequila, deep sea fishing, and money. With another week to go before Bryce's next race, the Mexico GP in Mexico City, he invited Nitro, her new boss, Glen Gunn, and Jack Madigan to go off-roading on the peninsula.

Every year, racers and fans that love off-road racing, the sport of racing against the terrain rather than on a race track or a paved course, flock to the region for spectacles like the Baja 1000. This is where racing vehicles resembling cars and pick-up trucks, as well as motorcycles, ATV's and dune buggies, race across the hills, valleys, deserts, and mountains between Ensenada on the Pacific Ocean and La Paz, far south and on the edge of the Gulf of California. It's a brutal race that runs at high speeds day and night. Considering the obstacles and deep drops offs the competitors face, it can also be a deadly one.

Many companies have made a business out of providing off-road racing vehicles, complete with protective roll cages, fuel cells to protect the gas tanks from leaking or exploding in the event of a crash, helmets, fire suits, driving gloves, two-way communications, guides and support personnel, so that enthusiasts can "drive" the hills, beaches, desert-like stretches, and avoid obstacles like cows in the road or twenty-foot cacti. At points along the course it can be very dangerous. If not taken seriously, the sudden drop-offs on the cliff sides and deep ravines can gobble up a vehicle and its occupants, leaving them paralyzed or worse when they come to rest a thousand feet below. Bryce had arranged a two-day ride for the four of them, and he couldn't wait to get going.

Madigan and Gunn had flown to San Diego on commercial flights from Charlotte and Washington respectively, the day before, while Bryce and Nitro flew in early Tuesday morning on a private charter from Park City. The two men had stayed up late the night before in the hotel bar, watching Monday Night Football's West Coast game go into overtime. They'd sat just a few bar stools apart from one another. Groggy from their late night, Bryce took pity on the men and arranged for the off-road excursion to start a day later, on Wednesday, and arranged for an ice breaking lunch instead.

The Hotel Coronado is a landmark in the area, having hosted presidents and movie stars over decades for fundraisers, weddings, and parties of all sorts. The Coronado was also a popular spot for the friends and families of the Navy's finest, who were quite often seen in the area undergoing BUDS - Basic Underwater Demolition/SEAL training at the Navy Amphibious Base there. Bryce had been at this hotel many times before and always made the effort to thank the men and women of the Navy for their service and sacrifice, while they were just as enthused to meet him and pose for pictures. When Park City was mentioned, the conversation would always turn to, "You must know…." or "Yeah, that guy from Seal Team Six lives there now."

Over lunch at a table set in a quiet corner and away from the crowd, the four talked about Baja, racing, travel, dogs, and football. Bryce and Madigan had both shown a fake interest in their new boss's career and family, hoping to develop a rapport that was better than they'd had with his predecessor. *Guy looks more like a nerdy desk jockey than a spy, glasses and all,* Bryce had thought at first sight.

"No wife, no kids, no dog, just work and Redskins football," Gunn told them.

Bryce teased him about a man named Gunn working in law enforcement but, as the man had heard that a thousand times before, Bryce could see it irritated him so he backed off.

"What's the fastest you've ever driven?" Matt asked Gunn out of curiosity.

"With beltway traffic, about thirty miles per hour," he replied. "But I used to race late models on dirt at Potomac Speedway in my younger days, so I know a bit about speed." Bryce leaned over and gave him a high-five, pleased and surprised to learn this. He then looked to Madigan who was nodding his approval. When the conversation headed toward business, Gunn brought up a newspaper article he had read in the Washington Post about corruption in Mexico's federal government.

Bryce opted out. "Come on, we'll have plenty of time to talk about what's next," he told them. "Let's save that for the dinner table tonight. For now, let's go have some fun!"

After lunch they all loaded into a black luxury minivan and departed for Ensenada, Mexico just a short ride south of San Diego and the starting point for their Baja adventure.

The welcome dinner Tuesday night in Ensenada had not gone as Bryce had hoped. When he had learned that Gunn had raced, although years ago, he thought that could make for a better working relationship and perhaps even a friendship he could leverage to win his freedom. When

Gunn leaned in alongside Bryce after dinner at the bar and told him he knew what he was up to, all bets were off.

"Bryce, I'm with the damn CIA," Gunn had told him in a slightly inebriated state. "We read people better than anyone. Don't let the clothing or the glasses fool you. I may look like a suit from DC, but I'm highly trained, highly skilled, and capable of things you can't even imagine. So, you *will* continue to do what we need when we need you to. Period."

Bryce smiled at the man. "10-4," was Bryce's only response.

The next morning, after a quick meal of breakfast tortillas and large quantities of coffee and orange juice, the four of them hopped in a white mini-van that had been sent for them by Baja Driving Adventures. Of the four, only Madigan was a so-called morning person. After he repeated a few things he'd heard on the Howard Stern show earlier that morning on SIRIUS, the rest of them livened up. Bryce could see from Nitro's expression that Gunn had shared his words from the night before, but when he smiled and winked at her he could see her relax. After the short ride, most of it down dusty roads, they arrived at BDA, and after suiting up and a thirty-minute orientation and instruction meeting with the guides, the four participants walked out into the bright Mexican sunshine. It was time to choose a partner, buckle up, and get going.

"Joan, you ride with me," Gunn stated. "We can talk business along the way." Bryce looked to her and then at Madigan and agreed. He smiled.

It took a few minutes for the crew from BDA to make sure everyone was buckled in and ready to go. Gloves, neck braces – check. They attached the breathing tubes to the side of their full-face helmets allowing for filtered air to be pumped into them. The dust and silt of the desert would make life miserable without them. Helmet communications were connected and tested, window nets meant to keep arms inside the cockpit and foreign objects out were latched into place, and then the two drivers fired up the Subaru engines and pulled out onto the road that would lead them from into the wild. Bryce had driven this course many times, so it was agreed that he would lead the way out of town and onto the course. To Bryce's surprise, Gunn bumped his vehicle hard from behind as if to remind Bryce he was back there and wanted to get moving. Bryce switched his radio setting from A to B so he could speak to his navigator who was riding shotgun.

"You know, I'd forgotten she had a real name," he said.

"Me, too. I thought for a second, who the hell is Joan," Madigan responded.

"This is going to be fun," Bryce said with a laugh.

"Let 'er eat," was Madigan's reply.

The moment the two vehicles cleared the city's limits, away from the children and the dogs playing in the streets, Bryce hit the gas and left Gunn and Nitro in his very dusty wake. Over the next two hours both teams ran hard and fast through the open desert. Eventually they began to encounter saguaro cactus, at least twenty feet high, that and had been growing for nearly 100 years. In the daylight it might be easy to avoid running into one of them, unless you were trying to pass or following a vehicle in front of you too closely and the dirt and dust kicked up obstructs your vision.

"We better back off a bit," Gunn told Nitro over their in-car radio. "Those big ones, if they're full of water, can weigh over three thousand pounds. If hitting one at speed wouldn't hurt enough, their barbs would make a porcupine jealous."

"Yes, please," Nitro responded, her tone of voice showing concern. "Anyway, I can't read this damn map with all the dirt flying around. Bryce said we'd encounter some cliff sides before lunch, and I'm not up for breaking my neck in Mexico."

The guides had shown the CIA staffers how the maps and GPS worked on the course. Dash-mounted satellite tracking systems were critically important in off-roading, especially when racing in the dust or in the dark. The map would show the hazards and the places where left or right turns needed to be made to stay safe and on-course, and the distance between them. There was the occasional straightaway that would give the navigator a chance to take their eyes off the map and enjoy the scenery for a short time, but as quickly as it had come break time was over and they were back on edge. Drivers or navigators couldn't make mistakes for if they did it could be a fatal one.

A few times Gunn had been able to leave the path the leader had taken and get alongside Bryce, intending to pass as he flipped his rival the middle finger. But sudden evasive maneuvers to avoid a rock or a looming cactus always sent Gunn and his shotgun rider back into second place. Bryce had driven all sorts of race cars in all sorts of conditions all around the world, and his reflexes and judgment were second to none. For a novice to desert racing, like Gunn, things could happen fast. The two-seaters they were racing would typically top out at 80 mph, but the guides, and Madigan, had cautioned Gunn and Nitro that at that speed they'd be traveling at over 100 feet per second – the length of an American football field in three seconds. On dirt and gravel that gives way, and with the challenges of steering and braking, crashing a vehicle and screwing up your day (or body) wasn't worth it. So, they had cautioned, "don't do anything stupid."

"Hey, Gunn, you tired of eating my dust yet?" Bryce crowed after switching his radio back to A so the two cars could talk.

"Copy that," Gunn stated.

"How long before a pee break?" Nitro asked. "I know that coffee's been sloshing around way too long, at least for me, and then it's my turn to drive!"

"Not long, maybe another twenty minutes," Madigan answered. "We have to make it around one more set of cliff sides and then the guides will be waiting for us with food and toilet paper for anyone who needs it."

Running out front in cleaner air was preferred, but to Bryce there wasn't much of a challenge to it and gestured to Madigan that he was getting bored. He let off the gas slightly and pushed the radio button mounted on the steering wheel.

"Hey, Gunn, you a betting man?" Bryce asked over the radio.

"Absofuckinglutely," he replied.

"Okay. I'm going to pull over and stop and let you pass. We'll wait five minutes and then if I catch and pass you before we get to the pit stop you have to burn my file and turn me loose."

Madigan slapped Bryce's right shoulder then shot his hands up in the air, as if to say, *When did you come up with that one?* Bryce attempted to shrug his shoulders but the four-inch wide shoulder harnesses wouldn't allow it. He waited for a response from Gunn and then radio checked to make sure he was still there.

"Winters to Gunn. You copy?"

"Negative on the fire, nice try, but I accept the challenge. We'll be waiting for you at the checkpoint." Bryce shook his head in frustration but pulled off the course onto a low hillside and waited. Madigan switched the in-car radio back to B so they could talk, but Bryce just shook his head, slowly this time, and turned the radio back to A.

Two minutes later, Gunn and Nitro blew past Bryce and Madigan's vehicle, leaving them in the dust for a change. Finally, Gunn had clear skies and air in front of him, with his foot hard on the gas pedal. The clock was ticking.

Gunn watched as Nitro switched the radio back to B and told him that within a mile they would have a sharp, ninety-degree right turn and then a slow ride along a very narrow and high cliff path before it opened up to where Madigan said the crew would be waiting.

"Tell me when we're a quarter mile out, and I'll slow it down," he told her. As they rode closer and closer to the spot where they'd need to turn, the gray mountain in front of them rose higher and higher into the sky. Closer now, Gunn could see rocks of all shapes and sizes strewn across its face.

"Half-mile," Nitro said. "Remember, there's a cliff coming."

Gunn didn't respond. He kept his foot hard on the gas and kept going.

"Quarter mile," Nitro told him, this time her voice sounding a bit more concerned.

"Eighth mile, please slow down," she begged.

"What did you say?" he joked, shouting over the whine of the engine. He knew the cliff side was coming fast, at this speed they'd be on it within seconds. But the urge to compete, to win, had overtaken him. He let off the gas, touched the brake, downshifted from fourth to third gear, and got on the brake pedal again as he turned to take a quick look at his navigator. He saw her white helmet falling forward with the deceleration and noticed she had let go of the clipboard holding the map. He pushed harder on the brake and shifted down into second gear as he looked back to the road. It seemed to end right in front of him.

Suddenly his hands fell from their grasp of the wheel. At 40 mph the vehicle continued on, straight off the side of the cliff.

Years before on a New Year's Eve, Nitro Circus star driver Travis Pastrana had travelled 269 feet over water in a Red Bull rally car through the air in Long Beach, California, from a pier to a barge. But the scene unfolding 250 miles to the south on the Baja peninsula was a polar opposite. The vehicle crashed onto a mound of jagged rocks and boulders that had fallen down the mountainside over the decades and collected far below. Something must have punctured the fuel cell as fire immediately engulfed the vehicle. A swirling wind carried the smoke away and through the ravine.

Nearly eight minutes later, Bryce slowed to a stop and pulled up to the edge of the cliff. Madigan tapped Bryce's shoulder again, gesturing with both hands as if to say, *What gives?*

Bryce flipped the ignition switch to kill the engine, lowered the window net and then removed his gloves, unbuckled the shoulder harnesses, lap and crotch belts, unplugged the wires to his helmet headset, removed the neck collar and unstrapped his helmet, placing it on the dashboard. Bryce climbed out and walked a few feet to the edge of the cliff and looked down, gesturing for Madigan to join him.

After his navigator had repeated the same steps Bryce had taken, he climbed out and walked toward the side of the cliff. A spot of bright light washed across Bryce's dust-covered driving suit and then Madigan's, causing him to stop dead in his tracks. Bryce looked across the canyon and up the mountainside at the source of the blinding light and gave a thumbs-up to the sniper who had decided the race.

"Well, that'll help get the CIA off our backs, maybe for good," he said without taking his eyes off the floor of the canyon.

Bryce pointed down to the mess that used to be two CIA agents and an off-road vehicle.

"What did you do?" Madigan asked as he turned his eyes from the sniper's location on the hillside to the site far below them. "What did you do?"

Having learned his new handler left no loved ones behind Bryce felt no remorse for what had just happened. He then turned his thoughts to the beautiful Nitro, who had played the good cop to many CIA bad cops since their arrangement had been made. She may have appeared sympathetic to his plight now and then, but she had also pulled hard on the leash one too many times. Her ambivalence about hits that left children without a father sealed her fate; he would shed no tears for her either.

"What's that saying?" he asked as he turned toward Madigan.

"Which one?" he asked dejectedly, still shaking his head as he stared at the accident scene below them.

"Live by the sword, die by it, too?"

With that, Bryce began to reverse what they had just done and prepared to move on to the checkpoint. Madigan stood quietly at the hillside until Bryce called out to him.

"We need to get moving now, bud. You good?" he called out. Madigan turned toward his friend, nodded, and walked back to rejoin the driver.

Once the engine was restarted the two sped off, Bryce driving as if they were on a qualifying lap, flying around the cliff side and headed for the refreshments and food that would be waiting for them. Bryce switched the radio to B and laid out the rest of the plan. They'd wait patiently for five minutes, then ten, and eventually feign concern for their friends when they didn't arrive at the rest stop that was marked clearly on the map.

"Why didn't you tell me what you had planned?" Madigan asked Bryce over the radio. When he didn't answer, Madigan asked again.

"It was a game-day decision," Bryce began. "I gave the guy an out. When he didn't take it, I fed him to the dogs. I didn't want to, but I needed a plan and he fell into it."

"No, *they* fell into it, Bryce, *they* did."

The two didn't speak another word until they arrived at the checkpoint, hydrated some plants and then themselves before washing the dirt and fine silt from their faces. They sat down to eat the tortillas and enchilada lunch that had been staged there for them but Madigan had pushed his plate away. Once Bryce finished his meal the acting began, and the concern for the two drivers late to the lunch was heightened. A satellite phone, the only thing that could reach civilization way out in the middle of nowhere, was used to call the tour's office in Ensenada. A quick check of the locater for the GPS device in Gunn's vehicle told the teams exactly where the car had come to a stop.

"They're in the ravine," the contact in Ensenada informed them. "I'll call for a rescue chopper right away."

When the rescue party discovered the crashed vehicle, it initially seemed as if yet another set of adventure-seekers had somehow messed up. Their charred bodies were removed from the wreckage. Only then did it become clear, from the condition of their helmets that something else had happened. There should only have been one opening – in the front for vision. But both helmets had new, larger openings in the back. In the following week, the news media around the world would describe the failed murder attempt on the famous race car driver and one of his engineers. The target the CIA had wanted Bryce to kill in Mexico City would never know just how lucky they were.

The FBI and Mexican authorities reviewed the crime scene photos that showed the remains of the occupants, still strapped in their seats. The face shields of the victim's helmets had melted in the ensuing fire and erased any trace of a bullet's entry, but the significant holes in the back of both helmets told investigators what had happened long before autopsies back in the States verified it.

In a secret arrangement made by the American State Department with their counterpart in Mexico, the true identities of the individuals found in the wreckage wouldn't be disclosed. What would the CIA have been doing off-roading with this F1 driver and his mechanic and who would have killed them? The Mexican government relied heavily on tourism and wanted no part in anything that might threaten even one of those much needed dollars and euros.

In the coming days, Gunn's boss at Langley would want answers while Bryce went about his business racing, waiting for the next handler to arrive. When they did, his story would be simple.

"Look what you bastards have gotten me into," he'd tell them when the call came. Only one of the two bullets, or what was left of it, was recovered after it was found imbedded in the fuel cell of the vehicle. FBI's ballistics experts identified it as the 7.62 type used by the Russian military, particularly snipers.

"You had me knock off a Russian oligarch. Now *they're* trying to kill *me*. The shooter obviously thought I was driving the lead vehicle. So, what are you going to do to protect me now?"

CHAPTER TEN

Mexico City rests at an elevation of over seventy-two hundred feet, nearly the same as Bryce's mountainside home two thousand miles northwest of there in Utah. While some foreign visitors to the Formula One event held at the Autódromo Hermanos Rodríguez circuit needed a day or two to acclimate to the thin air, Bryce embraced it. He ran, biked, and hiked the area around his home in Park City as often as he could and was ready and eager to get back to the pursuit of his second F1 Driver's Championship. The media, and others, had different opinions on how his week should go.

Immediately after Bryce and Madigan had been interviewed by the local police who had been called to the scene of the double murder in the desert, they flew back to Ensenada by helicopter, retrieved their luggage, boarded a small private jet there, and headed for Mexico's largest city. F1 management and the Mexican promoter hesitated but eventually agreed that the star driver would not participate in the customary media blitz of interview and photo sessions that took place on Thursday before the race.

But the media hounded Bryce at his hotel and at the track, shouting allegations ranging from conspiracy theories, that he'd been having an affair with the dead man's wife, and on and on. Bowing to pressure from the race promoter, and with Max Werner's encouragement, Bryce agreed to make a brief statement at a hastily arranged press conference in the track's media center. He insisted that was the last he would speak on it.

"They were a couple we met in San Diego who said they were there on vacation and asked me if I thought it was safe traveling to Mexico. One of our team engineers, Jack Madigan, and I had planned on running Baja for a few days to have some fun, so we suggested they come along. They were informed of the dangers of the course. Sadly, they messed up. Motorsports can be dangerous. My thoughts go out to their families and friends and that's all I have to say on the matter."

The local press persisted in shouting questions while the media that traveled the world with the Formula One tour let him go. They knew better. Pursue a driver too hard, and that would be the last interview you'd ever get—especially when your target was Bryce Winters. He had showed them that a year before when allegations of an affair with a married woman in Spain had been front page news on tabloids all across Europe. Bryce denied it, saying someone had set him up and was trying to blackmail both him and Werner to make it go away. Race fans are a very passionate breed, especially the Europeans, and the couple were hounded by protestors who followed them to work every day and played loud music in front of their residence every night. When the husband and wife were found dead in their home in Madrid in what was called a murder-suicide, along with a note admitting they had made the whole thing up, Bryce demanded an apology from the media and those who didn't repent were never spoken to again.

On Sunday morning, just like he had at Sochi and all the races he'd run in recent years, Bryce sought out the solitude and comfort of the private space the team always provided as part of his contract. When travelling outside of Europe the team shipped their race cars and container loads of parts, tools, support equipment, hospitality and meeting facilities via cargo aircraft from their headquarters in the Midlands of England to faraway places like Singapore, Melbourne, and Austin, Texas.

For Mexico, Bryce's private space came in the form of a rented pearl white Prevost motorcoach that would be his to use for the event in Mexico and then be driven back across the border into Texas for the F1 near Austin the following weekend. Three framed photos were always transported from race to race and treated with the utmost of care. Werner knew their sentimental and motivational value to his friend and employee; he'd had three copies made of each item to insure that these would always be there for the star driver.

As Bryce sat back into the brown leather captain's chair he savored every drop of the last cup of coffee he'd have before switching to his pre-race energy drink regimen. He looked to the photos as he always did before changing into his fire-resistant underwear, driving suit, and shoes and heading to the starting grid for the pre-race ceremonies and the battle to come.

The first photo had been a selfie taken with his father and his uncle back in Vermont, Bryce smiling at the nine-point buck. His first kill. His father's health hadn't been good enough to allow him to go on the hunt but he wouldn't have missed standing proudly with his son and brother as part of a passing of the guard at the Winters' household.

Bryce's attention then moved to the next photo. It was of him standing in victory lane after winning the Daytona 500. Max Werner, Jack Madigan, and the then President of the United States surrounded him and the massive Harley Earl Trophy.

Finally, he finished his coffee and got up, placed the bright yellow and red mug in the sink and walked to the third photo on the wall. There he stood in another victory lane, this one at Tom Curley's Thunder Road in Barre, Vermont, after his first win on an asphalt-paved oval track. He'd grown up in the area, so a lot of friends and family had been there to help him celebrate. But that night, with the winner's trophy on one side of him, Christy Hill – his girlfriend – stood on the other.

Bryce shook his head, still in disbelief all these years later, that she was gone. A drunk driver had crashed head on into her car late one night when she was driving from her job at the local VP gas station to meet Bryce for dinner. The finality of it all and the heartbreak that ensued crushed him. Other than saying goodbye to her closed casket at the gravesite he withdrew and didn't do much of anything for nearly a month. Since that time, he'd focused strictly on racing and swore that he would never let anyone in again. The pain had been too much, and he wasn't interested in ever running the risk of feeling something that painful ever again. Two weeks after Christy's funeral, the drunk driver, who was free on bail, was found dead in his bed of a gunshot wound through his mouth that exited very dramatically through the top of his head. Other than the fingerprints that were on it there were no ownership records for the silver .357 magnum pistol the police found lying in the man's left hand. The serial number had been ground away. Relatives and neighbors the police interviewed had expressed surprise that the dead guy owned a gun. But with no other paths to pursue, the police ruled the case a suicide and moved on.

"Hey, you got your clothes on?" Bryce heard a familiar voice call out after a knock on his motor coach's front door as it opened slightly.

Since the incident in Baja, F1 security had increased the number of persons shadowing Bryce wherever he went and stationed two guards at the door to his coach. Inside, Bryce shook his head to clear his thoughts and approached the coach driver's dashboard to push the button that would release the door for his friend. He knew his distinctive knock and would be happy to spend time with him. The security team knew Werner, too; a team owner. They weren't going to get in his way. As Max stepped up inside the coach, he greeted Bryce and turned to look back down the steps.

"Look who I found wandering around the paddock just now, our favorite nomad," Werner said, his German accent as strong as ever, as he gestured for the man to follow him in.

His second guest, Western mustache and all, had always made Bryce think of the actor Sam Elliot.

"Uncle Pete!" Bryce called out as his guests stepped up into the coach.

Werner stood back as the two hugged and greeted each other. Werner had VIP guests to attend to, and Pete's unexpected visit had cut into his time.

As Werner excused himself, he turned to Bryce. "Let's plan on dinner when we get to Austin, Bryce. We have to revisit what we talked about in Japan and I'm on a bit of a deadline."

Bryce nodded and then turned his focus back to his uncle. "You had me worried, I was thinking you weren't going to make it," Bryce told him as he stepped back and smiled at the man.

Werner took two steps down to leave and then turned to Bryce, pointing to his watch. It was near time for Bryce to get moving, but he had informed the team that he would wait until the very last minute to head for the grid, cutting down on the time the pesky media and camera operators could attempt to poke and prod him for more about the Baja incident. Another knock at the door brought yet another familiar and friendly face.

"Come on in, Jack," Bryce called out. "Look who's here!"

Madigan greeted Pete Winters the way he always had, with a big hug and a handshake. But this time he pulled away abruptly and stared at the uncle's face.

"Pete, you old son of a gun – where the hell'd you get that tan?"

The two made small talk while Bryce changed into his gear for the race. As he came back into the living room area of the coach he smiled at his uncle and his friend, but he saw something that concerned him. Madigan wasn't smiling.

As the three left for the grid, Bryce in the middle and Pete to his left, Madigan kept muttering something that Bryce couldn't quite make out. They entered the area of the paddock where fans, as well as sponsors, media and dozens of other interested parties, willing to pay a small fortune to get close to the drivers funneled into a choke point that would lead to the grid. People shouted, passed hats or photos for Bryce to sign. He smiled and obliged a few – focusing on the children who were calling his name.

He leaned toward Madigan. "What were you grumbling about back there?"

"Pete didn't get that damn tan in Vermont, not in November he didn't," he said.

Bryce didn't respond.

"He was the sniper on that hillside in Baja, wasn't he?"

CHAPTER ELEVEN

THE LAYOUT OF the circuit in Mexico City is unlike any other. It splits a grandstand full of spectators, allowing fans to look down into the cockpits of the Formula One drivers as they pass at speed between the two tall structures.

Bryce had demonstrated to the worldwide media, and the near four hundred million fans that watch race broadcasts around the globe, that the incident in Baja and the media frenzy that followed hadn't distracted him. He'd won the pole at record-setting speed in his Werner Industries-sponsored yellow and red entry, powered by Mercedes Benz racing engines.

At the start of the race he'd taken the first corner in dramatic fashion, pushing past a rival who had tried a kamikaze dive to pass him into the first corner, only to lose control and spin off the course. Bryce went on to command a three-second lead and held the margin lap after lap. He was headed for his first victory in Mexico until things changed in the blink of an eye.

A routine pit stop for four fresh tires normally took 2.3 seconds. But a problem with a pneumatic wrench used to remove a single, high-tech lug nut delayed the stop until a back-up unit was thrown into service. The 4.5-second stop, which in F1 racing is an eternity, cost Bryce the lead and left him with a second place finish behind the man closest to him in the point championship, Tony Bishop from Vancouver, Canada.

This was the same Bishop he had come close to fighting with years before at a restaurant in Monterey, California. The same driver he had beaten by a mere 11 points to take his first F1 Championship. Someday, somewhere, the rivalry between the two was sure to boil over. With only three races left—America, Brazil and Abu Dhabi—every single point, finishing position, and fastest lap award, would now be more important than ever and the increased intensity was palpable.

Hours later, as Bryce watched the NFL highlights on ESPN in the Presidential Suite at the five-star St. Regis in downtown Mexico City, he stared at the second-place trophy he had been awarded earlier that afternoon. When ESPN began to roll the race report from the event, one that over forty-five million fans in that country alone had watched, Bryce clicked the off button on the remote and reached for another Heineken from the bar. It had been a long week and a long race, and he was beat. With F1's plainclothes security stationed outside his door, Bryce called it a night. He fell asleep in the chair before taking another sip of his beer.

Just past midnight, a loud knock at his door woke him.

"Bryce, it's Jack – we need to talk."

Bryce rubbed the sleep from his eyes, recognized that

Madigan sounded as if he'd been drinking, and wondered to himself what the hell couldn't wait until the morning. The two security staffers who had just come on shift looked to Bryce to make sure he was okay and the visitor was welcome. Madigan was still wearing an All Access Pass but it was late and he *was* drunk.

"Come on in," Bryce said in a frustrated tone as he gestured for Madigan to enter.

With a nod and a smile, Bryce closed the door and followed Madigan from the marble foyer into the living room. When his guest turned to face him, his expression let Bryce know there was a big problem.

"What's up Jack?"

Madigan turned away and took a seat on a white leather sofa and suggested Bryce might want to sit down as well.

"You should have told me what you had planned out in the desert, Bryce. You should have told me!"

Bryce was tired and was trying to clear his thoughts so he could understand what the problem really was. *Whatever this is, it could have waited until morning*, he thought.

"Joan and I were having an affair," Madigan blurted out. "I was falling in love with her."

Bryce was even more confused now and tilted his head to show it.

"Who the hell's Joan?"

"Nitro, you dumb bastard. You killed Joan Myers. Not only that, you killed not one but two CIA agents. What the fuck!"

Bryce stood up, walked into the master bedroom,

and then returned with a small device in his hand that resembled a TV remote. He walked directly to Madigan and waved the device from his visitor's head to his toes.

"You think I'm wired?" Madigan asked with surprise.

Bryce stared at this friend and, after a long pause, shook his head to indicate he didn't. "You know the drill, Jack." He tossed the device on the sofa and took a seat in the matching chair across from him. "But for all we know, the CIA could have put a bug *on* you at some point tonight, if they are here and suspect something of us. You know that's how they work. If they are listening, I guess we're proper fucked now as they say back in the Midlands."

"Let's talk through this. But I would prefer to do it when we're back across the border in the good old USA."

Madigan shook his head, indicating he wanted to talk *now*. Bryce leaned in and grabbed a bottle of water from a service tray on the coffee table between them. Madigan pulled a beer from the ice bucket.

"First off, you should have told me about you and Nitro, about Joan. I had no idea. I can't say I'm sorry I got the CIA off my ass, off *our* asses, for a while but I am sorry I hurt you. You know that's the last thing I'd ever do – if I had known. How long has this been going on?"

Bryce watched Madigan's eyes as he spoke fondly of the woman, recalling how they'd become friends, kindred spirits traveling the world. As things do, one thing led to another. Whenever she came to a race she'd sneak into his hotel room and back in the states they had met in Vegas, Miami, and New York. He remembered how much fun they'd had together when he took her skiing in Boone, North Carolina one weekend.

"She kept an apartment in Arlington – Virginia, not Texas," Madigan continued. "But she lived out of a suitcase like we do. No family, no friends, just work and people she knew around the world."

"But why did you keep that from me Jack – we're friends – partners in crime for Christ's sake. If neither of you were in relationships why hide it from me?"

Madigan chugged down his beer. "She said it was against CIA policy to sleep with operatives and if she got caught they could fire her for it."

"I thought that's what spies did," Bryce said sounding surprised. "Sounds like they have lives much like racers do – traveling a sometimes lonely road, risking your life." The two sat quietly, lost in their thoughts until Bryce sat forward.

"Listen, let's talk more about this when we're awake and in a better environment. I was surprised Gunn accepted the team-building, camaraderie bullshit I threw at him when I asked him to do Baja with us. When I told Pete what we were doing, with them coming along, he gave me that shit-eating grin he has, you know the one, and the plan was hatched. He's always had my back. When he learned these two had a gun to it, he was there when I needed him."

Madigan sat quietly on the sofa, his eyes closing slightly.

Bryce walked back into the bedroom and returned with a blanket he'd pulled from the closet. Madigan was emotionally drained and needed sleep. Once Bryce threw the blanket on him, the man relaxed and closed his eyes. Bryce turned out the lights and walked to his friend, slowly taking the beer bottle from his grasp.

As he headed back to his bed, he heard his friend whisper something.

"We're not done talking about this, I hope you know that."

Bryce turned, his silhouette set by the bright lights coming from behind him. "I know, bud, I know. Like I said earlier, I am *so* sorry."

It took only twenty minutes for their chauffeured SUV to drive from the hotel to the charter terminal at Mexico City's International Airport. Madigan had returned to his own room in the middle of the night, and Pete had rendezvoused with them in the lobby just after ten am. On arrival at the terminal, Bryce walked back to the black SUV that had followed them from the hotel and thanked the two F1 security agents for their help over the weekend.

After the three men checked in, they walked straight through the one-story building and exited onto the tarmac where a dozen or more executive jets were arriving, being serviced, or taxiing toward the adjacent runway. Not seeing anyone he knew, Bryce assumed most were remaining in Mexico for a few days before heading north for the F1 event at Circuit of the Americas in Austin. Madigan hadn't said a word to Pete or Bryce during the ride. He climbed aboard the Bombardier twelve-passenger jet and took a seat in the back of the plane. Bryce and Pete stood at the base of the stairs and spoke briefly.

"I know what to do," Pete told his nephew and then climbed aboard, taking a seat that faced Madigan.

Bryce greeted the flight attendant, an attractive young Mexican woman with long brown hair and dark complexion, jade green eyes. She wore the charter jet company's red and white colors. He slid his sunglasses down on his nose and whispered, "Coffee, *lots* of coffee please." She smiled.

He stepped into the cabin and saw the two in the back deep in conversation. They were talking, not arguing or fighting. *Well that's a good sign. Let's see how long it lasts.*

As he stepped into the cockpit to greet the pilot and co-pilot, he heard someone calling his name from down on the tarmac. He excused himself and stepped into the doorway. There, at the bottom of the steps, were three men – all flat-top haircuts, ex-military types. One held out a credential, and Bryce recognized the logo right away – CIA.

The F-word immediately came to mind but Bryce put on his best smile and went down the steps to greet him. After the introductions and handshakes, one of the agents gestured to a smaller jet sitting two spots over. Bryce saw a man climb down those steps and head toward them. He was dressed in an olive-green polo shirt and khakis, a flattop cut as well, only he didn't have a military or intelligence service air about him. He looked more like a beaten man.

As he arrived at Bryce's position they shook hands and spoke briefly before Bryce gestured for him to come aboard. When Madigan and Pete saw two of the strangers following Bryce down the aisle, they stopped their discussion and stood.

"Uncle Pete, Jack – this is Billy Myers, Joan's husband."

CHAPTER TWELVE

BRYCE RELISHED THE relative anonymity of living in Park City; there were so many locals, tourists, and celebrities in sunglasses and ball caps that he found he blended in easily and he desperately wanted to be there now. At a race track in the US, or *anywhere* else in the world, for that matter, he'd be recognized and mobbed. In his homeland NASCAR might have the biggest fan base. In the rest of the world, including Monte Carlo where he and many other drivers and celebrities maintained residency for tax purposes, F1 and soccer were the ultimate sports followed by hundreds of millions of passionate and devoted fans.

The visit with Billy Myers on the tarmac in Mexico City lasted twenty minutes. Bryce, Jack and Pete sat back and listened as Myers described how grief-stricken he was. He told them he and Joan had met in college and both pursued careers in government, she with the CIA and he close by at the FBI. The only problem was, a year after they had both settled in at their desks at Langley and Washington, Joan became a field agent and was out of the country more than she was in. They'd talked about having kids but that was put on hold again and then again because of the travel, he'd said.

Bryce listened, he'd lost loved ones in his life too, but he wanted desperately to be landing in Park City rather than hearing how the couple's relationship had taken off. Once all the words had been spoken, Bryce looked past the grieving husband's shoulder at the agent who had followed him onto the plane. It was time. Bryce stood up and a few seconds after Myers realized that he had, he did as well.

The man shook hands with Bryce, then Pete, and finally Madigan. "Thank you for telling me about her last days. It helps me to know that she was enjoying herself until the end."

Jack Madigan had sat stewing through it all but was able to act and display a calm exterior. The last thing he wanted to do was raise suspicions with a CIA agent sitting across from him in the jet while Jack's lover's husband droned on about his feelings for her, the hopes of a family, and a romantic rendezvous they had earlier that summer in Quebec City overlooking the St. Lawrence River in Canada.

Jack wanted these strangers the hell off the plane, he wanted to get up in the air headed for home, and he wanted to throw Pete Winters out of the plane at 42,000 feet, for killing the woman he'd loved. As for Bryce, while they'd grown tighter than most brothers over the years, he still felt betrayed. With only Austin, Brazil and then Abu Dhabi left on the schedule, perhaps it was time for a change.

Circuit of the Americas, COTA, is a massive racing facility located in southeastern Texas, between Austin and Houston. Bryce had great affection for the track. Not just because it was the only U.S. stop on the global tour, and not because it was the site of Bryce's first podium in F1.

His hero 1978 F1 champion Mario Andretti - the man whose mark he was trying to beat, had opened the track in 2012. This was a race Bryce wanted to win just about more than anything. Covering the 3.4 miles in just ninety seconds, Bryce and the rest of the competitors reached speeds of over 200 miles per hour. On the flight from Mexico City to Park City, the itinerary provided for a quick turnaround at Phoenix to let Pete Winters catch his commercial flight home to Burlington. And Madigan hopped off for his ride back to Charlotte. Bryce had asked both of them to cancel their plans and continue on with him to Utah to spend a few days decompressing and talking through what had happened in Baja.

Pete hadn't said a word to Madigan after he found out what his second target had meant to him. He'd placed his right hand on Madigan's shoulder and shook his head slowly with regret. Madigan had tensed at first there in the jet, but a few deep breaths had deflated some of the tension - *some* of it. Madigan had been first to disembark and it was then that Bryce told Pete to give it time.

"His issue isn't with you Pete, it's with me."

With wheels up just ten minutes later, Bryce sat back and watched the golden-brown terrain of Arizona as the jet headed north to his American home and three days of peace and quiet. Early morning hikes down the quiet streets and hills close to his home and the cool mountain air and orange glow in the horizon reminded him of his years back home in Vermont. He stopped to admire the sliver of moon still shining off in the distance, only to look further down the street to see a bull moose, six feet tall at the shoulders and all 1,000 pounds of him out for a morning stroll, too. That had been another big reason for moving here.

Only one thing was keeping him from relaxing though. It was the question that kept popping up in his head. *When*, he kept thinking, *when will the CIA come knocking again?*

Texas. On Friday morning before the first practice session at COTA, Bryce made himself another coffee. He listened to BBC News on the satellite TV feed, waiting for Max Werner to arrive for their meeting. The motor coach had made the drive up from Mexico City without issue, except for one checkpoint. Two Policía Federal -Mexican Federal police officers – had insisted on coming aboard to inspect for undeclared passengers and anything out of the ordinary. It turned out that all they really wanted was to pose for a photo inside an F1 driving champion's rig, and make off with a few souvenir ball caps. The coach driver offered these to them, including some team t-shirts, to assure a smooth inspection.

At the track, this was D-Day, decision day, and Bryce was anxious to deliver the news and get out on the circuit to chase a championship. Werner had arrived, on time as usual. After exchanging their customary pleasantries Bryce got right to it. He told Max that he intended to win his second driving championship. The ability to clinch it was within reach that weekend if Bryce finished just nine positions ahead of his only rival at this point, Tony Bishop. But then he dropped the bomb and said that when he climbed out of the car after the last race of the season, Abu Dhabi, as long as he'd won the championship, he would announce his retirement from the sport.

"This makes no sense to me, Bryce," Werner protested. "I know you and love you like a son. What the hell is the matter with you? Why settle on two titles when your destiny clearly is to win many more. You're too young to quit. You have no wife or family pulling at you to stop and spend more time with them. What is this? I don't understand?"

Bryce spent the next ten minutes trying to convince his friend – the man who had helped him come all this way since their chance encounter in New York, years before.

Werner wasn't buying it.

"Are you signing with another team? Is that what's going on here?" Werner charged in frustration.

"That's never crossed my mind and I never would, Max. I just want to finish this season with a second title, give ole Mario a call to thank him for the inspiration, and then start cultivating the next American champions.

"Bullshit!" Werner swore. Without uttering another word he stormed out of the motor coach.

Bryce was disappointed he hadn't been able to convince him that this was what he really wanted, needed, to do. He also understood Werner's frustration that the big sponsors – global companies with huge advertising budgets and keen to have Bryce represent them – would need to be put off.

A knock at the door let Bryce know it was time to head for the garage. As he stepped down onto the asphalt, he greeted Jack Madigan, whose temperament had been shifted from still pissed-off to one of concern when he had passed a steaming Max Werner just a few minutes earlier. Bryce stood quietly for a moment, looking at his friend's face.

Madigan shook his head and slowly slid his sunglasses down a bit to reveal his eyes. "We need to sort this out Bryce, maybe after Abu Dhabi. But for now, let's just get to work."

From that point on, the weekend went nearly as perfectly as Bryce could have wished. There weren't any CIA agents sitting in his coach each time he boarded, he'd won the pole in qualifying, the stands were packed with excited race fans, a global audience of over 415 million people had tuned into watch the event, and Bryce finally won his homeland's Grand Prix.

Bishop had been a pest the entire race, though. Relentlessly trying to overtake his rival, refusing to give in and let Bryce take the title before the next stop on the circuit - Brazil – a track where Bishop had dominated the last two years. Uncharacteristically, Werner did not greet Bryce after the podium ceremonies and the playing of America's national anthem.

To his surprise, Bryce learned that Werner hadn't stayed for the race. He had left via helicopter right after the five red lights above the grid were switched off to signal the start. Late that night, after the crowds had gone and Madigan and Bryce were the last ones standing in the motor coach after the post-race party, Bryce suggested Jack accompany him to Las Vegas in the morning.

"They're testing at The Strip," he said, excited at the chance to see some of the fastest race cars on the planet.

"Let me sleep on it," Madigan said.

But, by nine the next morning, both men were showered, dressed and boarding a jet headed west to Nevada. Neither of them spoke much during the ride, opting instead to watch a movie, nap, or stare through a window most of the way.

At least he got on the plane, Bryce thought, *it's a start.* Bryce had decided to give Madigan a very wide berth, but he also wanted him to know how different things would have been if he'd only known about the relationship. They operated in a fast-paced, noisy world and Vegas would be no different. Soon they would need earplugs. But, for now, the relative quiet inside the cabin was a good thing.

Formula One cars have a distinct sound. Over the decades a variety of engine designs have produced high-pitched screams and whines, but in recent years they've become a bit less ear shattering – if such a thing exists when it comes to the sounds of a racetrack. The technology behind these exotic machines is stuff that space shuttles and weapon systems are made of. The sound of acceleration, especially as they shift up through the gears, most regard as a thing of beauty.

Conversely, while the race cars known as Top Fuel and Funny Cars are technological marvels in a much different type of competition, their sound is far from symphonic – perhaps regarded more as bombastic – as in a bomb going off. Standing anywhere near one of these cars when they accelerate will shake your chest, deafen your hearing, and alert your nose to something special in the air – sweet nitromethane.

Once Bryce and Madigan arrived at McCarran International in Vegas, they rode the half hour across I-15, passing the new NFL stadium and the dozens of massive casinos before seeing the signs for Nellis Air Force Base and finally Las Vegas Motor Speedway. The Strip, the dragstrip portion of the LVMS facility, had hosted a National Hot Rod Association, NHRA, drag race the day before. Many of the top teams had remained there to test. With only one race left on *their* schedule – the World Finals in Pomona, California—the racers were focused and Bryce had no intention of interrupting them. He and Jack took seats in the empty grandstands and watched, their ears plugged with the same orange foam pieces he and Uncle Pete had worn years before when hunting to put food on the table back in New England.

After the first car thundered past, Bryce shook his head and uttered the f-word under his breath.

Bryce felt Madigan tap his shoulder once and then a second time.

"We'll go say hi to Force and Capps and the rest when they're done," he said to Madigan, who seemed more interested in talking to other mechanics than watching cars scream by – reaching 320 miles per hour on a 1,000 feet straightaway in just under four seconds.

He felt Madigan tap him again. Frustrated, he turned quickly to see Madigan holding his phone up for Bryce to read the breaking news.

WERNER DROPS WINTERS; SIGNS
BISHOP TO THREE-YEAR DEAL

CHAPTER THIRTEEN

BRAZIL. Most people might think of Carnival, the 2016 Summer Olympics, Rio, or the massive 100' tall statue of Christ the Redeemer that stands on the summit of Mount Corcovado, looking down upon Rio de Janeiro and the more than seven million people who live in the region. For racers, Brazil is recognized as the birthplace of one of racing's most successful and beloved drivers, the late Ayrton Senna.

The Brazilian who won three F1 driving championships had died as a result of injuries sustained in a crash while leading the 1994 San Marino Gran Prix in Italy. During that same weekend in Northern Italy, another driver was also killed and another gravely injured. As Bryce's ten-hour flight from Dallas to Sao Paolo landed at just past nine in the morning, he gazed out the window from his seat in first class and thought of Senna, one of his idols.

Time, and the throngs of mourning fans who flocked each race weekend to Senna's grave not far from the Autódromo José Carlos Pace – Interlagos - had never allowed

Bryce to visit and pay his respects. At Imola each year, Bryce always went to the spot where Senna struck the concrete wall, suspension parts crashing through his protective helmet and fatally wounding him. He remembered watching the accident live on television and turning it off when he realized one of his heroes was surely gone.

Maybe I can get there this time, he thought. *I may never be back here again.*

As the jet taxied to the gate, Bryce thought of the career choice he had made. He was glad he didn't have a wife or children whose hearts he could destroy if he were ever taken from them. Race cars, private jets, and helicopters all crash. He'd had moments like this before and considered the loved ones of the people the CIA directed him to terminate. As the jet came to a stop, he thought of the look on Billy Myers face as he spoke of the woman he loved, now gone forever.

Maybe the CIA will forget about me, he thought – he hoped.

An escort greeted him as he stepped onto the jetway that led him down a set of exterior steps to a waiting armored SUV. Kidnapping was a huge concern and the track and race organizers treated the F1 drivers with the utmost care and shrouded them with armed security 24/7. A short time later, Bryce fell onto the king-size bed at the five-star Unique hotel, named for its truly remarkable architectural design. Thursday might be media day at Interlagos but there was so much news surrounding Werner's announcement of a driver change for the coming season that Bryce opted to forgo the excitement and focus on sleep and mental preparation for the race. Bishop would be on his best game. There was little time for mistakes and less time to make up for any. Abu Dhabi would be their last stand, Winters versus Bishop, if the championship wasn't decided this weekend in South America.

Bryce's eyes opened long after dark. He got up to make coffee, ordered room service, checked his phone for emails and messages, and then sat down in front of the 80" flat-screen TV in the suite's living room.

He and Werner had not communicated since their meeting in Austin. Bryce thought it was time for them to talk, to at least clear any bad air and wish each other well. Judging from the way Werner had handled the situation though, with a major announcement to the press that had blindsided him, Bryce stopped the text he had begun and tossed his phone on the bed. *Fuck 'em.* In his moment of anger and frustration, unable to tell his friend the truth, he vented for a moment and then sat quietly waiting for his food to arrive.

He turned on the news and saw images of the newly elected U.S. president and smiled. Here Bryce was, the proud American representing his country in international competition but compromised by one of his own government's clandestine agencies. If he won the title, surely the new president would invite him to the White House for a photo op and to offer congratulations, just as his predecessor had. If he could get a moment alone, perhaps he could ask the Commander-in-Chief to call off his CIA dogs.

Now, of course, all he had to do was win.

Weather often played a part in racing, and the Brazilian GP wouldn't disappoint. The forecast was hot and humid, very humid but dry. The temperature in Bryce's private lounge at the track was near boiling.

"That was a chicken-shit move, Max, and you know it," Bryce charged.

Max had known Bryce for years, had spotted his raw talent and grabbed him up, trained him, refined him, and gave him the experience and the other elements required to win championships, all to their mutual benefit. Not many people could talk to Werner in such a manner. While his business acumen was outstanding, Max—like so many other well-moneyed power players—also had an ego and a temper to go with it.

"You left me no choice and you know that. The sponsors were sitting at the table, documents ready to be signed, and laptops set to transfer the initial fifty million euros to my account. All we needed was to write down your name as the designated driver. But you couldn't give me one good reason for not moving forward. You weren't being honest with me. The first time I think I've ever felt that way – ever –so I reacted in kind. Live with it but don't take that tone with me or I'll park that fucking car and send the team home on holiday until the first of the year!"

Bryce knew that was a bluff. Werner wanted this second F1 championship almost as much as he did. Nothing was going to get in the way of that. Plus, showing his new sponsors what a wild card he could be might scare them even before the honeymoon had begun.

Werner had seemed too agitated to sit and discuss anything. He remained near the doorway, leaning back against the wall but tensing to a stance whenever he spoke. Bryce got up from his leather chair and walked to his friend.

"The damage is done, naming my replacement before the season is over. I'll just need to deal with it. But Bishop? Of all the bastards you could have signed, you had to do it with the only driver who hates me as much as I hate him. What the fuck, Max."

"The sponsors wanted to make an announcement then and there, and I needed a driver. Would you turn down two hundred million euros?"

Bryce shook his head. No, he wouldn't have.

Max walked toward Bryce and stopped two feet from him. "Are you sick? Are you dying? That's the only way any of this could possibly make any sense. What is it you aren't telling me?"

Bryce thought for a moment and made sure to not let his expression or his eyes give anything away. He had always known that for every action there is a reaction. He wondered, vindictively, if he shouldn't piss on the Werner-Bishop parade right there in the media center in front of the entire world.

"Yeah, that's it," he began. "I'm dying and have a year to live. And after I told you the news you found a new sponsor and replaced me without even blinking. Yeah, that's what I'll go tell the media right now. The sponsorship will be tarnished. Fans will shit on the companies that couldn't wait to announce their new driver and partnership. I'll say I asked them to wait until the season was finished and allow me to fade quietly into my last days, but they said sod off!"

Bryce had hit a home run and he knew it. He watched as Max's eyes grew as big as cue balls with surprise. Bryce prepared himself for the next sentence. It would show him who Max really was. Care more for his friend and driver, or more for his new sponsor?

"You wouldn't do that, Bryce. That's not you," Werner charged. Bryce stepped to the closed door and opened it.

"Get out," he demanded, loud enough for the dozens of people in the hallway to hear.

Formula One races typically offer practice sessions for the drivers on Fridays followed by an elimination-style qualifying session on Saturdays. All the cars try to move on from Q1 to Q2 and only the fifteen fastest can do that. From Q2 to Q3, only the fastest ten cars will now have a shot at winning the pole. A handful, but usually only three or four, have a real shot at the pole or even the front row.

The start is everything. Passing, depending on the car, the track, and the driver you are trying to pass or hold off—all of that can make a huge difference in the outcome of the race. Many a heart has been broken in the first turn of the first lap, while a great start can propel you to a win, a new contract, a championship, and all the money and accolades that come with it.

On Sundays, drivers strap in for a formation lap around the track and then stop in the marked start position on the grid. Five red lights above the grid are lit one by one then they are turned off simultaneously, and the drivers race from a standing start into the first corner. Usually within ninety minutes, the cars that have survived the competition and occasional mayhem will pass over their starting grid positions one final time to take the checkered flag.

At some events, before drivers are strapped in to take

their formation lap, they talk with their engineers, sponsors, celebrities and officials until the announcement is made to clear the area. Rarely do drivers, even teammates, chat out on the grid. But this morning at Interlagos, Tony Bishop made a point of finding Bryce Winters. As their team assistants politely kept the media and others away, the two drivers leaned against the concrete pit wall and exchanged words.

"Max says you might be sick," Bishop began. "But I know what you are up to. You want to use that as an excuse when you lose the championship to me and go home with your tail between your legs."

Bryce smiled. His sunglasses hid his eyes from Bishop, not allowing him to know if he'd struck a nerve. Bishop continued. Getting under a driver's skin, getting into his head, could cripple some. In champions, it makes them tougher, meaner, better, giving them extra motivation to win.

"Max doesn't know this," Bishop said, "but as part of the personal services contract I signed with the new sponsors, if I win the championship *this year* they will pay me a five-million euro bonus. They don't want to start the new season hoping they have a championship coming. They want to advertise and use me as THE Formula One champion."

Bryce smiled. "Don't fuck the team you'll be with next year and take the title from them by taking me out. If you want to win the title, then win it by driving a better race here and in Abu Dhabi."

Bryce could read Bishop's eyes. It was clear he had never considered the ramifications of pissing off the team he'd be driving for next year. His only thoughts had been about the title, the bonus, and beating his archrival.

"Don't forget this either, Tony," Bryce added as he stood up from the wall and turned to put less than a foot between them. "I can knock you or block you, too. If you're going to beat me then go for it, but if you race dirty then it's on."

The fact that these two were now nose to nose on the grid wall had gone viral through team radios and social media. A crowd was forming around them and their assistants had lost all hope of holding back onlookers. Media called out questions. Fans shouted for photos. Organizers and race officials converged as did team principals. Before the confrontation could escalate any further it had been diffused, the fighters separated until the bell. At exactly noon local time, the red lights shut off and the race was on.

CHAPTER FOURTEEN

Diversify or Die. The top oil producers in the Arabian Gulf - at least those who understood and agreed with the slogan - took steps to turn their countries into tourist destinations. As global demand for oil fluctuated and the frustration and intolerance for high crude prices escalated they knew they needed to act in order to survive. If people from all over the world flocked to the deserts of Nevada to play in Las Vegas, then Dubai, Bahrain, and Abu Dhabi knew what direction to take.

Parts of those cities began to resemble Beverly Hills with its mansions and high-end shopping and dining. Watersports on the Gulf took off, and someone actually built an indoor, very cold, skiing attraction. Now locals and tourists alike could take to the slopes in spite of the 120° F temperature outside.

Motorsports also became a big draw. Tracks rose up and secured dates on the Formula One calendar, at a $40-million per race price tag. But with only twenty or so dates available each calendar year, even more money or many other things can go into securing such a date.

With the unrelenting desert heat of Abu Dhabi and intense competition that had come down to the last race of the season, it seemed fitting that it take place at the Yas Marina Circuit with ample water to cool things. Two weeks earlier, in Brazil, Tony Bishop had driven a clean race as Bryce had suggested. But Bishop's teammate hadn't. With three laps to go, Dickie Jones, a back-marker and lackluster performer since he'd signed on to Bishop's team, knocked Bryce off the track in what he later claimed was, "just a racing accident." Bishop had taken the lead by a mere five points, and that put Bryce in pursuit mode.

NASCAR's Dale Earnhardt, Sr., had been regarded as The Intimidator for bumping bumpers and fenders and pushing his foes into making mistakes or finally, once frustrated, just moving them out of the way entirely. In open wheel racing like Formula One, that's a bit riskier. Every item on an F1 car may be made of space-age materials that cost a fortune to produce, but a wing meant to direct and force air down to increase weight on the tires for better adhesion, steering, and acceleration, can become fragile when confronting a spinning wheel and tire going into a tight turn at 100 mph.

Bryce had a reputation for being relentless in pursuit. He'd fill an opponent's mirrors, pushing hard turn after turn, lap after lap until his prey either grew weary and made a mistake or simply dove into a turn too fast and washed out, allowing Bryce to strike. But today would be different.

Jones had just allowed his car to lose its position by letting centrifugal forces carry him up into Bryce. Both cars ended out onto the gravel meant to slow errant cars that have gone off track. They sat spinning their tires in the stones as Bishop flew past to take the victory.

Once the two drivers had climbed out of their cars they were escorted to a waiting ambulance for a quick examination by the medical team, standard procedure whenever there was a crash. The two might have climbed into the ambulance together, helmets still strapped on, but when TV cameras followed the vehicle into the paddock they captured Bryce exiting the ambulance first and, moments later, Jones was seen holding what seemed to be a bloody white cloth to his face. Later, before the media, Bryce said he knew nothing about how Jones could have injured himself. "Racing accident I guess."

The Abu Dhabi GP takes the green flag nearing dusk, and the race continues on into the night under the lights, a soothing break from the intense sun and heat of the region. Bryce had flown to his home in Monte Carlo from Sao Paolo. He took the ten days between the events to relax, train, and sit quietly on the 120' motor yacht he kept in the marina each year during the Monte Carlo Grand Prix. Other times the vessel named *Lucky* might be found with Bryce and friends aboard off the coast of Mykonos, Capri, or Ibiza. Now in Abu Dhabi, he was ready to race.

Rather than stay at a five-star hotel, of which there were dozens, he opted to rent a yacht much like the one he had just left on the Mediterranean. He would stay on board to avoid the crowded downtown. He hadn't spoken with Max Werner since their confrontation in Brazil, but his one-million-dollar fee for November, the last payment of his contract, had been received in his bank account, so he wouldn't have to chase him for it.

Bryce had talked with Jack Madigan once or twice, but only about car-related issues. Now, with time for the final formation lap of the year coming close, Bryce had just strapped on his helmet and was preparing to climb aboard his Werner Special one last time. He felt a tap on the back of the head and turned to see Madigan standing close.

"Come to wish me good luck one last time, Jack?" Bryce said sentimentally but the look in the man's eyes signaled something different.

"No. I came to tell you I saw Pete twenty minutes ago and he was in one of those moods."

"Holy shit!" Bryce uttered and pulled away from the crewman who had taken his arm to guide him to the car. Helmets might save lives, but the restricted field of vision can hamper simple movement at times.

"You mean Baja mode?" Bryce asked as he moved close enough to Madigan that his helmet bumped his head.

"Two minutes, Bryce, we need to move," the crewman said in a loud voice.

"You've got to find him, Jack, you have to stop him!"

Madigan stared into Bryce's eyes. "You didn't arrange this?" Madigan asked. Bryce shook his head no. Jack smacked him on the helmet for luck and headed for the garage.

Madigan expected to find Pete, perched in a sniper's stance, hidden somewhere around the 3.3 mile track.

Locating him would be nearly impossible until he shifted back into Army Ranger mode and considered where *he* would take a shot from if he had to.

He brought up the track diagram on his smartphone and stared at it, enlarging one spot, shaking his head no, enlarging another, no again. Finally, he hit on a yes. The marina – Pete had to be on one of the yachts!

Trying to move as swiftly as possible without drawing attention to himself, Madigan worked his way through the maze that was the team's garage area, past the computer center where the team would monitor everything on the car and the driver for the duration of the event. Feeds would be shared with the staff back in the Midlands of England and split-second decisions made when even the hint of something going sour was detected.

As he exited through the back he swerved to the left and to the right to avoid the hundreds of fans, celebrities, and the dignitaries wearing the customary flowing robes and keffiyehs held by agals, a square cotton scarf over their heads held in place with a cord, now headed for their grandstand seats or VIP suites. He heard the cars fire up on the grid for the formation lap. In minutes they'd take the green flag and be flying past the marina. Down into the pedestrian tunnel just past the fan zone, under the track and now out by the West Grandstand, he turned to get his bearings as the cars drove past. It was then that he realized he'd screwed up, bad.

Trying to get from his location behind two sets of grandstands, and then a very long walk along the water to the dozens of yachts resting in the marina, he'd taken a wrong turn. He checked the map again and then doubled back, down into the tunnel, emerging just as Bishop and Bryce began their chase for the win and the championship.

The cars were now screaming by, fans on their feet cheering, and Madigan was running out of time. He back-tracked toward the paddock and snaked his way left and then right and left again until the line of motor yachts docked at the marina were in clear view. He tried not to run but picked up the pace, almost to a jog. His all-access credentials flew back and forth on the lanyard around his neck. If anyone tried to stop him he'd just say Bryce left something on his boat.

Who is he going to take a shot at? Madigan wondered. Would Pete take out a driver or just disable a car? Would he nail Jones for pushing Bryce off course in Brazil or perhaps take out one of Bishop's tires to cost him a lap, if not more? *If he leaves lead – leaves a bullet anywhere or someone sees him then in time, we could all be found out.* "Damn it Pete!" he said out loud. Suddenly, he slowed his pace. He needed time to think.

Pete is Bryce's uncle, not mine. If he shoots anyone or anything here and gets caught it's on Bryce, not me, not the team. Maybe. He stopped walking and turned back to look at the track. *Bryce ordered the hit on the two CIA agents in Mexico and Pete carried it out. If they both go down there's nothing on me - unless one of them talks.*

The sounds coming from the cars on track were all he could hear. His other senses picking up a slight smell of rubber from a smoking tire mixed with just a hint of race engine exhaust. Madigan had lived in this world back into his teenage days in North Carolina and loved it, until now. Here he was chasing down a sniper, a known killer, at a Formula One race on the Arabian Gulf, 7500 miles from home. He watched for two laps as the cars raced by and could see Bryce was in the lead but with Bishop hot on his tail.

With everyone on the property focused on the race, Madigan turned back toward the marina and saw the green glow of a laser brushing across the path in front of him. He focused. He'd found him - third boat from the right. There was Pete, standing on an open bridge, two levels above the deck, enthusiastically waving for him to come join him.

Madigan paused and then headed for him. The yacht was a beauty. The two men standing guard at the base of the gangway checked his credentials, which included access to this vessel – Bryce's rental. He rushed on board, saying he didn't want to miss a lap. Once up on the bridge, he tapped Pete's shoulder and they got into it.

"This isn't Baja, Pete," Madigan shouted over the sounds of the track. "You can't take a shot – at anyone!"

Pete looked around the bridge, laughed, and leaned in to speak into Madigan's ear.

"What are you talking about, Jack? I'm just here keeping Bishop and Jones honest. If either of them interfere with Bryce tonight, I'll give them a green shot through the visor and set it right for our boy." He held up the green laser pen, the one he'd used to paint Madigan minutes earlier. "You actually thought I was going to shoot someone from up here?"

Madigan nodded. "Yes – and when I told Bryce you were on the property he said to stop you."

Pete laughed again and turned his focus back to the

action on the track. He slipped the laser pen into his shirt pocket and placed a set of noise-cancelling headphones back into place. Like Werner and the crews in the pits and those back in England, Pete could listen to communications with their driver. He related that Bryce was happy with the way the car was running and, as was customary, spoke very little as lap after lap sped by.

A lap later, two cars collided on the track and brought out a full-course yellow and the safety car to pace the field while the mess from the incident was cleaned up. Pete took off the headphones, but almost lost his balance as he sat down on the captain's chair and unscrewed the top from a bottle of water.

With still waters beneath them Madigan wondered if Pete had had a beer or two already, which was very uncharacteristic of him during a race.

"This isn't Baja, Jack, but it isn't America either. How the hell would I have gotten a damn rifle here for Christ's sake?"

Madigan smiled and sat down beside him.

"On the water, Pete. We both know how these things work. You probably motored in here on a boat, maybe in from Dubai. I'll bet you fished for Barracuda or sailfish in the gulf for cover, showed your ID here, got on board with a small bag, and was planning on reversing the move after the race ended."

Madigan looked around and then continued.

"If it were me, I'd have taken a boat across from Doha. There's a lot of retired military personnel, assets, private operators – friends of mine, and boats of all kinds there. Long guns can break down and fit into tiny bags these days. Like that little black one sitting against the wall behind you." With the short caution ending, the sound of the 19 Formula One cars still in the race cranked up again, and Pete placed the headphones back on to follow along. Madigan sat back and focused there, too. Before long it would all be over.

CHAPTER FIFTEEN

ABU DHABI. PODIUMS at race tracks are set up much like Olympic award ceremonies; top center step for the winner, second place stand is lower and to the winner's right, and third place to the left. At the Yas Marina circuit, Bryce Winters proudly stepped to the winner's stand and waved across the track to the massive crowd cheering him from the main grandstand. Then, his heart sank as he heard the announcer proclaim the second-place finisher, Tony Bishop of Canada, as the new Formula One World Champion.

Bryce had driven his heart out, but there were only so many points to be claimed. When the checkered flag waved the season, and Bryce's dream of taking a second title, were over. Once the third-place driver, Juan Valdez from Mexico, was introduced it was time for the customary musical interlude.

After the anthem for the United States of America was played, recognizing the race winner's homeland, the three on the podium stood with ball caps at their sides or over their hearts, as God Save The Queen sounded – Britain's national anthem, played for the U.K.–based Werner team. The dignitaries from the United Arab Emirates presented trophies, the corks from the faux champagne flew, and the three drivers drenched one another and then turned it to their crews standing a level below on pit road. In respect for local customs, non-alcoholic bubbly would have to do.

For the first time ever, Bryce couldn't locate his friend and teammate in the cheering crowd. Valdez pulled Bryce away from the rail and guided him back to center stage for the traditional photo taken of the top three finishers. All three smiled, waved to the fans and cameras, and the global feed broadcast nearly everywhere.

As their pose broke down, Bryce removed the yellow-and-red Werner Industries hat one of the team's media people had handed him before he had taken the stage. He stepped to the rail again. Holding the hat in front of him, he pointed to the Werner name, placed that hand on his chest, and took a slight bow before throwing the hat like a Frisbee into the crowd. His time with Werner was now over.

He'd ignored Bishop on the podium but came upon him in the staging area at the base of the steps. Bishop's people were cleaning him up from his bubbly shower before he faced the press as the new World Champion. Bryce stepped in front of him, extending his hand to offer his congratulations. To his surprise, Bishop seemed to return a sincere smile and a word of thanks just as the series and organizer's staffers jumped in to affix the two drivers with microphones for the post-race press conference.

"No thanks, I'm done. The spotlight's on the champ," Bryce said softly, waving off the mike. Without another word, he left the area and headed back to the garage. There, he spent the next twenty minutes shaking hands and thanking every one of the forty-seven men and women who traveled the world with the team and had made his past championship and the six victories of this season possible.

A few tears were shed, handshakes turned into heartfelt embraces, and when it was time to go he called out to everyone, "Hey – I plan on continuing the tradition, one last time. Invitations go out soon for my Christmas Party in the Midlands. Hope to see you all there next month!" And then, he walked away. He'd never discussed the Werner announcement with any of them nor they with him. Business was business. Time to move on.

The two security staffers who had shadowed him the entire weekend continued to do so. Bryce quickly changed into a red polo and blue jeans and black Skechers, grabbed a black Pirelli tire hat and kept his head down so he could b-line it to the boat. He wasn't in the mood for a party and he'd left his trophy, a shining vase made of silver and gold with the crew. He'd retrieve it back in England. Something special had come to an end and could never be replaced.

While he processed his mixed emotions, thoughts returned to Pete and Jack Madigan. Where the hell where they? Having managed to get all the way to his gangway with only four people stopping him for selfies or an autograph – most everyone else was still gathered, no doubt, below the podium on the pit road to experience the crowning of a new champion. Those who missed out on the glory had all quietly found their way from it.

Bryce thanked his two shadows and said hi to the two

still standing watch at the yacht. Unsure whether Madigan had ever found Pete or where either of them might be he opted not to ask the guards.

"Nobody comes aboard!" he said in a tone that made it clear he was serious.

He texted Madigan and then Pete. No response from either. He called both; again no answer. After a quick, cool shower and change into shorts and a light blue Olympic Park t-shirt, he grabbed a beer from the fridge and took a seat on the tan, leather sofa that faced a massive flat-screen TV in the main salon. He turned the air conditioning down to 65° F – despite the shower and the brew he was still hot to the core. He was pissed at them both for not answering but even more so for distracting him from the significance of the evening. It was his last race with the man and the team who had helped propel him to great success and fortune. He'd won the race but lost the championship by fewer points than fingers on a hand, and he didn't have a care in the world – other than where the hell these two were.

It had been quite some time since he'd had any contact with the people who had leveraged him into doing their dirty work. Maybe they'd forgotten about him, he mused. After all, it was a government agency with people climbing career ladders and changing assignments. In the shuffle, maybe they'd simply lost interest or had forgotten him and he was now free of them once and for all.

He tried both phones again and then checked his watch. It was nearing midnight. After a long, hot race and a long, tiring season it was time to call it a night and start tomorrow's scheduled adventure at mid-morning. As the partying on some of the other yachts docked there subsided, the quiet finally came. He checked the BBC news feed, watched the sports headlines of him taking the race win but passing the champion's baton to Bishop. He felt a twinge of regret, and then helpless and resigned. He peeked out through the break in the window shade to confirm the security team was still there. Time for sleep, finally.

It might have been a minute after he pulled the covers up over him, the master bedroom now chilled to perfection when he heard it.

Someone or something was knocking banging, somewhere in the vessel.

❧

"I'm going to kill that son of a bitch," Madigan swore. He stood in front of the bar, downing his second beer and a shot of Jack Daniels. The bleeding from the gash over his left eye had finally stopped. "Damn it's freezing in here!"

Bryce and Madigan had been through a lot together, like brothers only without the occasional brotherly brawls. They'd seen the world, stood in victory lanes together celebrating wins at Indy, Daytona, Silverstone, and so many others historic tracks. But now, things were different. Bryce had made a decision Madigan couldn't forgive or forget. Pete Winters had killed Joan Myers, Nitro. The season was over and tonight Pete had done something just as unforgiveable, something Madigan could never let stand.

"He tased me. That bastard. We were on the bridge and I came down to take a leak. When I came out of the shitter the bastard tased me," he told Bryce.

"Seriously?" Bryce asked. "Pete did this?"

"When I wake up, he's got me hogtied and gagged on the bed. I got so pissed I fell off the damn thing, hit my head on the night table, and wound up where you found me. Did the prick shoot anybody?" Madigan asked. Bryce shook his head no.

"I don't know what he did or where he went, but I'm going to find that fuck and put a bullet in his head. No debate, no excuses, just a summary execution like he did to Joanie." Bryce grabbed a hand towel from the bathroom and moved to attend to Madigan's cut but Jack knocked his hand away.

He glared at Bryce. He knew what these words meant. It was over between them. Pete had gone too far, and Bryce had been a part of it.

"I don't know where he is." Madigan raged. "Hiding on this damn boat for all I know! But when I find him, Marine against Ranger, it's on. I'm not going to be a chicken shit from a distance with a sniper rifle either. I'm going to do it face to face." He drew a deep breath then shouted, "You hear me, Pete? You're a dead man!"

Bryce looked at his friend with regret. He'd lost Werner and now with these words, Jack. He knew that there was nothing he could do to fix this now. Someone was going to die.

"He's not on board, Jack."

"You better hope he isn't."

CHAPTER SIXTEEN

KRUGER NATIONAL PARK covers over 7500 square miles, perhaps a bit smaller than the state of New Jersey and is located in northeastern South Africa. Bryce had visited there three times, once after hiking the 19,000' Mount Kilimanjaro, a dormant volcano in Tanzania. He'd done the climb to draw attention through his media contacts to the lack of clean water in the region. His plan had been to push for contributions to a charity he'd learned of after his favorite NFL football team, the Philadelphia Eagles, had won the Super Bowl and a star player made the trek to drive awareness.

After an eight-hour flight from Abu Dhabi to Kruger's Mpumalanga International Airport, his favorite guide, an outgoing twenty-four- year-old local named Tommy, drove the 25 miles on decent roads to the Nkambeni Safari Camp near the park's Numbi Gate. The camp was spectacular, just as he had remembered it, with incredible views of the hills and plains of the region. Flowers were abundant, as were all the comforts his hosts provided. If you wanted to connect with nature and wildlife, it was here. You could hear an elephant's call or watch a giraffe pick leaves from a branch twenty feet overhead. Predators of all sorts were in abundance, too. Lions and leopards were plentiful and, despite everyone's assurances that the more dangerous animals kept away from the camp, Bryce never – ever was without a sidearm, his American-made .45-caliber Sig P220 at the ready.

"I don't hike where bears and mountain lions live without carrying this back home. Why the heck would I leave my gun there when the king of the jungle roams here, licking his chops and waiting to take a bite out of me?" he always reminded Tommy and his hosts at check in.

On this evening, as Bryce sat in his chair, rocking it back on its rear legs, he listened for a moment to the sounds of the wilderness and something man-made that he'd picked up on.

"Like I said," he shouted, "there are things out there can kill you, Uncle Pete. Big cats, buffalo, elephants, and what I came here specifically for this time – rhinos. Hell, most have claws, teeth, tusks or horns. The rest have size. But none of them have God-damned tasers!" He waited, hoping for a response.

"Come on out, Pete. I know you're back there." Bryce kept his focus on the view as the sun faded in the west. Before long, the sounds of night stalkers would replace those of the singing birds.

He could hear his uncle coming toward him but didn't move. As the chair beside his began to slide from the table, Bryce looked up and shook his head as Pete smiled and took a seat. They didn't speak except to order a round of beers – local brew Castle Lager for Pete and Heineken

0.0 non-alcoholic for Bryce, and then another, and then another.

After a bit, Pete finally broke the ice. "NA beer – why bother?" he asked, for perhaps the tenth time that year.

"Need to get up really early tomorrow. I want to be sharp as a tack, Pete," he replied. "When did you get in and what the hell are you doing here?"

"Just a few hours before you. Tommy came and got me. Made him promise he wouldn't spoil my surprise. Abu Dhabi to Doha and another stop then here. Didn't sleep a wink. I knew you'd be headed here after the race and I wanted to take another run at a water buffalo down south of us."

"Don't expect a pity party from me, you old bastard," Bryce said, only half-joking. "Jack told me what you had planned – to screw with those two assholes if they played dirty. I get that. I don't agree with it, but I get it. But why did you have to tase him and tie him up? What the fuck, Pete?"

His uncle leaned toward him. His expression was one Bryce didn't think he'd ever seen before. Considering Pete's recent behavior, post-Baja, he grew concerned.

"If I needed to put a shot in either of those pieces of shit, I would have. Jack would have tried to stop me. He might even have turned me over to the police to pay me back for Baja. Abu Dhabi isn't big on retired military like me playing with suppressed sniper rifles. I would have gone to prison forever."

Bryce listened but something was off. He pushed harder. "Pete, you know how I feel about you - you old coot," he added, "but we can't – I guess I have to say I can't keep doing this. It all started with us cleaning up messes, *your* messes. The CIA's had Jack and me by the balls because they caught us dumping bodies; they didn't know we were cleaning up after you. They've always thought Jack and I killed those shitheads. We agreed to work with them and keep up this charade to keep *you* out of jail, and this is how you repay us, Jack? One of these days you're going to get caught. Jack's done with the both of us. He's gone. The CIA might be gone, too. I haven't heard a damn thing from them since Baja. My point is—you have to stop killing people. I know they gave you a reason to, but every time you kill someone, we have to clean up the mess. You've jeopardized not just my career but also my freedom. Maybe *you* should work for the CIA and leave me out of it. Maybe it's time we told them it was you who did the killing." Pete shook his head, saying "But they've still got you dumping the bodies."

Pete Winters was as tough as nails and had taught his nephew well, stepping in for a father who was emotionally unfit to raise anything, let alone a young man. He'd always had intolerance for bad behavior and been in enough fist fights in high school, the Marines, bars, and parking lots whenever he felt someone was being wronged or abused, or unable to defend themselves. In Singapore he'd watched a rich punk, son of a wealthy banker push a girl around in an elevator. She got off, he didn't. The body was found in a laundry chute the next morning.

Pete rarely made a move on someone in Bryce's presence, but when someone made a move on Pete, Bryce used everything his uncle had taught him about fighting, and killing, and went from witness to accomplice as quickly as he drove. Bryce liked winning races more than anything but what he learned of himself, thanks to Pete, was he felt he had a purpose when delivering justice and helping people. The son of a policeman and raised by a Marine, it was in his blood.

Under the heavy yoke the CIA had placed on him, sometimes he delivered justice to a corrupt politician who enjoyed assaulting women, or a rich playboy who sold arms to bad nations, or the international drug kingpin who made a living ruining American lives. These were the same people who used their money, influence, and connections to party with the rich and famous. When the Formula One festivities came to town, they wanted in and when the CIA pointed out a target, Bryce always insisted on knowing why.

It wasn't always a death sentence though. Sometimes it was accepting an invitation to an exclusive affair where people would pose for photos and then identities could be discovered, fingerprints or even DNA retrieved. Once he attended a birthday party at the elegant Ritz Hotel in London. The CIA and England's MI6 used him as bait, hoping a Czech contract killer would attend his niece's extravagant birthday, unable to resist the chance to meet the special guest, an F1 champion.

Bryce refused to take out, to eliminate, as the CIA would say, someone who had children – that was non-negotiable. But a hit was much more palatable if he felt he was doing some good. What he hated about the CIA arrangement, *the only thing*, was that they had control over him, and that was nearly impossible to stomach. Bryce was a control freak, in control of his life behind the wheel at over 200 miles per hour, and everywhere else except with *this* arrangement. For his trio, Bryce had gone from helping Pete, then working for the CIA and needing Jack's help at times, then Pete had been called in to help them both but now Pete had gone too far.

"I don't think this is fixable, Pete. I think you're going to have to watch your back the rest of your life."

Pete smiled. Bryce already knew his uncle's response.

"Well, I could put the bastard out of his misery if he's still heartbroken over that woman. Guess he forgot when he was in deep that she forced him to kill people and was cheating on her husband. He sure can pick 'em. Reminds me of someone else I knew." Bryce didn't understand the last reference but that didn't matter now.

The sun was long gone now. Darkness swept over the camp. With no moon to be seen but an incredible blanket of stars surrounding them in the sky, Bryce said he wanted to walk a bit before turning in.

Pete stood up and gave Bryce a hug, tighter than the usual. "I love you, boy," he whispered in Bryce's ear and then broke off and headed for his cabin.

As Bryce stepped down onto the ground from the deck and began to walk away from the lights of the open dining room, he heard a movement behind him. It was Tommy, and he was carrying a rifle.

"Always watch your back, BW," he whispered when he caught up to Bryce, using the nickname the American didn't mind at all, at least not from him.

"You have mountain lions in Utah, yes?" he asked.

"Yep. People don't think they're out there, but they are. They're usually just too smart to be seen."

They kept walking, listening to the sounds of dark Africa.

"Same for leopards – all cats for that matter," Tommy continued. "I will stay behind you so you can enjoy your walk and the surroundings."

Bryce wouldn't hear of it and gestured for the guide to walk alongside him. They went one hundred fifty feet from the main building and stopped at one of the many bonfires the camp kept lit every night to ward off unwanted intruders. Bryce had done this many times before and came to a stop between two fires. All he could see was the darkness in front of him, his peripheral vision lit with the orange glow to his left and to his right. Then as his eyes adjusted, and he saw them he called Tommy in closer.

"I'll never forget the first time I saw the fire's reflection in a lion's eyes. It's primal."

The animals knew there was plenty of food, a buffet of tourists, guides, and camp employees just waiting to be taken in the dark, if it weren't for the damn fires. The camp knew, as well, an animal's tolerance for the flames. They never, ever allowed the bonfires to die out or to be moved a foot from where they were set 365 nights per year.

The next morning, Bryce had drunk a half-gallon of coffee before he'd gotten the energy to get moving and the clarity to engage the day. He hadn't seen or heard from Pete but figured if he wanted in on the day's plans, he'd turn up at some point. If not, that was fine. Bryce needed the space.

Racing season was over but he was exhilarated to set out with Tommy to meet up with the rangers of another sort – Kruger Park Rangers, who were assigned to the anti-poaching force. Today they expected to hunt down and capture a group they'd been chasing for weeks. The group was thought to be from Russia, well funded and very skilled in avoiding detection by drones, night vision technology, and anything else the force threw at them. Their treasure - Rhino tusks.

According to what Bryce had read in National Geographic, on the black market in South Africa, the horn of the white rhino sells for up to $3,000 a pound. But on Asian black markets it wholesales for 5 to 10 times that, and from there retail prices can go up astronomically. There's serious money in killing rhinos and cutting out their horns.

Elephants were in great jeopardy as well. Bryce had seen this firsthand on a previous trip. But today the focus would be on saving rhinos and instead of using technology to track the Russians the rangers would rely on one species of animal to save another – dogs. In some parts of the world not only are they regarded as man's best friend, but this particular breed of hunting dogs had been trained to smell out poachers and track them. Some risked being shot as the pack chased down their prey. But most times, when successful, they'd tree a poacher until the force could get there to bring them down and to justice.

And so it was that, after a full day in the African heat, Bryce found himself standing face-to-face with three poachers the dogs had chased down.

"I think putting these three in jail is too good for them," he suggested to the rangers as he stared at their captives with contempt.

"Why don't we have some fun, give them a taste of

their own medicine." Tommy had seen Bryce in action before, taking a gun butt to the head of a poacher that had killed an elephant, and even more needlessly its calf.

"I say we cut *their* noses off and leave them out here without weapons. If they survive the night, we set them free." One of the rangers played along and pulled a knife from its sheath with a shine as bright as his smile. He held up the knife, almost a mini-machete in size, sleek blade on one side, the other serrated for those really hard to cut through moments.

Two of the poachers knew they were screwed. Bryce could see it in their eyes. For his part, he was smart though – wearing a Kruger Park ball cap, sunglasses, tan t-shirt, tan shorts, brown socks in Merrill boots as if he was part of the force. No need to draw unwanted attention from these three, any tourists, or perhaps those waiting for the poached goods to arrive. Bryce *always* preferred being the pursuer rather than the prey.

Most times, a captive's behavior would dictate how Bryce would proceed. Take it like a man and it would be over in an instant without pain. Curse, spit, threaten – like the drug kingpin did the year before – and die of a massive, convulsive overdose. Bryce did have a dark side, but it only came out when someone pushed him there

Unlike in his homeland, there were no Miranda rights to be read in Africa to poachers. They were cuffed and would be driven to the nearest lock-up where, within 24 hours, a magistrate would hear their side of the story, often with a well-paid attorney up from Johannesburg representing them. A huge fine would be levied and paid, with that money being used by the force to chase these same men down again. Bryce's frustration at remembering that was poking at his temper. But when the third poacher used Russian slang, something Bryce had learned a long time ago, to suggest the late Mrs. Winters may have enjoyed doggie style, literally, he snapped. Two of the three were able to walk into their jail cells while the third, somehow left behind for a time, was found unconscious and with the shape of a rhino tusk carved into his forehead.

Late that night, sitting back at the same table where he'd last seen Pete, Bryce drank down his second Castle Lager. He'd received a text along with a photo when he returned to camp and picked up a WiFi signal.

REMEMBER ME? CONGRATS ON THE WIN.

It was from Kyoto, the woman he'd met on the flight from Japan back to the States. The photo she'd sent was the selfie she had taken with him in the terminal at LAX. That made him smile. He remembered her very, very well. She was intelligent, funny, beautiful, and a world traveler. Before he had a chance to respond to the text, the manager of the camp approached the table, handed Bryce an envelope, and excused himself.

The bill already – but I'm not leaving. As quickly as the thrill had hit when he saw Kyoto's photo, his heart sank when he opened it and began to read. It was from Pete.

Bryce, there's no easy way to deliver this message other than the way I have chosen to have it done. We will talk about this once you are back home in America. For now I want you to enjoy Africa, I know you love it here. Forget about me and Jack and Werner and all the crap that doesn't really matter.

I've been lashing out for some time now, and you and Jack got drawn into something you didn't deserve.

A few years back, I was having some health issues, and the doctors told me it was cancer. I got a second opinion down in Boston. They agreed. Now I've managed to outlive their projections but I can feel the cancer moving in the fast lane now. I have just a short time before your dad and I get together again and get to tell the folks at the pearly gates, "It's us – Peter and Paul!" They say I will be lucky to make it past Thanksgiving. Don't rush home on my account but come to Vermont for some dead bird this year. I'm happy I got to see your last race. My killin' days are over now, boy. It's time for me to go home. Love, Pete

CHAPTER SEVENTEEN

By the end of November in Vermont, the vibrant red, yellow, and orange leaves that signaled summer's end were just a memory. Nothing more now than a mess to rake up or perhaps a massive pile for children and dogs to play in. Goodbyes can be brutal, especially around the holidays, and Bryce would have no part of it. He wasn't going to let go of Pete just yet.

Together they drove out to the cemetery to say a prayer at Paul Winters' gravesite and then Pete stood quietly and leaned against the gray stone monument that would soon bear his name. He watched Bryce take the short walk to Christy's resting place and bow his head for a time. Heading back to the car he kept in storage at the Burlington airport, Bryce chose his next words to set the tone for the rest of the day. "You look like shit."

They spent the next forty-five minutes busting balls and laughing as Bryce sped east toward Stowe. The plan was to spend the rest of the day at Pete's get-away cabin up in the mountains, but Bryce had something planned first—a fast, illegal white-knuckle ride to the summit of

Mount Mansfield. Bryce's black Subaru WRX was an all-wheel drive, 310-horsepower turbocharged vehicle built for this sort of excursion. But his friends at Vermont SportsCar, the team that fields rally cars for driving champions like Travis Pastrana and David Higgins, had spent some time bumping up the horsepower, altering the suspension, and adding tires that made this version want to climb for the clouds fast - really fast. They'd even bolted in a roll bar that reached up over the driver and rider seats in the event things got dicey and the car suffered a rollover.

With everyone focused on the Thanksgiving holiday and the massive meals being served, nobody was guarding the entrance to the 4.5-mile road to the summit. Built in the late 1800's to allow horse-drawn wagons and carriages to reach the hotel built at the pinnacle, the road was unpaved after the first hundred feet. As Bryce drove around the barriers, he tightened the aftermarket shoulder harnesses that had been added as he came to a stop. He looked to Pete, who was grinning from ear to ear with anticipation, and watched as he did the same.

The hotel was long gone, and passenger cars normally took the drive slowly, cautiously, admiring the view, but this car was built to climb and soon it would. Bryce checked his watch, hit the timer button, and popped the clutch. Just short of five minutes later, after countless switchbacks, short straights, above dangerous drop-offs, he slid to a stop at the top by the closed Ski Lift and abandoned First Aid Center.

Looking at each other, both men began laughing and then Bryce's expression turned serious. He whispered, "I've always wanted to try this. Hold on. It's pucker time!"

Bryce threw the Subaru into reverse gear and sped backwards at full speed toward the path they had just raced up. He saw Pete close his eyes and then threw the car into a controlled spin, coming to a stop with the nose of the car facing the way down. "Maybe next time Pete," he shouted and then popped the clutch again and ran down the road pitching dirt and gravel as he had on the way up.

At the bottom Bryce drove around the barriers again and stopped before pulling back out onto Route 108. He looked to Pete who was catching his breath. "Smuggler's Notch or time for beer?" he asked.

Pete smiled and pointed to the right. The tight drive, weaving between massive rocks, would have to wait for another time. Hours later, after they had enjoyed a Thanksgiving dinner his friends at a local restaurant had left for them, Pete dozed off in his worn, leather easy chair as Bryce stared at him fondly.

"I'm not dead yet. Watch your damn football!" Pete said without opening his eyes.

CHAPTER EIGHTEEN

To many teams, racers and fans in America, Indianapolis is regarded as the center of the motorsport universe, hosting the Indy 500 since 1911. The city has seen Formula One and NASCAR compete at the Indianapolis Motor Speedway. In early December, when the famous track is cold and lonely, things move inside for the annual Performance Racing Industry trade show held at the convention center downtown. Cars, parts, and equipment are on display. Racers, crewmembers, engine builders, manufacturers, resellers, and celebrities attend from around the world.

Bryce had taken in the show for years, first coming out of curiosity as a young racer looking for connections. Once he began winning the big races he became a much sought-after celebrity, paid by companies to park in their booths to sign autographs and pose for photos. The year he won the F1 championship the show invited him to make remarks and do a Q&A at the opening breakfast. He'd entertained the audience with jokes and anecdotes about the season he'd just had. The standing ovation, given in the United States to the first American driver in forty years to win that championship, gave him goose bumps.

This year, he was happy the new NASCAR champion had been tapped to address the crowd. Bryce was able to walk through the aisles of the show before the breakfast concluded and the doors to the attendees were opened. In the past, Jack Madigan has walked the aisles with him. This year was different. Jack hadn't returned any of Bryce's calls so he went it alone and without security. He stopped by the NASCAR booth to shake hands and pose briefly for a photo. A few journalists spotted him making his way through the show and pestered him about his future and the coming year.

"Not sure what I'll be doing next year," he told them. "You've already seen me at the NASCAR stand. I was just making my way over to the IMSA group. I might be spending a lot of time in Florida after the New Year, maybe running the Rolex 24 or the Daytona 500. Maybe both so stay tuned."

That was all he had to say to them and moved along, quietly but firmly reminding them how it worked with him and the media. He'd rarely ask for space but when he did, most obliged. Keep after it when I've asked you to stop and you'll never get another question answered again.

He stopped at another booth, shook a few hands, and then another but kept up a quick pace so he couldn't be swept into any one space where a crowd might quickly congregate and impede his progress. This was what he called a hit-and-run, something he wanted to do, thank the companies and people who helped him get to where he was, but not spend all day doing it.

He stopped at the racing fuel booth where, years before, someone at the company had recognized his ability and potential and sponsored him with free fuel. All he was asked to do in return was display the company decal on his cars and his driving uniform, up close to his face where it would show up in most photos.

"You know some day this will all be electric but they'll never be able to replace the sound of a race engine or the smell of the fuel. Some of the exotic stuff I've run into over the years smells like skunk but yours always smelled sweet," he offered.

He shook hands, posed for a few pictures, thanked them, and then left – disappointed that the people he'd known there had retired or were no longer with the firm.

With his mission accomplished, he saw the exit signs and headed for the taxi stand and the ten-minute ride out to the airport and his flight back to Park City. Just as he got to the outer doors, he heard someone call out his name. He turned. Two excited young women approached. One asked for a selfie while the other looked for something he could autograph. He obliged, he usually did, but as the three of them smiled for a photo, he heard someone call out, "Know where I can find some Nitro?"

Coming toward him were two men dressed in gray suits, red tie on one, blue on the other, both looked fit and rigid—either law enforcement or former military.

The two greeted Bryce and suggested he had a plane to catch. Bryce smiled, thanked the women for the selfie, and said simply, "Bodyguards. Can't leave home without them."

Blue tie moved his arm to the right indicating the way

out. Bryce followed red tie through the doors to a waiting white Dodge Charger. He didn't sense they were a threat and assumed they were there to replace Gunn and Myers. He also appreciated the photos onlookers had taken as they recognized him leaving the building. If he went missing, someone would have at least captured their faces. Blue took shotgun and, after red opened and closed the door for their guest, hopped in the other side. The car sped off.

Halfway to the airport, the driver took an exit off I-70 and pulled into the parking lot behind a Cracker Barrel restaurant.

"You boys buying me lunch?" he joked. "I'm starving."

They hadn't said a word during the ride. Bryce just rode along as if this happened every day, but now it was time to get to it.

"I'm Bill Brownell with the Central Intelligence Agency," he told Bryce as he showed him his credentials, including a blue-and-gold badge with CIA stamped in a semi-circle around a shield. "That's Agent Russo and Chadwick. We wanted to connect to follow-up on what happened in Mexico. We've read the file, spoken with the FBI and Mexican officials who were on scene, and interviewed you and your friend Mr. Madigan. We just have a few questions for you." Bryce smiled. For the next ten minutes they reviewed the notes, asked Bryce to retell what had happened, asked him a few follow-up questions, and then suggested that was all they needed.

"What next?" Bryce asked, hoping above all hope that they were actually finished with him. That someone at Langley had closed his file and he was free to go.

Russo in the front seat turned to face Bryce. "One of

our desk jockeys, the same one who tagged you as suspicious before you first met with Joan Myers and her team in the U.A.E., was reviewing the Gunn-Myers murder case. He must be a race fan or something. Anyway, he took a look at your travel and activities and found it interesting that the Russians who allegedly were trying to take you and Madigan out as payback for Sochi haven't made another move on you. Everything around you has been quiet. He also brought up the fact that you appear to have taken no evasive maneuvers, changed your routine in any way, enhanced your personal or property security in Utah or in Europe. We all know you race car drivers are cool characters under pressure. But if Russian hit-men were after me, I'd have changed quite a few things immediately."

Bryce had been ready for this. "The desk jockey, and you I guess, are assuming whoever the shooter was in Mexico knows he messed up – that he, or the people who sent him, are race fans and saw me show up alive and kicking in Austin and then Brazil and back to Abu Dhabi. If they don't know he failed, then they'd have forgotten about me."

Russo shook his head and began to speak but Brownell cut him off.

"I have to call bullshit on that train of thought. If you had been killed in Mexico it would have been on all the news feeds around the world – not just the sporting news but headline, breaking news. Someone involved in the hit on you would have learned pretty quickly that it failed." Bryce shrugged his shoulders.

"Hey guys, this is all new to me. I don't know how these things really work. All I know is someone tried to kill me and Madigan and to be totally honest with you, and not trying to insult anyone, I was under the assumption that you were watching me, that I was regarded as an asset that needed protection. And since you guys are really good at not being detected I actually thought you were on me, watching out for me, just without saying so. My mistake, I guess. No need to ramp up security if the CIA is already providing it right?"

Brownell looked to Chadwick and said simply, "Airport."

On the final leg of the journey nobody said a word. Once the car pulled up in front of Signature Jet Service and Bryce thanked them for the ride, he got out of the car and headed inside. But the CIA wasn't done with him yet.

"Bryce!" Brownell called out from the car, gesturing for him to come back. "Just so you know, we don't have anyone tailing you or watching your properties."

Bryce shook his head. "Great. Maybe Russian hit men work the same way you guys do. It's been quite some time since I had contact with anyone at the CIA. Three races and not one call, not one assignment, no new handler, nothing. Maybe things just move slower in the spy business. Maybe I'll get shot dead at my front door tonight. Watch for me on the news."

Bryce grinned, turned, and walked inside. Five hours later he stepped out of a black, chauffeured SUV, entered the code to open the main gate, and walked toward the front entrance of his mountain retreat.

The man who maintained the property driveway had plowed it earlier in the day, but a light snow was falling and had dusted the area. As Bryce stood at the oak door, the grizzly bear head carved into it snarling at him, he thought back to his last words with the CIA in Indy. It was very quiet now. Everything was still. He could hear wind in the high trees brushing through the woods. Then he heard it. Crack. Then another.

He placed his backpack and small suitcase on the ground and turned, slowly. There, on the hill across from his iron gate, was an adult female moose. She took another step, a piece of brush cracking under her weight, and looked toward him. He let out a breath and smiled back at her. He turned back toward the door and took another very deep breath and let it out.

They had monitored his heart rate when he was driving a race car and found he maintained an even, steady keel of 60-65 beats per minute, everywhere except on the streets of Monte Carlo during the F1 race there. That drive always had him on edge and pushed his heart rate much higher. Tonight it had jumped up again. He never thought of dying in a race car, just feared screwing up and losing a race or getting hurt and not being able to compete. Death would come later in life, he hoped. Tonight, he thought, it had come knocking.

CHAPTER NINETEEN

Central England is home to Britain's second largest city, Birmingham, William Shakespeare's hometown of Stratford-upon-Avon, and the universities at Cambridge and Oxford. Known as The Midlands, it's also the home base for most if not all F1 teams, the historic Silverstone auto racing circuit and Santa Pod Raceway, a quarter mile long dragstrip built on an old runway used by U.S. and British forces during World War II.

As promised, Bryce was there this week to host his annual Christmas party for all of the employees and their families of Werner Industries' F1 complex. But first, he had a press conference to attend in the media center at Silverstone. It was scheduled for 11 am. With over 135 journalists, photographers, and camera operators in attendance, the news he delivered surprised nearly everyone, especially Max Werner and Tony Bishop who were watching from Werner's office, just down the road. As the white-on-red Breaking News banner scrolled across the bottom of the television screen, a few cheers could be heard from offices and mechanical shops throughout the building.

BRYCE WINTERS RETURNS TO FORMULA ONE

INKS THREE-YEAR CONTRACT WITH PROFORCE

ProForce was the team that had just won the Formula One Championship with Tony Bishop at the wheel. The move immediately stunned the racing world. Based on Werner's signing Bishop most thought Bryce was retiring, win or lose, at the end of this past season. Now, in a three-year deal, the former F1 champ was back. And he'd be driving for the team that had just won the title. It was racing's version of musical chairs. Bryce had enjoyed every second of delivering the news in such dramatic fashion. After all, this was how he'd learned he was out of a ride just two months earlier.

⸙

The cheers that reverberated within the walls at Werner's HQ were met with a chair thrown by him at the flat screen TV in response. Werner was furious that his former friend had refused to extend his contract only now to sign with Werner's biggest competitor. Even worse, he was enraged that any of his employees would cheer for Bryce's news, especially with him and their new driver sitting just overhead in the executive offices.

Within minutes, he'd sent an email to every employee stating that anyone attending Winters' Holiday Party, he refused to call it Christmas, would be violating their confidentiality contract with their employer and be terminated and left unable to work for two years in the industry. The email also reminded them of the date, time, and location of the Werner Holiday Party and his expectation that everyone attend.

Bishop voiced his concern, telling Werner he thought it a mistake. But Werner's expression, and the last words he spoke to Bishop before storming out of the office, was clear. "I pay you to drive. I don't pay you to do anything else."

~

The Toby Carvery in Stonebridge was always a special stop for Bryce whenever he was in the area. There was nothing like it anywhere else he'd traveled. The classic British pub & family restaurant's design was warm and inviting, but the main attraction was the hand-carved buffet.

For a reasonable fee, patrons could load as much hand-carved turkey, beef, or ham along with all the fixings – three types of potatoes, four types of veggies – all roasted, and then take a return trip for a piece of pie. He didn't do much with the meats, but the stuffing, potatoes, and veggies alone would fill him for a week.

He sat quietly in the rear of the restaurant, surrounded by ProForce's media manager and her assistants. They had some planning, a lot of planning, to do before Bryce headed out in the morning for the U.S. He stopped listening to them for a short time to take in the atmosphere – especially the aroma of the feel-good food. He wouldn't be back in England until the Autosport International trade show at the NEC, just up the road at Birmingham airport, until early January. After that he would be off until pre-season testing began in Spain in mid-February.

There was much to be done. Fitted for the cars, new custom fitted fire-resistant driving suits to be acquired, and media photos to be shot in them, and on and on. His day, and night, had been busy and fulfilling. His only frustration was the cancellation of his Christmas Party. He'd received enough calls and texts from former co-workers that pressure had been applied that he sent a message to all saying he understood.

He did two things right after that before heading to dinner. First, he organized three buses to transport people from one of the homeless shelters in the area to the venue so they could eat to their heart's content. He closed the bar, but the night went on very well and was much appreciated by the church he'd contacted to make it all happen. Second, he arranged for the gift cards he would have handed out in person at the party to be sent via courier to the home addresses of every employee at Werner. The gifts were significant in value and came with a personal note thanking them and wishing them the best. The next morning, he was back on a jet, high over the Atlantic, headed home.

This was the first Christmas Bryce had spent at his home in Park City, ever. In recent years he'd either been sitting on a barstool alongside Jack Madigan somewhere in the Keys or standing before a roaring fire at a ski lodge in Zermatt with Max Werner. He was at odds with them both now and, without suggestions or an invitation from either of them, he opted to go it alone and embrace his solitude. He reflected on all that had happened in recent months, and all he expected might come.

Days before, he had invited a dozen local athletes and

two coaches he had met at the Olympic training center to come to his home for a buffet-style dinner of southern specialties of fried chicken, ribs, corn on the cob, corn bread, baked beans, pecan pie, and soft drinks. To keep the coaches happy, he'd added something green to the menu at the last minute and laughed afterward when he noticed the green beans hadn't been touched.

The food didn't come for free, though. Bryce had made a deal with them. "Help me decorate my first tree, and I'll lay out more food than you can imagine." Now, at just past ten on Christmas Eve, Bryce's phone vibrated in his jeans' pocket. He didn't recognize the number, but as the hours had drawn closer to midnight, Bryce discovered how truly alone he felt. A caller, any caller, might do.

"Bryce Winters?" an unfamiliar voice said, "Billy Myers here – Joan's husband."

Bryce was shocked to hear the name and equally surprised that Billy, of all people, was reaching out to him.

"Hi, Billy. This must be a very difficult time of the year for you. What can I do for you?" Bryce waited but didn't hear a response. "Billy?"

"I'm out by your front gate. Can you let me in?"

Bryce spun to look at the monitor on the iPad on an end table. Security cameras covered every inch of the exterior of the residence, even where the floodlights that remained on from dusk to dawn he had coverage. Night vision cameras kept an eye on any movement in unlit areas. Bryce had always been amazed at the number of animals who wandered through. Moose mostly, but the occasional mountain lion always received extra attention.

There was Billy, standing at the entry gate, a light

snow dusting his shoulders. Bryce stared at the image. *You've been a bad boy Bryce Winters,* he thought, *maybe this is a ghost of Christmas past coming to collect.*

Bryce considered his options and pushed the button to open the gate as he ended the call. After taking a quick walk through the great room and kitchen, Bryce headed to the door and invited Myers in. The two men stood quietly looking at each other until Bryce offered to take his guest's coat and offered him a drink.

"Just coffee if you have it, thanks." Myers followed Bryce's lead into the kitchen and stood quietly taking it all in. The floor plan was an open one, allowing a full view of the kitchen, dining room off to the left, great room with the massive tree and trophy display to the right. Myers pulled a high stool from the island and returned his focus to his host.

"That's where she sat, the last time she was here," Bryce told him.

Myers blinked, as if the words had knocked the wind out of him. After a moment, he said in a soft tone, looking at Bryce through sad eyes. "Is this where you fucked her?"

Bryce leaned back against the counter and shook his head no and paused to let his response sink in. "Billy, we had a working relationship and that was it. I never touched her." He waited for a response but when none came he turned, poured a mug of coffee and slid it across the island to his guest.

"Well, she was fucking someone. I found enough in the notes and things she left behind. Stupid shit. A CIA agent, and she left evidence behind to let the guy she lived with discover there was someone else."

Bryce was shocked and related where they had met and

that she had only come there to prepare him to meet her new boss.

"We worked for the same boss. That was all. You know that I can't discuss any of the details other than to assure you that it was just that. Nothing more."

Myers drank down the hot coffee and stood up. His posture seemed, at first, threatening, but as he turned toward the tree in the great room Bryce watched as the man's shoulders fell.

"Do you know who she was with?" Myers asked, his back still to Bryce.

Race drivers are known for quick reflexes and millisecond decision-making. Bryce knew what he would say he just waited to deliver the news.

"No, Billy, I don't. She traveled the world for the CIA. I wasn't her only assignment." Myers shook his head.

"I still don't understand why they chose you to pass messages to foreign dignitaries. Thought the state department did that shit." Bryce shrugged his shoulders as if in agreement.

Myers turned to face him. "She spent more weekends away than weekdays, and she spent more time at auto races than anywhere else. I may not be the sharpest tool in the box, but all indications are to racers."

Bryce shook his head in agreement. "Racing is a magnet, Billy. It feeds on money, hype, fans, competition, and excitement, but it also sends a lot of lonely people to bars and beds. If she was with anyone else, anywhere else, it could have been at a race but it wasn't with anyone I know." He paused. "This might hurt but you need to know this, Billy. Until that day you turned up at the airport, I never even knew she was married. Never even noticed a ring." He watched as Myers stepped further into the great room, staring up at the vaulted ceiling and then to the fireplace before approaching the far wall, covered with winners trophies claimed across the United States and around the world.

"I believe you, Bryce," Myers began. "I believe you didn't fuck my wife but I'm not sure about the rest of it." *Well, I rarely saw her at races so there's that,* Bryce thought and saw this as a chance to shove the spotlight, an unwanted one, off of racing and onto something else. "Have you considered she might have been with someone she worked with at the CIA? Everything they do is so secretive, so need-to-know. Maybe she had a fling with someone she spent a lot of work hours with. If I were you, I'd look there. Go back East, go back to Langley and see what you can find out there."

Bryce walked to his guest and stood directly in front of him.

"Or, you can realize you and Joan had a good thing for a time. And, like life, shit happens. You can spend a lot of time banging your head on a wall and trying to catch someone and make them pay for what they did. But if it was an affair, she would have been a willing participant. Have you considered you might have played a part in that – maybe working too many hours yourself or taking things for granted?"

Myers was listening. Bryce could see that he had planted the suggestions well. Maybe it was time for the widower to pursue self-awareness instead of revenge.

"You're a smart man," Myers told him. "Is that why you aren't married?" he said with a laugh.

Bryce stepped closer. "The only woman I ever loved was killed in a car crash, years ago, back home in Vermont. For me, falling in love again would hurt too bad. Dealing with that loss felt as though I had been in a violent car crash of my own and needed years to physically and emotionally recover. No, sir, not interested in *ever* getting that banged up again." Bryce saw a change in Myers eyes.

"Makes for a lonely life though doesn't it?" he asked.

Bryce nodded. "Well, look around. Kind of quiet isn't it?"

The two men just stood there, silent in their grief. Talking about Christy had been a gut punch even after all these years. Christmas had been their favorite holiday and none of them had been very joyous ever since she died. He wondered where Myers would head next. *Bars in town would be closing early. Did he have a hotel room? Was he going to just drive away?*

"You have somewhere to go now, Billy?" Bryce asked.

"Yeah, I have a room in town," he answered as he walked past Bryce back into the kitchen. He stood by the stool his wife had sat on and put his hand on the back of it. Without saying another word, Myers walked to the door, took his coat down off an ornamental gold hook that looked much like an antler, and left.

Bryce walked back to the iPad and released the front gate, watching Myers pass through it and then get into a car parked twenty feet down the hill. As the car drove off, Bryce walked back into the kitchen and opened one of the dozen drawers under the island. He stared down at the Sig .45 caliber gun, one of five he kept in various spots throughout the house.

He'd had enough unwanted visitors show up at all times of the day and night; overzealous fans, crazy ones, and then there was always the paparazzi. For him, the 45 was the ideal gun for dealing with a pissed off moose or a fence jumper with bad intentions. Whenever he traveled, he'd lock his weapons away in the gun safe behind a fake wall in a walk-in closet just off the master bedroom. There, with a bullet-proof vest, night vision goggles, ammo, stacks of cash, and another half-dozen weapons of all shapes and sizes, "Something for every occasion," he'd joke.

He looked to the coffee pot and then the clock above the doorway. It was getting late but he poured a mug, added a healthy shot of Bailey's and took a seat on one of the brown cloth sofas facing the fireplace. The smell of the sweet Irish cream liqueur made him smile, and he looked forward to every drop.

"I miss anything?" a raspy sounding voice asked as the footfalls in the hallway came closer and closer.

"Nope, Uncle Pete, all quiet here. Grab some grub. I was starting to think you were going to sleep all night. You want to watch *It's a Wonderful Life*, *Ford versus Ferrari – again*, or *Full Metal Jacket*?"

Pete shuffled around in the kitchen for a time, dropping a knife and then a spoon that Bryce heard but ignored. Pete plopped down across from him with a huge plate of food and a bottle of beer.

"Nope my ass," he stated as he picked at a piece of leftover chicken and then locked eyes with his nephew. "That guy comes anywhere near you again, and he'll be with his wife under six feet of dirt."

CHAPTER TWENTY

New York truly is the city that never sleeps. It has something on offer any time of the day or night. The excitement, the electricity generated by tourists from all around the world who flock to Times Square, is a perfect complement to the neon lights and huge billboards touting everything from Jennifer Lopez's next album to Calvin Klein underwear.

Bryce looked forward to his visits there, taking in a play on Broadway, dining at one of hundreds of great restaurants, riding the boat out to the Statue of Liberty, or watching a group of school kids standing in awe of the *Tyrannosaurus rex* during a field trip to the Museum of Natural History. So far today, he'd spent an hour at the Sirius studios being interviewed by Howard Stern then boarded a taxi to visit with Kelly Ripa on her live TV show before he could take a break and grab some lunch.

His trademark blue jeans, gray sport coat, blue dress shirt, and Merrill shoes assured him of total comfort and a good look. Bryce didn't spend much time on fancy or expensive clothes and jewelry. He waved off inquiries from any company wanting to pay him a ridiculous amount of money to wear their goods. He wore the same TAG watch his uncle had given him years before after he won his first NASCAR race, passing on the offers from every high-end watchmaker in Europe. Media tours like this were a necessary evil, but Bryce had the luxury of picking and choosing who he spent time with. Today, it didn't feel much like work and he'd laughed the entire morning.

He had one more stop on his schedule, but of everything on his itinerary, next on the list would be the icing on the cake. Despite his best efforts not to he hadn't stopped thinking of her since they first met. When their schedules finally synched he'd invited her to come along to watch him tape an appearance on the Tonight Show at NBC in Rockefeller Center. It wasn't meant to impress Kyoto. He simply wanted her to enjoy their long-awaited rendezvous to the max, a memorable first date.

The taping went as he'd hoped. The video Jimmy Fallon played of himself and Bryce racing go-karts at one of the indoor fun centers in the area was a big hit. Finally, after reuniting out on 49th street they walked to a spot Bryce had told Kyoto had sentimental value to him. It was December, though, and despite the chilly temps and occasional wind gusts funneling through the streets they talked and laughed during the brisk walk to Sardi's.

She looked stunning in her tailored gray suit, heels, and red and black scarf, and he told her so. After grabbing a table he explained the place's significance and proudly pointed to the spot on the wall where they had placed his caricature after he had won the F1 championship. He introduced her to Joe the bartender who had told him years earlier, "Maybe someday you can be on one of these walls."

Kyoto was just as beautiful and intellectually engaging as he had remembered from their flight to LA a few months earlier. They had hit it off from the start and talked nearly the entire trip, save for watching a movie during dinner. She related how thrilled her father had been when she showed him their photo. Over the next hour Bryce got to learn more and more about this intriguing woman until she dropped a bomb.

"You know, Bryce, I really like you. But trying to have any sort of relationship with you would be impossible with me living in Tokyo and you in Utah or Monte Carlo and racing around the world."

Bryce looked at her, an expression of disappointment replacing the permanent grin he'd felt until this moment. Bedding a beauty like her might have been all he had been interested in during his younger years. He'd had no interest whatsoever in falling in love, lust and plenty of it had been okay then. But since that first meeting on the plane, he had thought about Kyoto, her brain, her beauty, and their connection more than he had thought about anyone in years – since Christy, his first love. Now this.

"So," she continued, "not that you had anything to do with my decision, because you didn't, but I've taken a transfer to my employer's headquarters in Washington. My brother has worked there for years. With things changing at home, the move makes sense. The job will require a lot less travel, and I'll be closer to my brother now. He helped me pick out a condo overlooking the Potomac. Do you know DC at all?"

He was thrilled at her news. If there were going to be anything between them this could help it along, despite her choice of venue. Bryce would love to have shared his thoughts on the area, in addition to the truth about the intelligence service that had him bent over a barrel. Instead, he went along.

"Been there many times. Love the monuments and the history. I got to meet the President in the White House and have been to a few events there. If you're moving to DC I can be your tour guide if your brother doesn't mind."

She smiled but then frowned. "Here you are showing me a good time. I move to the States and cut down on travel and you're off to Europe till who knows when."

He laughed but then *his* expression changed. "Today was a good day, a very good day and I've really looked forward to seeing you again. Putting my uncle Pete in the ground up in Vermont and doing it on New Year's Eve was a bitch." He paused in thought but then smiled when she placed her hand on his. "I spent the night up in his cabin in the woods and started to go through his things. I found a journal he'd kept that went all the way back to his boot camp days in the Marines. I had no idea he'd kept one. I started to read it but just couldn't – not yet. After I watched the ball drop sitting in his chair at the cabin, I went outside and stared up at the stars. I got up the next morning, shook off last year and then, out of the blue I get a text from you wishing me a Happy New Year. I took it as a sign of good things to come." She leaned toward him and kissed until a server cleared his throat once and then again so he could continue service. They laughed.

They talked for another hour. It was during that time

that Kyoto shared why she had been so willing to move from Japan to the United States. Her father had been dying of cancer for some time and had finally passed in early December. Without any remaining family there, and all the international travel her job entailed, she told him that she had found it hard to maintain even casual friendships there. Just as Bryce was looking to the New Year as a new beginning, so was she.

"Tell me about your dad, and your mom. You haven't said much about either of them," she suggested.

He shook his head. "Nope, I'm having too good a time with you. Those are two sad stories we'll save for another time."

They both went quiet for a moment but then Bryce broke a smile and looked to the future.

"Okay, so you'll get settled into your new digs in DC and I'll fly over to England for some work. I'll be gone a week and then don't have to be anywhere but the gym until pre-season testing starts in Spain in February. Usually I hang in Monte Carlo. You probably know this, but the government requires you to live there a day over six months to qualify as a citizen and be tax exempt."

"And I thought it was because of the nude beaches, the casino, and the Mediterranean," she joked.

He grinned. "Maybe I can sneak back here, or you'd consider meeting me in Barcelona for Valentine's Day."

She smiled. "We do things differently back in Japan. It is the woman who gives her love a gift of chocolate or something more in February. Then, a month later, we call it White Day, the love must return the sentiment. Maybe we need to set some rules – like we do whatever the locals do?"

"Deal. That could be fun." Bryce checked his watch. They had sat down at just past six o'clock and were only one of two tables still occupied at just past eleven. "Let me get you back to your hotel and then I'm off to England."

She gave him a look of surprise.

"I see that look, young lady. You're not getting into these pants all that easy!" he joked as he stood up and extended his hand.

They walked to her hotel, the Millennium Times Square, where he accompanied her to her room on the 12th floor. They leaned against the hall walls and talked for another ten minutes until the door across from hers opened abruptly. A visibly annoyed and rather obese bald man in boxers and worn out t-shirt suggested they keep it down, go in, or go elsewhere.

The couple laughed and apologized. Suddenly the man's door opened again. He'd put on a hotel robe and had his phone with him. Busted, Bryce stood with the man as Kyoto took three photos of them standing together like old friends. Once the fan shook his hand and said goodnight, Bryce took hers and pulled her to him, kissing her once, and then giving her a slight bow. Their first date had now ended. Both would always look back on this evening as something very special.

Bryce walked out onto 44th Street and headed west. He hadn't gone far when a voice came from close behind him.

"Give me your money, mother fucker!"

Bryce spun around to see an imposing figure. The man was at least 6'5", 300 pounds and wrapped in an assortment of sweaters, outer coats, torn pants. A filthy NY Jets wool hat was pulled down to his eyebrows.

Bryce did as Pete had taught him decades ago. *Look to the hands. Check the stance.* No visible weapons. And this character was flat footed, neither foot set back to support a punch or launch an attack.

Bryce stepped his right foot back and reached for his wallet. "Look, fella, times are hard. I'll give you a twenty for some food. Then you're going to walk away and there won't be any more trouble." The last thing he wanted after such a remarkable evening was to end it by sending some poor slob to the hospital.

"I said hand it over!" the man roared. "All of it. Now!" He lunged for Bryce.

Bryce sidestepped him. "Is that what you want? It's cold out tonight. You want a free trip to a warm hospital bed? I can tell you the slab in the morgue is colder than it is out here. Take the twenty and—"

The mugger swung at him. Bryce ducked away. Now, his conciliatory tone changed. "You know, on second thought, I don't give a shit if you're homeless, crazy, or out of a job. There's no excuse for hassling people out here on the street. Problem is, if I call the cops you'll be back out here doing this to someone else. And if I let you go—same deal, you'll scare or hurt someone less able to take care of themselves."

The man's expression showed Bryce had confused him.

"Don't just stand there." Bryce motioned to him. "Come at me once more so I can end this and get back to where I was headed."

The hour and the winter cold had made this block a quiet one with very little car or pedestrian traffic. This city might never sleep but Bryce and his companion were very alone at the moment. Bryce looked both ways down the street then up at the buildings for security cameras. Good. Not a one.

"Ain't askin' again. Give me your money."

But Bryce wanted the bastard to throw the first punch just in case there were witnesses or cameras he'd missed. "Come on you prick. You be the aggressor just one more time and I'll just have to defend myself. You want it come take it, you piece of shit!" Bryce paused and smiled at his attacker. "I always wanted to say this movie line so here goes, Yippee-ki-yay *mother fucker*."

The incident was over with one lunge by the attacker and a well-placed punch to the throat thrown by his victim. The big mugger dropped in his tracks. Bryce was as good in hand-to-hand combat as he was behind the wheel, thanks to Pete and the two trainers from the CIA who taught him in private sessions overseas.

Early the next morning, Bryce woke from a sound sleep and smiled at the text that had just landed.

> STILL IN TOWN? HUNGRY? NEED COFFEE?
>
> GOT TIME FOR BREAKFAST?
>
> I CAN BE IN YOUR HOTEL'S RESTAURANT IN 30 MINUTES
>
> LMK. KW

He smiled and took one of the quickest showers possible. When the elevator door opened, there she was, a big smile and another tailored suit, this one a deep brown with a yellow scarf. In contrast, his blue jeans, button-down dress shirt, sport coat and hiking shoes were standard operating procedure on long–haul travel days, and every other day for that matter, whenever possible.

Over breakfast they picked up where they had left off, as if nothing but a good night's sleep had happened since they'd said goodnight. When Bryce called for the car that would take him to JFK for his flight to Heathrow, they waited together in the lobby until the black SUV pulled up and a familiar driver he requested whenever he was in town, came in to grab his luggage. Another kiss, followed by a long embrace, and then he was off – until their next rendezvous.

CHAPTER TWENTY-ONE

The CIA's headquarters in Langley, Virginia has gained recognition in recent years, its star-bearing marble wall honoring the lives lost in service to their country portrayed in TV shows and films. Charged with foreign intelligence and restricted to conducting clandestine operations outside the United States, the CIA is home to techs, researchers, foreign language translators, administrative personnel, bureaucrats, and operatives also known as spies. Some of these dedicated individuals have been known to hold a grudge and seek revenge. To these few, justice wasn't just a building in DC named after Bobby Kennedy. To them, it was their mission.

Agents Brownell, Russo, and Chadwick believed their supervisor Gunn and their friend Myers had been targeted and assassinated in Mexico. They were intent on revenge. They got the face time they had wanted with Bryce Winters at Indianapolis and came away wanting his head. While waiting for Gunn's replacement to be named, *they* decided what they would focus on. Sitting around a small white table in a small white meeting room at HQ, the trio discussed their options.

"When I was shadowing Winters at that trade show," Brownell said, " he spent a lot of time with some racing fuel guys. I wonder if there's something we can put in his fuel to blow him up – make it look like a mechanical failure or a plot by a competitor?"

"Maybe some Nitro. I can check with our chemists," Russo suggested. "Or we could contaminate his fuel and get him disqualified a few times; take a few wins away from the guy and brand him as a cheater."

"Too many people involved with those options and too much collateral damage," Brownell said. "Why not just put a bullet in him when he's out on the track – maybe at Sochi. Put it on the warring mobs that we lit a fire under – that Winters lit a fire under."

Chadwick nodded. "Maybe. One thing for sure there's something brewing between Winters and Madigan. Not sure what it is but I can go visit Madigan, see if we can exploit it and turn him. Turn them against each other."

"That's it – Madigan's a computer guy. Forget the fuel idea – get him to sabotage the car," Russo suggested.

"Maybe there's another way. His friend Werner – we've had eyes on him the past two years. He's been up to no good with the Iranians and the Russians. What if we send Winters to take him out and then send the police in to catch him with the murder weapon in his hands. Kill two birds without firing a shot."

The three talked for another twenty minutes and agreed on an action plan. Brownell would dig deeper into Werner, and Chadwick and Russo would go to Charlotte to pay Madigan a visit. They'd need to work fast though, as word had come down from the top floor that Gunn's replacement would be seated within ten days and there were no assurances he, or she, would share their enthusiasm for putting an end to Bryce Winters.

CHAPTER TWENTY-TWO

At the Catalunya race circuit just outside of Barcelona, the silver safety car, a sleek Mercedes AMG coupe, screamed down the front stretch. It was media day, twenty-four hours before any of the F1 cars would take the first lap of preseason testing. As Bryce gave the car all it could take without spinning out, his shotgun rider held tight and laughed nervously to camouflage his panic. He'd challenged the F1 driver to scare the hell out of him, and Bryce was doing that and then some.

The G-forces of the sweeping turns, the acceleration, the heavy braking, then next turn coming on so quickly, and then another, and then another. Living on the edge was what Bryce loved to do, at least on the track. But he had no idea he was slowly killing the man riding with him.

As he brought the car back onto pit road he looked to his right and raised his hand to give the VIP a fist bump. Shocked by what he saw, Bryce made an erratic turn and stopped in front of the silver Medical Car and the two trauma doctors who were leaning on its fenders. The man's head was down and his face a dark blue, in stark contrast to the shiny white of his open-face helmet.

It took only seconds for them to react to Bryce's gestures and pull the man from his seat and lay him out on the concrete. The team administered CPR and used their portable heart defibrillator as Bryce stood by ready to help if needed. From the primary doctor's expression, Bryce knew the ride had been the man's last.

Journalists and camera operators had converged on the scene, startled by the unexpected move by the American driver. Bryce had ignored their questions as he watched the medical staff do their work and spoke briefly to the safety car's race-weekend driver expressing concern for the man. Once the body was placed on a stretcher and loaded into the ambulance, he turned to the crowd. Everyone was shouting questions, all of it going out live and around the world.

First, he explained that he didn't know the man. He said that he was just one of many VIPs scheduled for a hot lap, a thrill ride, around the circuit. He then offered his condolences to the man's family and told the press he had nothing more to say. Journalists continued to call out questions as he headed for his team's hospitality area, but then he caught himself and turned away from the newly branded Werner livery and quickly course corrected for his new one. Only two persistent journalists continued to pursue him. One caught his attention, slowing him from a fast pace.

"You said you don't know the man who died while riding with you," she said. "You didn't know he was regarded as an enemy of the state, someone who challenged the government's rule? He was also a ex-convict who used to deal cocaine across Spain and Portugal."

Bryce kept walking but looked at her. "Nope, sure didn't."

She persisted. "This man had powerful friends and powerful enemies. Are you at all worried that some may find you at fault for his death?"

Bryce shook his head. "Lady, the excitement killed him. He was a big man; maybe he had heart problems. Maybe they should post warning signs like they do on roller coasters. That's all I have to say on the matter."

He suggested to her that he needed to get something to drink and time to decompress. By this time one of the new team's PR people had intercepted Bryce and escorted him into the private quarters they had set up for him on the second level of their hospitality area. Once inside he drank an entire bottle of an orange sports drink and sat down to take in his new digs.

There on the wall were the three photos that followed him wherever he went. Photographs of his father Paul, his uncle Pete and his first and only girlfriend Christy. All three were gone now. He looked to the Daytona photo, of him standing alongside Max Werner in victory lane. Bryce shook his head. His relationship with Werner had come to an end, and he felt very lonely standing there in Spain.

A knock at the door brought him back to here and now. His two bodyguards, earpieces and lightweight jackets to hide their hardware were on duty now that he was on site in his suite. A member of the PR team, a cute brunette with a South African accent, knocked and then stuck her head in and advised him that a representative from the American Consulate in Barcelona was there to greet him.

"You saw their credentials? It's not another journalist, you're sure?" he asked. She nodded in the affirmative. "Do me a favor, find out how the hell I wound up driving around with a damn drug lord. Doesn't anyone screen these people?"

She smiled, made the money gesture with her right hand, and then stepped back and motioned for the diplomat to enter. A plain looking middle aged man, receding gray hairline, eyeglasses, plain blue suit and striped tie but with an American flag lapel pin in place. *Someone just wants a photo I'll bet*, Bryce thought. The man presented his identification, shook Bryce's hand, and then looked to the staffer with an expression that told her she could go. She glanced at Matt who nodded and closed the door behind her.

"Thanks for stopping by. I can't think of—" Bryce began but was cut off in mid-sentence by a hand gesture from his guest. He watched as the man flipped the lock on the door and pulled an object from his coat pocket, placing it on the table in front of them. It was a small square black box, measuring perhaps 2" per side. A little red light on the top began to glow confirming it was functioning.

"Not a problem, Mr. Winters. I'm not actually with the consulate." The man reached inside his suit coat pocket and presented another form of identification. Jason Ryan, CIA.

"I was wondering when I would hear from you guys again," Bryce said, gesturing for his uninvited guest to take a seat. "This isn't my first rodeo. I've seen those jammers before. But you need to give me more before we talk any further. I don't know you."

"Certainly. You used to report to Glen Gunn, and your handler was Joan Myers, codename Nitro – your choice, I'm told. Both were killed in Mexico. Back at the shop we've all been waiting to see who would replace them and what they'd decide to do with you."

Bryce let out a sigh. He had hoped somehow that the bureaucracy in Washington might lose him in the shuffle and forget about him, but this visit ended that dream.

"Who did I last meet and where was it?" Bryce asked.

"The three musketeers, that's what we call them back at Langley. You met them in Indianapolis in December. They're old school, knuckle draggers as far as I'm concerned, but they come in handy when that sort of medicine- outside of the United States, of course, is prescribed. What they lack in stealth capabilities they make up for with effort. They were pretty tight with Myers so, to be frank, I'm surprised they didn't have someone take you out or at least have you roughed up. Some people don't think that happens, that it's not that easy to make someone disappear. But it happens every day. Sometimes it's a car crash, sometimes – like today – it looks like a heart attack."

Bryce did a double take at his guest.

"Yes, *we* did it – you and the CIA. We've had eyes on that fat bastard for some time. When we saw he was on the guest list for your ride-along we had someone drop a little something extra in his orange juice this morning at the media breakfast. Then you took him out and scared him to death. His heart was on the edge already. We tuned it up and you put the finishing touches to it. The coroner will rule it a heart attack with contributing factors like his obesity and high blood pressure. Case will be closed before the casket is. Much more creative than just blowing the lid off a Russian animal in a bathroom, don't you think?"

"But you've put me at risk. A journalist suggested I should be concerned - that someone might have a hard on for me since I was driving when he stroked out."

"I doubt you're in any danger, except for maybe the musketeers. They've been known to go off book from time to time. Once you're back in the States the new boss wants to meet you, the sooner the better. Until then, I'll be your go-to. Now tell me about Jack Madigan. I understand you two are at odds. He's been a good resource from what I've read in the file. His being on another team, he stayed with Werner I understand, makes your working together much less convenient. But we can work with it if you two can. Is the relationship repairable?"

Bryce shrugged. "I think time may heal those wounds, but you'd have to ask him. He's not talking to me."

Ryan looked around the quarters that would be Bryce's mini-suite, his sanctuary over the next three years whenever Formula One was racing in Europe. Then his focus turned toward the three photos on the wall. He stepped to them and stared.

"He didn't call you after your uncle died?"

Bryce shook his head. "Listen, you know what really got this started don't you?"

It was his guest's turn to shake his head.

"I never killed anyone," Bryce began. "Uncle Pete was a great guy, former military, raised me like a son and taught me volumes, but he also had his flaws. He was nomadic, coming and going as he pleased. Hell, half of that was my fault since I put fifty grand in his bank account every year and got him an all-access credential so he could come to the races whenever he wanted. He also had a temper and a zero tolerance. I'm talking not an ounce of tolerance, for assholes. Jack and I cleaned up after him four times, and somebody caught us on tape dumping bodies. We never killed anybody – at least not until your employer, my own government, blackmailed us into it."

Ryan just listened but didn't respond. Bryce was lying and realized he might be better at driving than acting. The guy sitting across from him was a professional, and Bryce didn't want to give any indication there might be dirt on him they knew nothing about. Nothing to look for, like the death at the speedway in New York all those years before.

"There was no way I could let Pete go to jail, especially in some of the countries where he lost his temper."

"Okay, if all that is true and he's dead now – I assume that really happened and he's not hiding on some island you bought somewhere – why not just refuse to help us anymore?"

Bryce felt his temper start to rise. "Don't insult my intelligence. You guys have had me by the balls for years. You have incriminating videos of me, and Jack. Other than me just asking to be cut loose I don't have much leverage. We're about even on that score."

His guest smiled. "Bingo. I can't tell you everything that we've discussed about you but I can tell you this – if you *had* retired at the end of last season they probably would have forgotten about you. When your new contract was announced the agency went back to reviewing the race schedule and discussing operations."

Bryce sat quietly for a moment. "You just can't make this shit up." He reached back for a bottle of water and tossed one, fast and without warning, to his guest and then reached for another for himself.

"Let's get one thing straight right here, champ. I'm here doing my job but don't think I won't shove the next thing you toss at me up your ass if you show an ounce of aggression towards me again."

Bryce laughed and checked his watch.

"It's a date." They stared at each other, sizing things up.

"So, I'll play along. Guess I have to, for now, like the patriot I am. But only as long as you brief me on why someone needs to be terminated. For the record, Pete *is* dead and buried. Also, for the record, I've been keeping notes on all the shit the CIA has asked me to do, forced me to do. If anything does happen to me off the track, the international media will get it all."

"You're watching too much television. That's a bluff. Remember, we have a file on you, too."

"I feel like we're playing chess so here's my checkmate. The next time I'm at the White House posing with the president and a championship trophy, I may have to mention this little arrangement you've boxed me into."

"I'll let you share those thoughts with the new boss once you two meet. You can direct your hostility toward her too if you'd like but from what I've been told, she has something better in mind for you. For now, we need to talk about Max Werner. We've intercepted enough of your conversations to know you are clean. But Werner, he's another story. Perhaps we can get together in Barcelona before you fly out and I can share some information you might be interested in."

"You're kidding?"

"About Werner?"

Another knock at the door interrupted them and Bryce spoke with someone without letting them enter.

"Time to get back to work. I'm sure I'll hear from you again. You guys always seem to know how to find me."

The man smiled, handed Bryce his card and assured him he would be in touch. Bryce took a minute to check his hair in a mirror and then looked at the man's card again before sliding it into his money clip.

JASON RYAN

FIELD AGENT

CENTRAL INTELLIGENCE AGENCY

Bryce followed the staffer down the circular steps and then toward pit road to resume the VIP and Media Day activities. In the distance he saw Max Werner giving an interview and shook his head as he walked. *What have you gotten yourself into now?*

CHAPTER TWENTY-THREE

Regarded by many as a spectacular city—the European center of fashion, food, wine, desserts, and artwork—Paris had much to offer, and Bryce had experienced all of it on many trips before this one. His journey had begun just two hundred miles north of the city, a few short hours before. The plan had been to attend the launch of a new associate sponsor for the race team, a breakfast at the Royal Automobile Club's Pall Mall location in central London. A British watchmaker was paying dearly to have its name on Bryce's car, fire-resistant driving suit, and left wrist. Most of the other big names in racing had watch deals, but Bryce had held out and finally received an offer truly too big to refuse.

"I know they'd like me to refer to this engineering beauty as a time piece," he said to the assembled media, holding up his wrist as he smiled. "But in all honesty, *this* is the best damn watch on the market."

Bryce collected watches and had at least a dozen in various sizes and shapes—Rolex, Patek Philippe, Omega, TAG Heuer—all gifts or awards for winning races and championships around the world. At home, he wore a simple Timex Ironman and kept a half dozen of those in a kitchen drawer. He'd ruined too many expensive watches over the years, working on race cars, and knew this one could take a beating. For the money he'd just now been given, by contract they'd all now have to sit idle and gather dust. He had agreed to wear, out in public, only the sponsor's watch for the next three years.

He posed for photos with the principals, team owner Ameer Kazaan, and a few male and female fashion models. Then his new assistant, Vicki Dini from Milan, introduced him to a journalist who was going to accompany Bryce for the rest of the day. She was writing a *Day in the Life* series of articles. She already had followed soccer, boxing, golf, and film actors, but she told him as they were introduced that this interview was one she had been most looking forward to.

Her name was Susan Lee and she had flown in the day before from Shanghai. She was also there to cover the press conference as part of a publicity effort for the upcoming F1 race in China. Her English was excellent, which Bryce always appreciated. He was accustomed to being interviewed by journalists in countries all over the world and, while English might have been a second, third, or even forth language for them, sometimes he struggled to understand them. Not so much their words but their accents and the manner in which their sentences were asked.

Lee, the daughter of a Chinese diplomat, grew up and attended schools in London. She spoke the Queen's English as if she was a Brit, which would make the day much easier for him. The fact that she was nearly deaf as a result of a childhood illness impressed Bryce. Lee learned to read lips at a very early age, she told him during the ride to the train station. She confided that this helped her excel in school and her profession. All she requested to make the interview a great one was for candor and eye contact. Bryce promised to oblige.

A quick limousine ride to the St. Pancras train station and Bryce, Lee, and two bodyguards (casually dressed and staying at a distance) boarded the tunnel train bound for downtown Paris. Not long after their departure, Bryce and Lee sat in opposing seats and began the interview as they made the two-hour ride that included a thirty-mile trip under the English Channel.

"You joked about Vicki being your latest assistant?" she began. "Does that mean you go through assistants very fast?"

He smiled and leaned forward. She gestured for him to sit back. "Lip reader," she said. An attendant operating a beverage cart placed coffees and waters they had requested on the mini-table that jutted out from the train car's window.

"No, that's not the case at all," he explained. "They keep getting pregnant and go off to start their families. A situation that I had nothing to do with," he assured her with a smile. But then his mood changed as he reflected on the women he had grown close to in his life but had left to pursue theirs.

"When I raced NASCAR back in the States, I worked with a great girl by the name of Melissa Steck. She and I hit it off from the get-go. She took great care watching out for me and keeping me on schedule, caffeinated, and out of trouble. Her husband was a great guy, is a great guy, but when they decided it was time to start a family, she quit the racing game. Then I found another assistant, and she was great but got pregnant. Max Werner hired someone for me who said she had no interest in having kids but wound up falling in love and starting a family. She was from Iceland. Jenni was her name." He smiled and watched as Lee jotted a few notes, even though she was recording their words on her phone.

The interview continued and covered a great deal of Bryce's life, from his earliest days in racing to riding a high-speed train bound for France.

"I have heard," she corrected herself, "I have been told that, despite all the fame and fortune, the type of life you live can be a lonely one. I could see from your eyes when you were talking about your various assistants that you were fond of them and miss them. What about the rest of the people close to you – the racing teams? Does the camaraderie that you share, the goals, the wins and the losses, all make you one tight family?"

Bryce finished his coffee then tossed a piece of chewing gum in his mouth to counter the aftertaste. He looked out the window and just then felt the shudder of the train moving at speed into the tunnel opening. He turned to answer after considering his words.

"I've had the best of pals and the worst of enemies in this sport. But, yes, at times, it can be a lonely proposition," he began. "There are some great people in motorsports. I'd say ninety-nine percent of them are. We share a passion for an incredible sport that we are all lucky to be part of. But things happen. People change teams – I just did.

Loyalties have to be to the car owner, the crew chief and the engineers and teammates and the new driver, not the people from the previous team." He paused for a moment to think. "Trust is huge, but that's the case in any relationship. In racing, we share technology, knowledge, and experiences—despite the NDA's and confidentiality agreements—and all of that has a way of flowing into a new team. That can cause issues. But to a man, and woman, I can say that no matter what team you are on, when someone is in trouble, people respond.

"I remember two drivers in NASCAR who hated each other's guts. But when they were involved in a big crash at Daytona one year, their cars came to a stop within twenty feet of the other. When one car caught fire, the other driver was the guy who pulled the hot driver, his sworn rival, out of the car."

She smiled. "There are rumors that there is much more to what happened in Mexico when you were off-roading and two people died. What can you tell me about that incident?"

Bryce's mood changed, and he had no problem showing it on his face or with his words. "Vicki told you anything regarding Mexico was off-limits," he glared. He'd seen this move so many times before. The interviewer lets you settle in, get comfortable, and then they throw a curve ball and ask you something out of left field.

"Let me rephrase my question, Bryce, please. My apologies." She leaned forward and placed her left hand on his knee. She left it there as she continued. "What I am trying to say is that while you put your life at risk in race cars, you walk around with bodyguards. Your life obviously must be at risk from other threats. Can you speak to that?"

He stared at her for a moment. "Yes and no," he began. "Mostly I have people around me to help maintain distance between me and an overzealous fan who's had a few too many Heinekens or perhaps the fan that's angry because I passed his favorite driver on the last lap to win the race. That happens. Race fans, like soccer fans, are *very* passionate. Not as much as the American football fans back in Philly though." From the look on her face Bryce thought she wasn't buying it. Her next question confirmed it.

"Is that why you and all the other drivers ride around in armored cars followed by car loads of armed bodyguards in places like Brazil?"

"You're persistent, I'll give you that," he told her and looked across to the two armed men sitting on the other side of the aisle, who were now staring at her. Security was a huge issue and one most prefer not to discuss.

"I'd just say we live in different times and precautions have to be taken." He gestured for her to turn off her phone, which she did. He leaned in, for effect not because she couldn't hear him. "We can end this right now or we can change the subject. My security and the security of all the other drivers and people you've been interviewing for your series is very important and confidential. That's the last I'll say on this. So, you can turn that back on, Miss Lee, or you can move to another seat."

She looked at Bryce and then the two men sitting across from them.

"I understand one hundred percent," she said, nodding to Bryce and to the guards.

She pressed record on her phone and then threw him another question, one he'd been asked more than most. "So, what do you do if you have to go to the loo?" she asked with a grin.

The rest of the train ride and the interview went as planned. Once they worked their way out of the station in Paris, to a waiting black Mercedes limo van, they headed to another publicity event scheduled for four o'clock at the Four Seasons Hotel George V. As part of the appearance a suite had been arranged for him for the evening before moving on.

Remarks about the rumors he would compete in this year's 24 Hours du Le Mans endurance race, a few photos with members of the racing associations there, and then he would be free. When that little happy hour event had concluded, and Lee witnessed first-hand how a few gregarious fans that crashed the gathering had to be escorted from the hotel, she told Bryce she understood now.

"I only have a few brief questions left," she told him.

He was amused by the way she used her tone and her eyes to attempt to charm him into spending more time with her. He turned to his security team and said, "Frisk her." They moved toward her. She tensed and looked worried.

"Just kidding. Come on – come upstairs. I'll give you ten minutes more and then I have other things to attend to," he said.

His suite was an elegant white-and-blue space with a white sofa, lit fireplace and a spectacular view of the Eiffel

Tower across the room from it. He carried his own bags. That was just the way he preferred. After dropping them in the bedroom he came back into the main room to find the journalist in a much different mood.

She had a gun, and was pointing it straight at his face. A race driver's reflexes and judgment require not a split second but tenths of a second to make decisions. Pole positions are often decided by such fractional moments in time, but tonight the next move he made might be Bryce's last.

He stared at the purported Chinese journalist. He knew the gun. He had a Sig 365 compact just like it. Small, accurate, clips to carry 15 shots. He'd never seen one with a sound suppressor, though, and was intrigued.

He knew that, even if he called out for the two security guards posted just twenty feet on the other side of the ornate door, the woman with the gun could put a decent amount of lead into his head before they had time to react. He thought it best to ride this one out and see where it took them. If she wanted him dead, he'd know soon enough.

He started to speak but she raised her other hand and placed her index finger to her freshly painted red lips. *Shhh.* She gestured for him to sit down and then sat across from him while reaching for a pad of paper and pen on the coffee table. She switched the gun to her right hand and wrote with her left, then slid the pad across to Bryce as he leaned in to read it.

He moved too quickly. Her hand extended the gun toward him again. At this range she couldn't miss.

WHY DOES THE CIA HAVE A
BUG ON YOUR PHONE?

She removed her ID from her small bag and held it out for him to see. Despite all that he had been through, this was the first time anyone had pointed a gun at him and was still breathing. Paris might be regarded as a romantic, beautiful city but for Bryce, sitting across from an armed Chinese agent from the MSS, Ministry of State Security, romance was the farthest thing from his mind.

Whenever Pete Winters had drawn him into something risky, it had been in tight quarters. The training his uncle had given him, combined with what the CIA had taught him for close encounters, weren't going to be of much help here. The suite was over 1600 square feet, bigger than the house he grew up in back in Vermont. The weapon was a good one and the woman with her finger on the trigger, who had played her role as a journalist, a deaf one at that, was deserving of a Golden Globe for best acting.

Bryce reached into his jeans pocket, slowly, and pulled his phone, placing it on the coffee table. He noticed, as did she, the screen was lit with missed calls and unread texts. She reached and turned the phone toward her, reading what she could, and then writing another note.

IF I WANTED YOU DEAD YOU WOULD BE

THE TWO IN THE HALLWAY
WOULD BE DEAD TOO

I JUST WANT TO TALK

I HAVE A PROPOSITION

TURN OFF THE PHONE

She'd hooked him. Between his uncle's bad behavior and what came out of his encounters with the CIA, he'd thought he'd seen and heard it all. Now he was curious. Pissed off, but curious.

He took the phone back, turned it off, and then sat back and waited. He watched as Lee studied the room and then stood up, gesturing for him to follow her to the balcony. The sun had set, and the Eiffel Tower was all lit up and pointing to the stars. Bryce laughed to himself, remembering the couple in Tokyo. The view was spectacular, but she shook her head no and went back into the suite. She'd moved to within a foot of him, but he opted not to pounce, remembering what she'd written. He followed her as she headed for the master bedroom and was surprised when she tossed her weapon on the bed. She continued into the bathroom, a space where marble and mirrors covered every inch. He followed her in, and she closed the door. She turned on the sink spigot and turned to him.

"Before you say another word," Bryce began, "if this is a practical joke of some kind, it's a bit over the top, wouldn't you say?"

She wasn't smiling. This wasn't a joke and she cut to the chase. She told him that the MSS was aware of the deal he had cut with the CIA. "We have analysts watching everything, everywhere, 24/7, rain or shine, day or night. We saw what they saw, but were slow in deciding what to do with the intelligence."

Bryce stared at her. He wanted to know what she did.

"You and your crew member, Jack Madigan. We saw the video of the two of you placing a dead body in a trash receptacle behind that hotel in the U.A.E. We know the CIA approached you in Abu Dhabi and cut a deal. You work for them now. But perhaps you can do something for us, too."

Bryce answered her, moving his lips but not making a sound.

"I can still read lips, even though my hearing is fine," she paused, smiling. "You are coming to race in our country very soon. There is a chance the CIA will want you to make a move on someone there."

Suddenly the bathroom door kicked open, tearing it apart at its fine French hinges. Bryce's two guards had their guns drawn. The one now down on one knee aiming at her torso. The second standing upright, his gun aimed straight at her head.

"You okay Bryce?" the kneeler called out.

Lee didn't move. Bryce smiled. "I'm fine, but ten minutes is ten minutes, boys," he said checking his new British-made timepiece. He watched as she turned her attention away from the gunmen and back to Bryce.

"Don't like surprises either?" he asked and then followed the guards' direction to slowly walk past them and into the bedroom. He stepped over the demolished door. Splinters and paint chips had fallen like snow in the doorway.

Bryce looked to the bed for the gun, but they'd already discovered it and taken control of the weapon. He listened as he heard the security experts spin Lee around to secure her wrists behind her back with zip-ties. Not the hardware store ones that can snap with the right leverage, these were heavy duty and staying on her as long as needed.

Bryce continued into the living room of the opulent suite and retrieved his phone, flipping it on and placing it back on the table while watching Lee being led into the room and shoved down onto the sofa. She cried out as she landed hard, twisting an already compromised wrist. Bryce noticed the room service cart the hotel manager had sent up, champagne, flowers, chocolates, and a fruit and cheese presentation fit for a king.

"You said ten minutes, Bryce, and then this showed up at the fifteen-minute mark. We texted you: AOK? But when you didn't respond, we used the cart delivery as an excuse to come in. When we saw the gun on the bed, it was time to party."

Bryce looked at her, at them, and then took a few chocolates from the cart and sat down across from Lee.

"Have you called anyone yet—hotel security…F1… the police? Anyone?" he asked. They both shook their heads, no. Bryce smiled. *Good.*

"Okay, you've eliminated the threat," Bryce began. "Give me another ten minutes with her. I'm intrigued."

The men stared at their protectee.

"I know, I know, I can see the concern all over your faces, but let me see what this is all about. We were just getting to it when you kicked down the damn door."

The two men had already holstered their weapons.

"Let me talk to her for a few minutes and then we'll decide if we throw her off the balcony or, well, I'll leave the other options to you boys, okay?" He saw the reluctance in their eyes, but they agreed.

"Where's the gun?" he asked as they headed for the door. The guard that had taken the knee pulled his suit jacket back. He'd tucked it in his waistband for safekeeping.

"It *wasn't* loaded," he said as he followed his partner into the hallway to stand guard there again, door slightly ajar, just in case. Bryce retook his place on the sofa across from Lee, as if to continue the interview. But now, he'd be the one asking the questions.

"Where'd the silencer come from? I didn't think they were made for that model."

She grinned. "We make *everything*." Satisfied, they moved on.

They spoke about the MSS. Bryce had heard of them before and learned it was set up as one service, essentially combining the Chinese version of their FBI and CIA under one roof. Lee insisted that her story, raised in London and working as a journalist was true, not just a cover. The MSS had leveraged her much like the CIA had done to Bryce and so they had that in common.

"Listen," she told him. "You and I are both under the gun so to speak. So please, I ask you, to listen to what I was going to say."

Bryce smiled at her. If she was telling the truth then yes, they had something in common. But she was pressed into the service of a ruthless government controlled by the Chinese Communist party. The holders of his leash were at least working in the best interests of his country, allegedly for freedom and democracy.

"Okay, so I cut you loose and we forget this ever happened. Those guards out there have seen a lot, a lot of things that rich people get to do because they can do what they want. They'll forget this ever happened if I ask them to. But you're paying for the door and I'm keeping the gun."

He watched as Lee processed the situation. She looked to his phone.

"They listen," she said. "I saw from the look on your face when I wrote that note that you never considered that."

"If they are listening, they've heard enough that someone else should be kicking in the front door at any moment, right?"

Lee shook her head no.

"They're as curious as you are. They want to know what I was sent here for."

Bryce looked to her bag. "And your phone? Anyone listening in from back in Beijing?"

Now she smiled. "I turned it off. I wanted to talk to you, just me to you. I thought we established a rapport on the train. It is against protocol, but I can talk my way out of it. I could say it lost power but they can tell that was a lie. I'll just tell them you insisted. That you thought we were going to have sex and wanted any recording devices clicked off."

"Guess I blew any chance of that happening now," he said with a laugh.

"Not necessarily, but we'll need more than ten minutes," she said as she looked to the front door.

CHAPTER TWENTY-FOUR

Winchester, West Virginia. Driving race cars can be exhilarating, but they can also scare the daylights out of a person. When things go wrong they can snuff out life in the blink of an eye. Today, with the brisk winds of late winter still blowing and a chilly 40° F outside the vehicle, Bryce sat behind the wheel of an entirely different animal than he was accustomed to. Over the years he had proven he could drive anything, but this had given him a run for his money.

Later, sitting in a small classroom that was set up for watching training videos and instructors, he sat back and thought through the day while sipping on a hot coffee. The driving academy was located adjacent to the historic road course at Summit Point Raceway. Here, they specialized in training professionals from federal, state, and local law enforcement and protective services. Learning how to drive smart and fast, getting to an incident or rushing a protectee from one was a challenge. Learning how to do it behind the wheel of a tank on tires was even harder.

Bryce had always wanted to give it a try and had suggested today's activity as cover for the meeting that would soon take place. He'd ridden in this sort of vehicle many times before, particularly in countries where kidnapping VIP's is a regular occurrence. His celebrity made the academy jump at the chance - the photos of him behind the wheel would wallpaper their social media. With members of the U.S. State Department there for training, it all fit together nicely. Then he heard what would normally have intrigued him, a set of high heel shoes clicking down the hallway. As the sound came closer and closer he looked forward to seeing who was driving them. When the woman entered the room his sense of intrigue vanished.

"I heard it took a while for you to get used to the weight of an 11,000 pound armored SUV out on the course. Did you have any fun?" she asked through an awkward smile as she approached him. She exuded confidence but his celebrity tripped her up. He'd seen it before.

Bryce stood, extended his hand, and introduced himself. The woman shook his hand, passed him her card, and took a seat opposite him at the table. *This one's all business, no cleavage, nada,* he thought. *Not a field op, I bet.*

"Sandra Jennings, Central Intelligence Agency," he read then stopped when he heard another set of footsteps approaching. When Jason Ryan entered the room, he nodded at Bryce and closed the door behind him. Out came the little black box he'd used in Spain and after exchanging pleasantries very, very briefly their meeting got down to business.

"So, how'd you do out there?" Ryan asked.

"The damn things weigh nearly twice as much as a regular full size SUV, but after I got in some seat time I picked up the moves pretty quickly. While we were taking a bunch of photos I asked if I could take one of the president's limos for a ride sometime but they just laughed."

"Bryce, first off I want to thank you for your service to the agency and to the country," Jennings stated. "I know you feel compromised, blackmailed as it were, into doing some of the work my predecessors asked you to do. But that will change with me, I can assure you."

Bryce was encouraged but kept his optimism in check. Jennings was clearly a serious woman, probably a career one, and kept her look and dress pure business. Graying hair, chiseled features, fit and trim but in basic blue suit and shoes. Just a touch of makeup, her red lipstick matching the stripes in her lapel pin. No rings. "So that means no more terminations. Cool. Thanks for the play date. Now, can I get the hell out of here?"

Jennings frowned and shook her head slowly. No. "Actually, I was hoping we could forget the methods the agency used to secure your services and try to put that behind us. What I want to do, what I am hoping to accomplish here today, is for you to *volunteer* to continue to work with us. You put your life on the line out on the track, and do a great job representing your country while you're at it. I want to solicit your help, ongoing, in taking out some very bad actors and helping to disrupt their enterprises and the natural order of the underworld."

He stared at her. *This was incredible,* he thought.

"Let me get this straight. You want to remove the shackles but have me continue to put my life at risk? My name isn't Bond, and I don't drive an Aston Martin. With all due respect, are you crazy?"

"No, Bryce, I am not. I've watched you from afar and went through every page in your file, over and over. You are an American hero and a patriot. You are very good at what you do – a really cool operator under pressure, and your celebrity status does get you closer to people and invited into places where we would struggle to put an agent or enable any other asset to penetrate without suspicion. Every time you learned why we wanted a target taken out you went about it with focus and seemingly without remorse."

Bryce stared at them both without uttering a word and got up to pour himself another coffee. He paused at the window, peeking through the blinds, watching his classmates outside continue to pose for group photos in front of the vehicles they had just mastered. He'd enjoyed the camaraderie; it reminded him of the race teams he'd been a part of over the years. He walked back to his seat and stared at the two, shaking his head.

"It's not something I would normally admit, not something I am necessarily proud of – killing that is. But I *have* looked on this as serving my country. I never had the inclination to join the military. I admire those who have served just like I admire all the men and women outside. But all I wanted to do was race. Then you guys came along and bent me over big time. I like serving, just don't like being on the receiving end, not under duress."

Jennings shrugged her shoulders and gave an innocent smile. She reminded Bryce that she wasn't in charge at the time and that she was only interested in serving her country and wanted Bryce to continue to do so, through a more cooperative and collaborative relationship.

"You know, I've never met a race car driver before let alone a world champion," she began. "Do you know Matt Christopher?" Bryce shook his head no.

"Outstanding investigator. Only works overseas and I'm told he knows a lot of the crowd you race with. Perhaps some day you two should meet." Bryce shook his head again. "Don't change the subject." She smiled.

"Remember, Bryce, you put yourself in a position to be bent over as it were when you and Madigan were caught cleaning up after your own dirty work, dumping bodies in the dark. My predecessors leveraged you, yes. They found someone capable and many felt you seemed comfortable with killing and took advantage of the situation."

Bryce sat forward. He explained that he'd been killing since a very young age, first taking out rabbits and then graduating to deer, all under the tutelage of his Uncle Pete. He didn't particularly enjoy having to gut and skin them, but he'd been taught that was what you did to live, if you had to. And he also learned to show respect for the animal whose life he had taken. It was a way of life in the woods, it was what they needed to do in those alleys, and that seemed to be the case with the CIA as well – doing what needed to be done.

"Did Ryan here tell you that Pete was dead now and that we were only cleaning up after him? Jack and I didn't kill any of those dipshits." She shook her head yes.

"That doesn't change where we are today Bryce. I'm looking forward, not back."

"So, are you willing, are you capable of handing me a presidential pardon for all past and future crimes?" he asked.

Jennings looked to Ryan and smiled. *Got him.*

"That's entirely possible with a few conditions. In addition, although your uncle seems to have trained you extremely well, kudos to the old leatherneck for that, I would like to have the CIA train you further so you can become an even more valuable and capable asset overseas."

"Spy school?" he joked.

She didn't laugh. "Private instruction."

Bryce grinned. He'd enjoyed today's activity, and Nitro had taught him a thing or two in the field. But this interested him. If they could take the gun away from his temple then he might go along, for a time.

"I need to think about this," he began. "I have to watch my mirrors at over 200 miles per hour *a lot*. I'm not sure I want to be looking for someone coming after me, seeking revenge for something you've asked me to do." He paused. "How can you stop that from happening?"

"By being smart—you doing your part and we doing ours," she stated. "You've only done - what - four terminations for us? We don't ask very often. You come and go like at one of your pit stops but you don't leave any skid marks behind – no clues or evidence that you were involved. You're good at what you do, very good. If you are ever compromised, we'll put a protective detail on you."

Jennings got up to get a coffee and kept the conversation going, her back turned to the men.

"You're accustomed to being shadowed by security already. Terrorists would love to grab you or take you out to embarrass our country. You're protected now but we can enhance it."

"For life? What if it comes too late? What about

our new arrangement if I agree to it? You retire or things change at the top and I get a new contact and our deal comes under scrutiny. I can't have that. I need all of this in writing."

Jennings said she would work on a top-secret document for him. She reviewed Bryce's schedule of the next few months and then she looked to Ryan. "Any change in status on Madigan?"

Ryan nodded. "Yes, I met with him in Spain after I spoke with Bryce. He told me he wanted time to process what had happened to Joan Myers."

"And what does that have to do with his relationship with Mr. Winters here? I don't understand. Refresh my memory please." Ryan looked to Bryce who simply returned the stare.

"Madigan believes that Pete Winters was behind her death in Mexico, that Bryce's uncle was the sniper who took out Agents Gunn and Myers."

"Why the hell would he have thought that?" she demanded.

"Because he did," Bryce stated.

CHAPTER TWENTY-FIVE

WASHINGTON D.C. HAD always intrigued Bryce. As a much younger man he had visited as a tourist many times. There was so much history there, so much power in those three buildings – The Capitol, The Supreme Court, and The White House. On one of his earliest trips his Uncle had taken him to the Marine Barracks, to pay respects to the fallen at Arlington, and tour the Pentagon and many other sites.

Bryce had planned this trip with someone special in mind. Following the meeting with the CIA he drove the sixty miles east to Washington and checked into the historic Willard Hotel. Back in 1861, amid fears for the safety of Lincoln, detective Alan Pinkerton brought the president-elect into Washington ahead of schedule, by some accounts in disguise. He took up lodging at Parlor 6 on the 2nd floor of The Willard and Lincoln would reside there with his family until his inauguration on March 4, 1861. Four years later, just a five-minute walk from there, Lincoln was assassinated in Ford's Theater. On the drive to DC Bryce had thought about Lincoln and then of John

F. Kennedy, both shot in the head by someone with an agenda.

For tonight, Bryce had reserved the George Washington suite located on the tenth floor. He had stayed there the night the president had honored him with a dinner at the White House and remembered the room for its views of the city, including the Washington Monument and the Jefferson Memorial.

"Well, this is impressive," Kyoto exclaimed as she walked through the living room to check out the full dining room and the view from its window.

"That dress is what's impressive. Red flags in racing mean you have to stop but you – in that and off the shoulder? You look amazing."

"Thank you," she said as she continued her tour. "I see the sport coat and jeans are still your go-to. You don't sleep in those, do you?" she teased.

"No way. I switch into superman pajamas with a cape that hides the trap door in the back."

She played along. "Funny to hear that. I've been called kryptonite a few times. Tonight could get really interesting." She walked past him and stepped into the master bedroom on the opposite side of the suite. "Nice. Is this what you do with all the ladies you entertain?"

He laughed and guided her back into the living room where he popped the cork from a bottle of champagne and poured two glasses.

"Nope," he said and handed her a flute. "I told you in New York that I didn't entertain much. I have to be careful of the women, everyone I let into my life. I need to avoid frivolous lawsuits, paternity charges, blackmail, and all the other nonsense that comes with the territory. I've found it easier to just avoid getting too friendly with women. If you don't let someone you just met at a party into your hotel room, it's pretty tough for them to say something happened there."

Kyoto went to sip her drink, but he protested. "Not until we toast," he insisted. "To the future," he said as he raised his glass and clinked hers.

"You're saying since I'm in your room you've now left yourself vulnerable," she teased.

He grinned. "Not so fast, little lady. I've got a dinner reservation and we need to get moving." He downed the champagne and headed for the door. He turned to see his guest still standing by the plush gold sofa, glass in hand, staring at him with a questioning look.

"Come on – I've got the room for the night. It'll be here if you want to come back up for a nightcap or check out my PJ's." She smiled and followed him out the door.

Bryce was thrilled to find that Kyoto was up for just about anything. Days later, after he took her for a really fast rally car ride through the woods of Vermont she was up for a drink. He had finally gotten comfortable again racing at high speed through tree-lined courses, thanks to the introduction of ballistic windshields that kept tree limbs, or anything else, from crashing through and penetrating the pilot or co-pilot.

Fire is a race driver's worst fear. But when Bryce had seen a young deer impaled on a sharp branch, years before he ever raced, he never forgot that warning image.

After the car was loaded back into the hauler, Bryce

got Kyoto her drink and thanked the team by treating them all to a happy hour at a local bar. He stuck to Heineken 0.0 though as there was more driving to do. He wanted to show her that there was more to him than fast cars and private jets. A few hours later, with Bryce now sound asleep on the couch in Pete's mountain cabin, he was startled awake when Kyoto pushed at him.

"Bryce," she began softly. "I've been reading your uncle's diary. You said it was okay. But I've come across something I think you need to read for yourself."

He looked up at her, the orange flicker of light from the fireplace made her eyes sparkle, but her expression was sad, almost scared, and he sat up once his mind cleared. "What is it – can't you just tell me?"

She shook her head and handed him the diary. They were still getting to know each other, and this was a side that Bryce hadn't seen before. Her expression concerned him. Instead of diving right in he got up and made coffee, refilled her wine glass, checked his phone, and then sat back down. He motioned for her to sit with him, but she had returned to the rocking chair near the fire and shook her head again. He flipped the diary over and began.

> *Damn that woman. Paul always picked the worst of them. Even back in high school, no matter how hard I tried to convince him this one or that one was better looking, nicer, or had more potential for doing something with their lives, he always chose poorly. And it always cost him. After I retired from the Marines, Paul let me stay at his house until I got my shit together. She was there. I found a job easy enough and bought*

the old Johnson place down the road from where we grew up. Walk right into the woods, quiet, just what I wanted and needed after all I had done in the Corps.

Bryce took a moment from his reading and gave Kyoto a questioning look. She gestured for him to keep going.

Liz had been pretty enough, was a decent cook, and liked a well-kept home, but she had a temper, especially when she had been drinking. I couldn't understand why Paul put up with her bullshit, the verbal abuse, the drinking, and her hanging out with her friends down at Casey's Bar. Nothing good ever came of that place late at night. Nothing. Finally, I moved into my new digs. I hadn't finished all the painting and work that needed to be done, but I couldn't take listening to those two late into the night – every night. So, I moved out.

I felt bad for Paul. His mind had never been right after he'd shot that kid. Cops have to do a lot of tough things, but when a gun barrel comes out of the darkness at you it's time to eliminate the threat. He sure did with his service revolver. He could always shoot a pistol, even better than me.

That punk had always been a piece of shit in my book, most everyone's, but he was still a kid at fifteen. He'd been picked up more times than anyone could remember. I think the department even stopped logging him in. He'd bullied the other, smaller or timid kids in school, had been caught breaking into homes, stole a car, and then some. The kid's father was the mayor for

Christ's sake. That made keeping the kid behind bars where he belonged even harder.

So one night, he pulled a gun on Paul. Paul responded and did us all a favor, far as I'm concerned. The kid was headed for worse crimes. But Paul was fired from the force. Between losing the job he loved and taking that life, he crashed. Luckily, he was able to get disability payments.

But something broke in him, and that bitch just couldn't leave him be. She nagged him, poked at him, and one night when I stopped by to check on him I found Liz sound asleep in their bed with some truck driver she'd picked up at the bar. They couldn't screw in his sleeper cab – she had the balls or the utmost disrespect for her husband, my only brother, to humiliate him like that. Paul just sat there staring at me while I stared into their bedroom at the mess those two had made.

I walked into Bryce's room to check on him. He was sound asleep. I pulled his blanket up tight over his shoulders and I remember smiling at him. I didn't know shit about little kids, hell he was only four, but I loved this little guy so much. I closed the door to his room behind me and then I lost it. I never told anyone except for writing it here. I pulled that driver out of the bed, bare ass naked he was, and threw him through the screen door. He came charging back in, but I beat the shit out of him. This time he was smart enough to take the belongings I threw out the door behind him. He walked off with his tail between his legs. As to Liz,

I was done with her, even if Paul wasn't. The house was his, and she wasn't welcome there anymore.

Bryce stopped again. He didn't look at Kyoto this time. He just stared into the fire and then continued reading.

I grabbed her by the hair. I had never laid a hand on a woman before that, and I never have since. But she drove me past my limits. I regret what I did to this day but that night I couldn't stop myself. She fought back and threw a punch that missed. I yelled at her to knock it off. The party was over, and she was going to follow that shithead right through the door. When we got into the living room she started yelling at Paul. "Stop him – make him stop!" But he just stared at her with contempt, tears in his eyes.

Part of my heart broke right there for him, but the other part kept going with rage. I told her to keep quiet. She said fuck you or something like that and then she changed her pleas to insults. "I wouldn't have to fuck anybody else, Paul, if you could get your shit together and act like a man." The insults went on and on. She was fighting back like a wildcat. She swung at me, clawed at me, bit me twice, and then I saw her spit on Paul, right in his face. That did it. She turned toward me, and I hit her as hard as I had ever hit anyone, anywhere, ever. She flew back and landed right on his lap. I looked at her lying across him. Her eyes were open, her mouth was open, and so was everything else.

I looked at Paul and he looked down on her. He didn't say a word. He just shoved her body off him and onto the floor. I could hear Bryce crying in his room, but I just stood there looking at Paul and looking down on his dead wife. I'd just killed that little boy's mother.

Bryce shook his head in disbelief. He looked around the cabin, the place where he and his Uncle Pete had shared so many experiences together. Pete had been a stand-in father for Paul, and he'd been great at it, until now.

Kyoto began to speak but quieted as he continued to read.

I checked the body to confirm what I already knew. I shut the front door, got a dirty sheet from the bed, wrapped her in it and then slid her body back into their bedroom and closed the door behind me on the way out. Paul just sat there. He hadn't said a word. I looked into his eyes and he mumbled something I didn't hear. I got closer and leaned in. He shook his head and then whispered, "Thank you."

We both cried. The Lizzie nightmare was almost over. There was a little boy who needed attending to. But as long as the truck driver had climbed into his rig and left town without filing a complaint, we would be okay. I could bury her up in the woods and nobody, except for whoever she might have been banging down at the bar, would ever miss her. Bryce was too young. He would never remember anything about her. That's a good thing.

Bryce slowly closed the diary and stood up. He walked to the fireplace and stood in front of it, the diary dangling from his hand. Kyoto remained quiet, watching. He turned to her and let out a deep breath, a sigh of relief.

"Well, that was different."

"They told you she ran off with a truck driver?" she asked.

"Yep." Bryce walked into the kitchen area, and stared out the window into the darkness. He stood there for a few minutes while Kyoto sat quietly, waiting.

Finally, he turned to her, feeling a deep sadness from within. "I know it's late but feel like going out for a few beers?" he asked.

She nodded. "Of course - but this time *I'm* doing the driving."

CHAPTER TWENTY-SIX

Melbourne, Australia was the site of the first race of the new season and after a very good test session in Spain Bryce was optimistic about the New Year and the new ride. Having to attend team meetings and debriefs with his new teammate, Dickie Jones, was unbearable at first, considering Bryce wanted to beat the living daylights out of the guy for knocking him off track as he and Bishop had fought for the championship. Team Manager Mick Roberts, another Brit, hadn't pushed too hard to make them share a peace pipe just yet. He'd told them he'd let time run its course and encouraged them to bury their differences. Bryce had found that remark hilarious and had laughed, to their consternation, when he'd heard those words.

As luck would have it though, a crash on the very first lap of the race ended his day and meant the 8,000-mile flight from the U.S. was a waste, unless he included the work the CIA had planned for him there.

The private jet ride from Melbourne to Sydney was over

before his host could open another bottle of champagne. "Drown your sorrows or celebrate life, your choice my new friend," Alistair Marshall had said through his homeland's accent. Marshall was a billionaire, much like Max Werner. Passionate about everything but especially the young twenty-something beauty he wore on his arm like an expensive watch.

Marshall had his hands into nearly every field of business down under, from constructing skyscrapers and exclusive beachfront resorts to owning cable news networks and print media around the globe. Tonight though, he was focused on impressing his new friend and bedding the woman he'd met on holiday in Thailand just weeks before.

"Come with us," he'd told Bryce. "Spend a few days with us on Bondi Beach and give a few interviews. We'll drink, we'll eat, we'll sun, and who knows what trouble we can find. And we will look for it, I can assure you," he joked.

Meanwhile, back at Langley, Sandra Jennings had other plans.

&

"He talks a good game. He has the personality and the charisma to be an excellent covert field agent," she told her superiors at their Monday morning closed-door briefing. "As long as he maintains his celebrity and continues the global travel."

During their first encounter back at the driving school, after she had convinced him she had different intentions, Bryce bared his soul to her. While seeking attention is what so many drivers and race sponsors want, Bryce hadn't gotten into racing for the fame. He liked the competition, thrived on it, and had found he could make good money using his talents behind the wheel. If posing for pictures, doing interviews, and relentlessly traveling was the cost, so be it. Death wasn't a consideration, at least not his. At the CIA, it was.

"How sure are you that he was party to the hits on Gunn and Myers?" one of her superiors asked.

"One hundred percent," she replied with confidence. "Agent Chadwick paid Jack Madigan a visit. He reported that it took little leverage to get Madigan to spill what he knew about Baja. He *volunteered* that he'd been having an affair with Agent Myers and that Winters had flown his uncle, a former Marine sniper among other things, to Mexico to take out Gunn and Myers. Madigan said Bryce resented both of them for forcing him into taking out people, even if their targets were bad actors. He told Chadwick he thought the plan was actually a pretty smart one, saying it was retaliation for the hit in Sochi. If he hadn't been in a relationship with Agent Myers he would have backed it fully. He also told Chadwick that Winters, Bryce, had not known about the affair and claimed he wouldn't have taken her out if he'd known."

Jennings watched as the three superiors sitting across from her went quiet, lost in thought. The stark meeting room, the only decoration a photo of the president on one wall and the CIA insignia on the opposite one, was a place where decisions about taking lives, not on furnishings or décor, were made.

"Any corroborative intel from other sources?" one woman asked.

Jennings shook her head no.

"Maybe Madigan is making this up, for whatever reason, to get us to issue an action against Winters," another suggested. Jennings nodded. "Does that mean you agree with that assertion or aren't sure?"

"It's conjecture at this point. There is no other evidence to indicate that's what happened. Pete Winters is dead; we can't interrogate him. I would actually like to confront Winters with Madigan's statement, but then the big question is, what if he says it's true?"

"You saw Pete Winters' body? Did Madigan? Did anyone? You sure he's dead?" the woman pressed.

"No, I have not. I'm told Madigan has not spoken with Winters since the last race in Abu Dhabi. He told Chadwick that he confronted Pete Winters there and that he'd been tased, tied up, and left on a yacht. Bryce had found him and cut him loose, but that was the last for them – except for Madigan telling Bryce, according to Chadwick, that he was going to find Pete Winters and kill him. Not just as payback for Myers but for assaulting him," she reported. "Madigan used to be Bryce's body man, closest friend, tech consultant to the race team, and get this – a retired Army Ranger."

Jennings had been watching the expression of the third person at the table. The man sat between the two others doing the questioning but hadn't uttered a word, until now.

"So, let me sum this up. We put a famous race car driver, an asset, on a short leash, blackmailed him into doing terminations overseas, he ordered a hit on two CIA agents, and now we're talking about what to do with the damn bastard. Have I described this situation correctly?" he said sternly.

Jennings nodded.

"Okay, well, let me offer a few words," he stated in the strong southern accent he'd brought with him from South Georgia. "Bryce Winters is a national hero, for Christ's sake. He's a good-will ambassador. Hell, he's had dinner with the president at the White House, even took the boss for a ride. I think it was at Road Atlanta or somewhere up north. I don't know which son of a bitch at this agency had the dumb-ass idea to screw with this man, but it wasn't well thought out."

Jennings sat quietly until she saw the man's eyebrows rise to indicate he was waiting for a response of some kind.

"I wasn't part of the team that set this up or was involved in its execution, sir," she began. "They've either retired or are dead now. But I do see value in working with Winters. And it would have disgraced the country if what he and Madigan had been up to was exposed. One concern has always been that if we found the tapes, others could have too."

She went on to relate the details of the meeting she had with Bryce at the driving school, his response to the new tone, and the softer, non-lethal mission she had suggested for the Australian person of interest that he was now after.

"Well, young lady," sitting forward as he began. "Confirm Pete Winters is dead. Until further notice, keep using Bryce Winters in non-lethal behavior that he agrees to or, better yet, volunteers for. That man's a highly popular brand ambassador for our country around the world He's a damn national treasure as far as this old redneck is concerned. He deserves to be protected. Use him wisely, cautiously."

"Yes, sir," she said.

"Once he retires, he'll probably be found up on a slope after he's skied hard, really hard, into a tree somewhere. Until then, don't let anything happen to him or allow anything tarnish the good he is doing for the United States."

Jennings nodded.

"And if he doesn't ski?" she asked, half-jokingly.

"Well, I just read an article about mountain lions in Utah. There are maybe 1500 big cats out there. They can grow to be two hundred pounds, can sneak up on people really well, or eat something they find that's already dead. I'm sure there's something in the CIA playbook that'll work." The man closed the file folder in front of him and then looked to her.

"Sandra," he continued. "Other than Chadwick and Madigan, who else knows Pete Winters allegedly killed two of our agents, supposedly at Bryce Winters' direction?"

"I'm sure Chadwick shared his intel with others on his team, Agents Brownell and Russo. Other than those few, just us."

"Good. Keep it that way," he directed. "One last thing. I'm going to move the three musketeers, as some have come to regard them here – I think they're stooges but necessary ones, to another division with explicit instructions that we are on this case now and they are to stand down. I know those boys. They've come in handy, from time to time, but I've heard through my sources that they've been snooping around the race team. They're plotting something. I know them. They'll be told to bide their time and that they'll be called on to execute the justifiable action, only when *I* deem it is appropriate."

Jennings nodded and excused herself. She understood the directive completely. Bryce would be terminated, timing TBD.

CHAPTER TWENTY-SEVEN

Sydney's Bondi Beach is a beautiful stretch of sand facing the Pacific Ocean to the north and east, the Tasman Sea and New Zealand to the southeast. It is a popular destination for locals, tourists, and the occasional great white shark. The five-star resort Alistair Marshall had built there was equally popular with celebrities and anyone wishing to be seen in their circle.

Bryce's host had set him up with a suite on the hotel's top level. After dinner and drinks that lasted late into the night, Bryce thanked his new friend for his hospitality intended to help him forget the bad finish and relax for a few days.

At ten the next morning, a persistent knock at the door interrupted his deep sleep. He opened the door ready to pounce on the noisemaker but what he saw put a smile on his face.

"Achara!" he said with surprise. Marshall's latest girlfriend, a young Asian beauty who had followed her sugar daddy here from Bangkok, was equally surprised.

"You forgot?" she joked. "We're supposed to have

breakfast together and then I take you skydiving and then beer on the beach. You forgot me already?"

Bryce's thoughts had immediately gone to Kyoto. He had always appreciated and had a fondness for the exquisite, natural beauty of Asian women. For the first time in a very long time he had let his heart begin to open and let someone in. Kyoto was stunning and intelligent, but they were not attached. Achara, standing there with her long silky black hair, tanned and fit body, and a skimpy yellow bikini showing through a see-through cover, was a knockout. And she was giving him *the look*.

Bryce smiled. That was all he could muster until he had coffee and a shower. He marveled at the CIA's knowledge of how this would all play out. Marshall would use his money and women, of which he had plenty, to reward his newfound friend and keep him around long enough to show him off, take plenty of pictures, and brag to his friends. Bryce would have work to do, which would take a few days to accomplish. But, for now, he just followed as Achara took his hand and led him to the shower.

Over the next two days Bryce took in all that the area, and Achara, had to offer. With his host having suddenly jetted off to Singapore, Bryce was able to place the bugs the CIA had given him just about everywhere—except in the man's office on the top floor of one of Sydney's tallest buildings. He wouldn't be able to get in there without good reason, so he planned on waiting for Marshall's return and, perhaps, an invite to visit his downtown office before allowing Bryce to buy him a thank-you dinner. Then he'd head on to the next race in Bahrain.

Bryce couldn't suggest he'd like to see the office as that might raise a hair of suspicion. But from what he knew of his host, he'd want Bryce to come see it. After all, Marshall collected trophies as well, not from races and not counting the ladies. He was a big game hunter and, rumor had it, he had mounted a lion's head over his desk, which he was most proud of.

It had made sense for Bryce to spend at least several days at the resort. If he had placed the bugs and left abruptly, that might have told Marshall who had planted the devices if they, or the fruit of their surveillance, were revealed soon after. Eleven bugs in all, undetectable to electronic inspection, had been placed. Just a few more, and Bryce would be on a plane headed to the Arabian Gulf.

As soon as he learned Marshall was flying back on Wednesday morning, he extended the invitation to dinner through Achara. To his surprise, he had an encounter in the elevator back up to his suite after breakfast poolside.

"Eleven little birdies are singing just fine. Just a few more, please, if you can," said a man dressed in a maintenance department uniform. He got off on the next floor without another word.

With the sun setting in the horizon, Bryce knocked at Achara's door – the Marshall Suite. He held out his arm to escort her to the car waiting below, to take them on the short ride to the big man's office. In the elevator, their small talk was short lived.

"So, you leave for Bahrain in the morning," she said, "I will miss talking with you – among other things."

He smiled at her. "You look beautiful tonight – you

look amazing in blue - and I will miss you too." He paused. "But I drive race cars for a living. They're a part of me and make me feel alive. I can't wait to get back in the seat." She giggled.

"And I thought *I* made you feel alive. We'll have to try harder next time," she said as she took his hand and squeezed it. As the doors opened to let others board, she released her grasp and the journey continued.

The Lion was impressive, as was the rest of Marshall's office. The heads of animals that weren't quite kings of anything filled the room. Now they just gathered dust. The rugby trophies he'd acquired as the owner of a championship team lined mahogany shelves. Bryce didn't see the sense in the killing of animals just so the rich would have something to brag about. In other circles he'd suggested the big dollar, big game hunters should seek their prey like they did in olden times, to make things more of a challenge, with a spear or bow.

As he inspected the man's trophies he thought of the last time he and Pete had been in Africa together, not that long ago. Pete had indeed bagged the water buffalo he'd been after for years. They had toasted the animal, and its head, when he put it on display at his cabin. The difference between the two hunters was simple; Pete made sure the meat from the kill went to the local village. Bryce was unsure what happened to the rest of the magnificent lion but assumed it was left in the dirt and became part of the circle of life there.

Back home in Vermont, Bryce had killed for food back before he could afford to buy meat in any quantity at a store. Trophy hunting – at least this type – did nothing for him, but he faked his enthusiasm, not wanting to offend his host and bring the night to an early end. To him, killing needed to make sense, and he still had work to do.

Marshall's view from his office of the Sydney Bridge, the familiar Opera House, and the city skyline was very impressive. When Bryce first entered the space, he was startled by the sudden move of a man in a tailored dark blue suit who approached him with a wand, much like the ones used at airport screenings. This instrument appeared smaller and more sophisticated.

"No need, Julius," Marshall called out. "He's a friend." As he talked about Singapore, Achara poured a drink for both men; scotch rocks for Alistair and a Carlton Draught, a popular beer and Bryce's new favorite – at least down under. As she began to fix herself a drink, a cosmopolitan, Marshall called out again. "No need, my dear," he said, his tone softening with every word. "Our guest and I have business to discuss, so nighty-night for you, all dressed up in blue."

Marshall then led her to the door. She turned to tell Bryce that she had enjoyed meeting him and, a few seconds later, her black silky hair and tight figure disappeared from view as the door closed behind her.

Marshall turned to face his guest. Bryce sensed an immediate change in his demeanor. Sitting down beside Bryce on a massive sofa that was covered in hides, something perhaps from the plains of Africa, Marshall leaned in. His breath was of scotch, but his eyes were that of a hunter, eyeing his prey.

"So, what are you really doing here, Bryce Winters?" he asked without taking his eyes from his guest's.

"Meaning?" Bryce responded. "Dinner, I thought we were going to dinner. Look, I've had a great time here this week. Your hospitality has been exceptional and Achara has been—"

Marshall had put his hand up for Bryce to stop. "Listen, mate, I can hunt. I can sniff out a big cat like that one on the wall. More importantly, at least for right here and now, I can sniff out bullshit. And you're shoveling it."

He leaned in closer, forcing Bryce to lean away and consider getting up to leave. "You sought me out at the track, I saw it. I see that look all the time, people wanting to get close to me. That happens when you're bloody rich."

Bryce cocked his head. "Really? I thought I saw the same look in your eyes. I see that all the time from fans, stalkers, women looking for someone to give them the good life, or just a ride. Then there are the brokers, the land agents, you name it – and in every country. People who say they want to pay me to promote everything from deodorant to diapers, for God's sake. What was that look in *your* eye, Marshall? Why am I really here?"

The stare-down continued. Marshall leaned an inch closer, took a few sniffs, and then burst into laughter. "So, you didn't connect to ask me to sponsor you or the team?" he asked.

"And you don't want me to do commercials for your beach resort?" Bryce replied, continuing the laugh, more from relief than anything else. The two got up, fixed another round of drinks and gazed out at the skyline again, the sun now fully set.

"You still buying me dinner?" Marshall asked with a smile.

"Of course, Alistair, it's what I would really like to do to show my appreciation. You have my permission to publish some of the photos of me at the resort – the ones you had Achara take." They laughed again.

"Okay, down that beer while I go use the boy's room. It's a bitch getting older, nothing to look forward to, I can tell you." Marshall disappeared down the hall into what Bryce assumed was a toilet.

This was his chance, his only chance, and he moved about the man's office with the speed of a finely tuned pit crew. One bug here, another bug there, until four were placed. He was back at the window, empty beer glass in hand by the time Marshall reappeared. Bryce wondered if he'd get the chance to say goodbye to Achara properly but if not, she'd be a better memory than the racing disaster that had come at the start of this adventure

CHAPTER TWENTY-EIGHT

THE STORY GOES that His Royal Highness Prince Salman bin Hamad Al Khalifa, Crown Prince, Deputy Supreme Commander and First Deputy Prime Minister's passion for motorsports enabled him to have a vision for raising the profile of the Kingdom of Bahrain internationally. The Crown Prince had also wanted to bring Formula One to the island. In a chance meeting with former Formula One World champion Sir Jackie Stewart on a Concorde flight, much like the encounter when Bryce met Max Werner, the seeds for this idea were planted.

Years later, the Crown Prince's dream became a reality. But for Bryce, Bahrain was a disaster and ended prematurely under the lights and night heat of Bahrain. On the opening lap of the event, Bryce started from pole with Tony Bishop alongside him for the start. Dickie Jones was behind Bryce in third and, as the pack ran as hard and fast as possible into the first turn, all three cars tangled and washed off the asphalt into the catch gravel. Bryce's car wound up on its side, but he was able to climb out before help even arrived. When he saw Bishop remove his helmet and laugh about the flip, his temper red-lined and he went after him. Two lightning fast punches to the face and Bishop went down hard with Bryce jumping on him and shouting every curse word he'd ever heard. What made matters worse was Jones then attempted to help Bishop by pulling Bryce off of him.

Bryce and Bishop were close in driving skills and courage, but when it came to fist fighting, it was no-contest. When Jones managed to pull Bryce away, he made the mistake of shouting what Bryce thought to be, "Get the hell off of him," and that was it. Bryce turned and leveled Jones with one punch to the nose. Two down, pace car out on the track, medical car there to attend to the injuries, and the team owners and series officials demanding an immediate meeting of all the participants after the race's conclusion.

When the association's CEO stated through his Spanish accent, "Well, over four-hundred-million people just saw two Americans in a fist fight. Let me remind you, this is not wrestling, this is not your Wild West, *this* is professional racing. And all three of you are on probation effective immediately. One more infraction, and it's a one-race suspension. If you *are* going to fight, do it in a dark alley somewhere!" Bryce laughed at the remark but quieted when he caught the Spaniard's glare.

Max Werner had not made the trip to Bahrain, and neither had ProForce owner Ameer Kazaan. But texts from both to their drivers let them know they weren't at all pleased.

Bryce was still furious at Bishop and Jones. He went directly to the airport, boarded his charter and flew directly to Nice. Soon, he'd be standing in his summer home overlooking the Med. It had been hot in Bahrain and as a result of the poor finish and the fight he had simmered the entire way home but worked it off, finally, with dozens of laps in the cooler waters of his indoor pool. Later in the day, he'd call Kazaan to discuss the early retirement and the ensuing fight.

"Not much of a fight, mate," Kazaan told him. "You kicked his smug ass. Well done. He deserved it." Kazaan had calmed after watching his two cars crash out in the race. But he was still hot over Bishop's leaving the team and joining Werner's in the off-season without even attempting to negotiate a contract extension. "Now you and Dickie, going forward, that's another issue. You two need to get along for the sake of the team and our sponsors and fans." Once he heard what Jones had said during the fight and was reminded of how Jones had probably cost Bryce the championship last year, Kazaan relented. "I'll speak to Dickie boy. He's always been our number two, first with Bishop and now with you. If he wants off the team, if he won't support you 110%, I can think of a dozen names who would die to get a shot at his seat. I'll refund his father's money and the two of them can sit at home and watch on the telly, for all I care."

CHAPTER TWENTY-NINE

ON THE WESTBOUND flight high over the Atlantic Bryce considered his existence as a road warrior – people who travel their territory, the country, or the globe—are used to hotels, rental cars, and restaurants. It may sound exciting to some, not being glued to a desk or an assembly line, but to others it's strictly the cost of doing business or a chosen lifestyle. Racers, rock stars, traveling sales reps know it well. Then there are the bars and the loneliness that comes with it all. For many, the idea of a home-cooked meal is so rare that it makes such an occasion very special. For Bryce, this 5,700-mile flight itself was no big deal. What was waiting for him on the other end was much more than a home-cooked meal. These were unchartered waters. Bryce had accepted an invitation to dinner and he would head back to the United States and to his surprise, the scene of a crime committed by The White House.

Kyoto had finally settled into her new home in Washington, DC. For her, being able to look out over the Potomac made her feel close to home. She'd grown up in a loving environment with a view of a river and great city, and it brought her comfort and tranquility. She was so excited to see Bryce. He hadn't been to her new address even after all these months of jet-setting dating. Even so, she was comfortable with the way things between them had been going. He had his career; she had hers, and she was still settling into not just her new home but also the new job that had brought her all this way from Japan. Luckily, for her, she had her brother close by. He had sent her information about the job opening and did everything he could to convince her to make the move to DC. He was lonely, too. Working long hours in a job he couldn't tell anyone about, including her.

ᯓ

"This is awesome," Bryce exclaimed as he entered the sprawling condo. "But the Watergate?"

Kyoto laughed as they embraced and held tight for a moment. She stepped back and smiled, pulling at his hand to take him for a tour.

She looked stunning—hair pulled back, white t-shirt, tight jeans, barefoot on the plush grey carpet. It all worked for him. History remembered the Watergate for its role in the end of the Nixon presidency, back in the summer of 1972. Nearly fifty years later, Bryce and Kyoto's generation was familiar only with the name, not the history behind it.

When Bryce had first learned of her new address, he recalled a few details about the place from school assignments, reading about the scandals and Nixon's resignation, the man shamed into it because he had broken the law. Among other things, his re-election campaign had put former spies and fixers from the CIA and other intelligence services to work. They had broken into the Democratic National Party's offices located in the Watergate complex to obtain intel on the competition. Over time, more and more incriminating information, including audiotapes of the president himself, would bring his reign to an embarrassing end.

And now I'm working for the CIA, he thought as he followed Kyoto. *For that matter, I wonder how much spying has gone on in racing, to try to gain an advantage by stealing info on the competition.*

First, she led him to the cluster of windows that revealed a view of the river and the tree-covered banks over on the Virginia side. The rooms were full of new furniture and fixtures, some still in boxes or shrouded in bubble wrap. But the massive flat-screen was mounted across from an inviting large brown leather sofa.

Bryce laughed to himself, remembering how long it had taken him to set up his address in Monte Carlo. Once the television and sofa were installed, he'd lost his appetite for setting up a second home and went off to race, again and again. Suddenly, his senses alerted him. He smelled something wonderful and followed his nose straight into the kitchen.

"I was going to show you the bedroom but you're in here?" she joked.

He turned and smiled at her as he peeked under a few lids and then opened the oven to inspect the main course. She slapped him on the wrist and pushed him away from the food prep area but then dove back into an embrace with him. Bryce thought about turning down the dials on the stove and delaying dinner a bit, but a knock at the door brought his plan to a sudden stop.

"*Company?*" he asked curiously. He slid back into the kitchen while she went to the door. Bryce went about opening the wine he'd brought and then noticed there were three settings at the table.

He could hear Kyoto speaking with someone in the hallway and turned when he heard her say, "Bryce, I want you to meet my brother - Jon."

She was beaming, standing alongside a young man who could have been her twin. Bryce put down the wine and stepped forward to shake hands. He laughed at Jon's expression; his mouth and eyes wide open in surprise. Bryce had seen the look a million times when people recognized him. He wrapped his arms around Jon. Two brothers had raised Bryce; neither of them ever said, "I love you" or verbally expressed feelings for one another very often. But they *were* huggers.

Strangely, Jon seemed unwilling to return his embrace. Bryce could feel the other man's arms just hanging at his side. Bryce stepped back to see his face. The look in Jon's eyes wasn't that of star-struck awe. It was fear.

"Earth to Jon," Kyoto joked, poking her brother in the side.

"I remember the picture you sent to me and father," he finally said, his voice strained. "You and Bryce Winters the Formula One driver." He stepped back a foot. "I-I didn't know you actually knew him."

She laughed, as did Bryce who then turned his focus back on the wine. *Maybe the booze will relax him.* After a toast, Kyoto insisted Jon and Bryce sit together in the living room while she finished preparing the meal. When she checked on them a few minutes later she laughed when she saw them engrossed in a premier league soccer match from England on the TV.

"Good to see you two have something more in common than just me," she said. "Dinner in five minutes. And it won't be in front of the television on my new sofa."

❧

"That's god-damned Bryce Winters taking a leak in your bathroom!" Jon whispered in his sister's ear as she spooned the last bit of mashed potatoes into a serving dish.

She just smiled at him. "I haven't felt like this about anyone in years," she responded in a whispered tone and kept working.

What the fuck! Jon thought in frustration as he tried to process what was happening. His sister had no idea what she had gotten herself into. The fact that she'd fallen for the man Jon had identified as an international killer was something that only happened in the movies. This wasn't possible; the world couldn't be this damn small. *Not with my sister.*

By the time Bryce returned to the kitchen, Jon was near panic, inside. He excused himself and locked himself in her bathroom to try and process what the hell was going on and what to do about it. He knew he couldn't tell Kyoto what he had learned of the man she was falling in love with. That would likely cost him his job. Maybe even result in prison time. Even worse, if he revealed what he knew to his sister and destroyed her relationship with Bryce, the race driver might pay him back by throwing his body in a dumpster in DC. This was crazy!

What the fuck, he said to himself again. I'm just an analyst; this is way higher than my pay grade. A knock at the door snapped him back. It was his sister. "Dinner's getting cold, stop playing in there and come join us. He doesn't bite."

Perhaps it was the three glasses of wine that helped relax him. One was usually his limit. Soccer, the sites and the history of the city two of the three now worked in, and food consumed them during turkey dinner that came with all the trimmings.

"It's not Thanksgiving," Kyoto had toasted earlier. "But I have so much to be thankful for." She looked to Jon and then to Bryce while taking his hand in hers.

Jon returned an encouraging smile but knew, one way or another, he had to get her away from this man. Bryce Winters and Jack Madigan, had been flagged as killers, assigned to one covert assignment after another. No way could he allow his sister to continue seeing, and sleeping with, Winters. But as soon as they finished eating and adjourned to the living room, the turkey and wine began to take their toll. The room seemed to spin. He felt confused enough by the situation and now the alcohol was taking its toll. Finding a solution, he decided, would need to wait. He was done. He closed his eyes, leaned back into the sofa cushion.

He remembered feeling his sister place a blanket over him there on the sofa. She must have turned off the television and the lights. By the time he woke up early the next morning, his head nearly clear, Bryce was long gone.

He could hear Kyoto in the bedroom, rushing to get dressed. He poured a coffee from the pot she'd made, trying to think of what to say to her. When he heard her finally come into the kitchen, he turned to face her, the words prepared to break her heart.

She flashed him a huge smile, and his heart sank. That smile wasn't for him. She was in love, and he knew *they* were screwed.

~

Arlington, Virginia. When it came to professional assassins—whether a government agency, the military, or a freelancer employed by a wealthy criminal, Bryce had learned they were an eclectic bunch at best. In the case of the "three musketeers" as they were nicknamed at the CIA, they *were* professionals and while never willing to be labeled as assassins, they were known to do whatever it took- *whatever* it took – to accomplish an assignment or protect the United States. In the case of their orders regarding Bryce Winters, they were conflicted. Having received specific instructions from their new superior, Sandra Jennings, they sat in the back booth of a bar in Arlington and stared into space. As their server brought them another round of beer and shots, they made their traditional boilermakers and downed them in short order.

"We can't touch the prick now, not as long as she's in the mix," Russo said as Chadwick and Brownell nodded. "None of the directions we wanted to take were practical, or they violated orders, except the one. Since Madigan agreed to this long before we got the memo, it's game on as far as I'm concerned. We just won't tell him to call it off." Chadwick said, waving for yet another round.

"Plausible deniability has to be maintained," Chadwick stated emphatically. "I'm not giving up my pension or freedom over this." They waited until the server removed their empty glassware before continuing.

"So, we are in agreement?" Brownell said. "Once Madigan makes his move, he'll wind up as dead as Bryce Winters."

CHAPTER THIRTY

Twenty-four hours after their dinner at the Watergate and then a meeting at the team's HQ in the Midlands, Bryce typed in the alarm code and turned the key to enter his hillside condo overlooking the Med in Monte Carlo. It was late. Weather in England had delayed the departure of his private charter to Nice. Keys dropped on the tray on the table by the door, bags beneath them. He walked through to the kitchen, adjusted the thermostat to a cozier 72 degrees, grabbed a beer from the bar, and then spent a few minutes just admiring his home away from home.

He'd hired an interior designer to mimic what he'd loved about the Greek isle Santorini. The walls were painted a shade of pale white, the tile floors mostly blues and golds, and the furniture white and bright throughout. In daylight, if someone didn't know better, they could very easily believe they were above the water in Greece, until they looked down on the motor and sailing yachts in the marina below. Monaco's presidential palace tucked away on the far hill off to the right.

He'd slept on the plane so wasn't ready to call it a

night, not yet. Bryce spent a good ten minutes in the long hallway that led straight from the entry door to the patio overlooking the sea.

Monte Carlo was far from Vermont and even farther from Park City, but the photos he'd hung in the hallway made it all seem a bit closer. There were large, mounted photos by his favorite wildlife photographer Tom Mangelsen. Grizzlies from Montana and Alaska and a lion much like those he had seen in Africa, healthier and happier than those he'd seen in zoos. On the wall opposite the predators, he had mounted football and motorsport photography by Mark Rebilas from Phoenix. He'd never met either man but greatly admired their work.

After a few days of rest, biking and hiking, rest, time in the gym, and then more rest, he'd reset the alarm and board another jet. This one headed for Shanghai. But a text came through that threw him a curve ball. It was from Jack Madigan.

Got dinner plans?

CHAPTER THIRTY-ONE

AMEER KAZAAN'S BOMBARDIER 8000 jet was a pearl white beauty with a red-and-blue stripe that grew thicker as it spread from nose to tail. Bryce hadn't flown on this one, yet was thrilled when he saw it pull up on the tarmac at the private terminal of the Nice airport. With comfortable seating, tan leather captain's chairs, contrasting darker appointments and plush carpet, the accommodations for eighteen were spacious and comfortable.

The cabin was half empty until Bryce and the team's new technical consultant, Jack Madigan, came aboard. Most of the team was heading from the Midlands in the U.K. to China on commercial flights, via Frankfurt or Istanbul. Bryce's chief engineer Freddie Burns and his four-man team were able to fly private as part of their contract with Kazaan. And there was *always* to be an open seat for their star driver. Dickie Jones, Bryce's teammate, was somewhere over Europe at this hour, flying commercial but up front in first class.

After exchanging greetings and a few jokes, Bryce and Madigan left the engineers to the meeting they'd been in the middle of and headed to the back of the cabin to continue their dinner discussion from the night before.

~

Madigan hadn't spoken with Bryce in months. But, after being so close for so many years, the time they had spent apart reminded Bryce of how much he cared for and had missed his dear friend. Dinner the night before was pizza, delivered so they could talk without the interruption of excited fans hoping for a photo, an autograph, or in rare instances, pulling up a chair and joining the party.

F1's security team didn't shadow him at home unless there was a specific threat. But if he'd gone out, two highly qualified security experts posing as a young couple on holiday, would have shadowed his every move. They and a dozen others worked shifts on the local police force, were retired military, or both, and provided protection when called on by Bryce or many of the other drivers who called the hillside their home. His security didn't come cheap, but it was necessary.

While they had waited for the food to arrive, the two had caught up as long-lost friends, picking up where they had left off nearly five months prior. Madigan's temper had cooled but began to resurface as they fought over the last slice of pepperoni pizza.

"This whole thing could have gone so wrong," Jack had told him and then dug up the hard feelings he'd expressed in Mexico and later in Abu Dhabi. After pushing the empty box out of the way, Bryce gave in and let his guest have the last piece.

Madigan shoved his chair back and threw the food

across the room. "I loved her, God-damn it, and you took her from me!" he shouted. "Don't give me any of Pete's bullshit either, Bryce. He left a voicemail on my phone two days after the last race and apologized, if you want to call it that. Listen," he said as he played the recording he'd kept of the last words he'd heard from the assassin.

"Hey Jack," the message began, "I really am sorry that I ruined your love life. I truly am. But remember, she was cheating on her husband, so what does that tell you? That you were *that* special she'd leave him for you, only to leave you to wonder if she was playing hide and seek with some other swingin' dick out there, too? Long term, you're better off without her. Move on. Don't blame Bryce for this. He didn't know you had feelings for her. He thought you resented her for blackmailing you, just as much as he did. So anyway, sorry I used the taser on you. I needed to be able to do what I thought was right if either of those pricks decided to screw with our boy."

Madigan looked at Bryce, who was listening to every word as the recording continued.

"Listen, you boys get your butts out from under the CIA boot they've got on your necks. I'm here in Africa now. I just left a note for Bryce, but I'll tell you. I'm dying and will be gone before Christmas. Sorry I messed things up for you both. I never intended for either of you to get caught up in my shit. Find yourself a good-looking woman back there in Charlotte once you're done with the road. There's plenty of them out there looking for a good man. And you are one, even if you *are* a prick sometimes."

They heard Pete begin to laugh as he delivered those last words and they responded in kind, Madigan seeing a tear well up in Bryce's eye. He watched as Bryce got up from the table to grab two more beers from the bar.

"I'll say it again, Jack, and I mean it with all my heart. I am sorry. If I had known, Pete would not have been in Baja." He came back to the table and sat down, pulling a one Euro coin from his pocket. He stared at his friend until he saw a change, a very slight one, in Madigan's expression.

"Flip ya to see who cleans that up?" Bryce said with a smile that Madigan then reflected.

Having lost the bet, Madigan cleaned up the pizza he'd smashed against the sliding glass door. Then they sat and retold stories of their earlier days in racing. Madigan announced that he'd sold his modest home in North Carolina, as it had only been a spot for pit stops all these years.

"I was thinking about buying a place somewhere in the Mountain West, maybe Utah, out close to the track in Salt Lake. I hear there might be a driving school opening up there soon. Thought I could get a job there if they're hiring." He saw Bryce's face develop a grin from ear to ear.

"Oh yeah, one last thing. I joined the team this morning. Signed the docs and flew here to tell you I'll be alongside for as long as you keep chasing that second title."

Bryce's smile was exactly what Madigan had hoped for.

"Oh, and one more last thing. The CIA wants me to kill you."

CHAPTER THIRTY-TWO

THE RACE IN China went perfectly. Even though Bryce kept looking over his shoulder, he heard nothing from the CIA or Lee or the MSS. He did as Lee had asked back in Paris, behaved himself in her country and left without trying to terminate anyone. Luckily, the agency had not asked him to do anything or move on anyone there but she wouldn't have known that.

The next race took place at Baku in Azerbaijan – a street circuit off the shores of the Caspian Sea. To the north was Russia, to the south Iran. He thought for sure the CIA would have a job for him, the area was dead center between two of America's most dangerous adversaries. Bryce hadn't heard a word although he thought he'd seen Jason Ryan's face pop up in a crowd of onlookers but had disappeared as Bryce did a double take. Two weeks later the tour was back in Spain on the same track where the pre-season testing had launched the racing calendar. Bryce hadn't heard anything from his handlers prior to Catalunya either but thinking back to the man he had helped kill with the pace car ride, and fearing repercussions from any of the man's family or business connections, Bryce kept his appearance schedule light and the security around him much heavier. As they separated at the airport for flights back to England and Monaco, Burns and Bryce joked that Madigan had been a much-needed lucky charm. With back to back wins and a second place, the quest for another F1 World Championship for the team, and for Bryce, now seemed possible.

The schedule kept rolling and the next event, one that he had always found most challenging, would take place just a short ride down to sea level from his European home. A win in the Monaco Grand Prix was the most prestigious, coveted prize for any driver, second only to the series title. Bryce was thrilled Kyoto had agreed to make her first trip ever to Monte Carlo. He was looking forward to showing her the city. It would also be the first race she would attend in person; she'd always passed on her father's invitations to join him in Japan. The race itself was one of the most intense experiences in racing he had ever competed in and he couldn't wait for the weekend to arrive.

Kyoto was also excited. Her first trip to Monte Carlo, an F1 race, and finally a glimpse of the home this jet-setting friend of hers kept. To surprise him, she flew in a day early. After a short ride from the airport in Nice to his address, she stood in the lobby of his condo checking her makeup and waiting for him to answer his phone. Despite the jet lag from the long overnight flight from DC, she was full of anticipation. Coffee and the warm, bright sunshine had recharged her, for now.

She was disappointed Bryce hadn't picked up yet – *maybe he is in the shower*, she thought, *it is early*. She kept hearing something strange echoing through the air and finally asked the concierge at the front desk just what that was.

"Formula One," he told her with a smug response, as if she should already know, "they are practicing today."

She said something in response, putting her first language of Japanese to work, cursing herself for not knowing he'd be racing that morning and telling the concierge to stick his smugness in a very dark place. Switching back to English she told him who she was, who she was there to see, and asked what he might suggest she do. She gave the man, a tall and thin French version of Herman Munster but with a pencil thin mustache, a look. She meant business, the air had just been let out of her tires, and she wasn't in the mood for attitude.

"You must understand, mademoiselle," he began, "this is the race weekend. Everyone will say these sorts of things but regardless I cannot acknowledge or deny that Mr. Winters resides here. It is forbidden." She glared at him but then took a breath and calmed. *Okay, he's racing. I need a shower.*

"I bet there's not a hotel room available within fifty miles of here," she said.

The man looked down at her bag, noting the airline baggage ticket still strapped to the handle; NCE.

"There would be rooms in Nice, most certainly at the airport but not on the beach, not the five-star hotels," he told her.

Just then, her phone vibrated, and she smiled, turning away from Munster and stepping to the lobby window to watch the passersby. She laughed when she heard Bryce ask if she was still coming and told him where she was. Flying in for a big surprise had gone wrong.

After a few minutes of catching up she turned and faced the concierge, this time displaying her own smug expression as she handed her phone to him. Minutes later, after she entered Bryce's five-number password code to disable the alarm, the bellman turned the key and led Kyoto into the Winters condo. Tipped and excused, he closed the door behind him.

She walked down the hall, slowing to examine his collection of photographs, and then headed for the balcony and the sensory overload that was waiting for her there. She opened the sliding glass door and the scent of flowers on the balcony wafted over her. The sun stood high overhead in a cloudless blue sky. She heard the sound of the race cars far below running through the tight city streets and darting past dozens of magnificent yachts docked in the marina. It was spectacular.

Bryce had told her he was booked solid between practice sessions, media and sponsor commitments, and a driver's meeting he had to attend. He suggested she make herself at home, get some sleep, and he'd be there by four o'clock at the latest. The shower and more coffee woke her, and she perched back on the balcony but was soon surprised by just how hot the sun had become. She moved back inside to the sofa where Bryce and Madigan had made their peace not that long ago.

After a minute looking about the room, loving the

bright decor of Santorini Bryce had told her of, she sat forward and picked through the books and magazines he'd left on the clear glass coffee table. There were paperbacks by Dan Brown, Jack Carr, Mark Greaney, a copy of Autosport magazine, and a hard cover of My Greatest Defeat by Will Buxton. She smiled at what she had found so far – nice guy, nice taste, nice place – but then she picked up a paperback that scared her.

The book's title was The Mechanic's Tale by Steve Matchett. The cover photo was of a man, a pit crewmember, fully engulfed in flames. She dropped it and shook her head in fear.

Racing through the streets of any city can be harrowing but driving between massive, hard-as-rock concrete barriers at speed requires exceptional focus and luck to win at Monte Carlo.

"Imagine driving through a construction zone, single lane, with Jersey barriers and guardrails close on either side of you. Now do that at three times the allowed speed, through tight turns and the occasional bump, with someone close on your tail, chasing you – pushing you - the entire way." That's how Bryce described it to the international media assembled for the post-race press conference.

In the hours that preceded, he'd won his first-ever Monaco Grand Prix, his first pole there, led every lap, and posed with his new girl. Royalty – the sovereign prince, graced the podium ceremonies. When the focus was taken from the race and to the Asian beauty he'd kissed for the cameras, Bryce's tone changed slightly.

"She's a dear friend. Her father who passed recently was a big fan back in Japan, and that's the extent of what I'll say. Now let's get back to the race story."

After a quick shower and change of clothes, Bryce, Kyoto, Kazaan, Burns, and a stumbling Madigan made their way across the track to the parties and celebrations on yacht after yacht, hosted by millionaire after billionaire, movie and sports stars.

"First Madigan and now this lovely lady," an intoxicated Burns said as he raised yet another glass of champagne to toast the two and the weekend's success. "They've both brought us luck."

Bryce couldn't be happier, but knowing Kyoto had to leave early the next morning he called it a night. The couple headed back to his condo to do what lovers do.

In the car he teased her. "Forget work, call in sick, stay the week," he begged. She thought about it, at least that's what Bryce assumed as he saw her attention turn elsewhere.

"No can do," she said as she turned toward him. "Got a job to do. But I will be there in Montreal." He smiled as she said something, perhaps a tease, in French. He'd always found the language sexy but coming from the lips of this beautiful Japanese woman made it even better.

CHAPTER THIRTY-THREE

Summers in Burlington, Vermont were a stark contrast to the vibrant fall colors of autumn and winters there with the cold temps falling over the land and frozen Lake Champlain that separated the state from New York. Everything in the summer was green; the lake was warmish and full of sailboats and jet-skis. The region was now crammed with tourists, campers, and travelers.

On this week in June many would soon head north, driving the ninety miles to Montreal and the next stop on the Formula One calendar. Bryce flew commercial into Boston from Nice via Paris and then rented a car to drive across New England. For someone who risked his life behind the wheel and loved it, a scenic ride at a significantly lower speed across New Hampshire and toward the region he'd grown up in was pure pleasure.

He stopped at Montpelier along the way, Vermont's capitol, to say hi to the Governor, who used to race cars on the same tracks—Thunder Road, Lee, Thompson, and many others. After he posed for photos with Vermont State Troopers at the state house, he headed north again toward the one spot he had to visit before crossing the border into Canada.

Cemeteries are tough places. They are reminders of what's been lost and what's to come. For race car drivers, they are stark reminders of what could come very prematurely. For Bryce, visiting his father's grave, and now Pete's, was always sad. He longed for what might have been but always left them behind with a smile, choosing to think of the happier times than the days he shoveled dirt to cover their caskets.

The brothers were together again, forever now. Bryce laughed as he imagined the two giving the gatekeepers in heaven a hard time as they checked their credentials, demanding to be let in. Then he turned his attention to Christy. He walked the short distance to her gravestone and stared at the date. It had been nearly ten years since she'd been killed in that horrible crash. Nearly ten years since he'd felt the pain that would never leave him. He'd been in very hard crashes over the years, but he loved racing, more than anything. So much so that the risk of pain and suffering just couldn't keep him from coming back.

"Ten years is a long time," he whispered to her. He hadn't loved anyone since her, but now his heart and mind had healed enough to finally let someone else in. *I have to let you go Christy,* he said to her without speaking a word. *It's not fair to her for me to continue to miss you and hurt from what happened. I'll never forget you, but today will be my final goodbye.*

He stood over her grave, thinking of her for another few minutes. But sensed someone nearby and, fearing they might have recognized him, he walked back to his car before they had time to approach him.

CHAPTER THIRTY-FOUR

THE PLATE THAT flew across the kitchen and smashed into pieces against the sink was the last thing Kyoto threw before her brother Jon wrapped his arms around her to disable her outburst.

"Why didn't you tell me?" she had screamed at him, more from a broken heart than the mental rage she had felt just minutes before.

He held onto her until he could feel the tension release through her tears. Jon guided her to a chair at the kitchen table, moving the last remaining plate from her reach.

She sighed. "I'm done. I'm done with plates, I'm done with love, I'm just done," she told him.

He had wanted to tell his sister, his only sibling, sooner—but hadn't been able to until he'd seen the race. He'd watched F1, just as he had with their father, growing up and inherited his dad's passion for it. When he saw Bryce Winters standing in his sister's living room a short time ago, he was excited but conflicted. The joy he'd seen in his sister's eyes as she stood beside her new beau, holding his hand, had put him in a bad way.

"I wanted to tell you. I knew I should," he'd said. "But that would have put my security clearance, even my job, in jeopardy." He leaned in, whispering, as if someone might hear. "There are some serious hombres at the CIA and even more serious operators working as contractors for them. I do not want to get on the wrong side of anyone affiliated with Langley. Period."

She looked up at him, her eyes still red from the tears. "So why now? What the fuck! You tell me that the guy I was falling in love with is a murderer. You got to keep your job for a while, but you've left me in bed with a guy that kills people? Is that job more important than me to you?"

They spent the next hour going over and over everything he'd told her, everything he knew about Bryce, Madigan, and their escapades. He told her about Baja, how two CIA agents had been assassinated in what some suspected was retaliation for Bryce's hit in Sochi. Others felt he'd orchestrated something in an attempt to free himself from the CIA.

"You're saying he not only kills criminals and enemies of the United States, he's taken out CIA agents? He's killed CIA agents?" she shouted.

"There's no proof he took out his handler and her boss, but that's what the team they worked with believes or at least that's what I've heard."

"Are you at risk – are we at risk?" she asked, her anger turning toward panic.

He tried to quiet her but watched as his sister's mind raced. She specialized in International Law and was brilliant at it. *She'll figure something out*, he told himself. He hoped.

"Now that your face has been plastered all around the world kissing a killer, how do you think this will impact you? Will you ever see him again or not?" he said as he placed a tall glass of vodka, no ice, in front of her.

She took a few breaths and stared at her brother. She didn't say another word but sat quietly and drank down the alcohol without flinching. Her eyes blinked as she shook her head and coughed in response to the liquor's bite. He watched her expression change from anger and frustration to a smile.

"Who knows, maybe I can get a Revlon contract or one with Chanel," she joked as she wiped away the few remaining tears. Then Kyoto got up and walked to the bar, poured another vodka and returned to the table.

Jon protested. "Don't you think one was enough?"

She smiled again. "No – this one's for you. Now down it or I'll kick your ass for not telling me!"

He made a face but swallowed the vodka. He'd never been able to drink hard liquor from anything more than a shot glass.

She was pleased. "Glad to see you still can't drink – one of us needs to keep our shit together while we sort this out."

"What's to sort?" he asked, pushing the glass away and getting up to look for something in the kitchen to wash away the taste.

"Well, from a legal standpoint, you've breached your CIA clearance. That puts both of us at risk from the CIA, not just Bryce. I've also got to tell him we're done and *that* he won't understand."

Jon looked at her and shook his head slowly. "This

can't be happening. He's developed a relationship – a working one – with his new handler Sandra Jennings. *If* he wanted to, he could ask her to check into you and perhaps even surveil *us* if he thinks the break-up is bullshit." He tore the lid off a tin of potato chips he'd found in a cabinet and began to inhale them.

She reached for the tin and pulled it away so she could share.

"Can you get protection from work?" he asked.

"Yeah, sure," she said with a sarcastic tone. "I just moved here from Japan, not even fully settled in yet, and my boyfriend is killing people for the CIA. I need to break up with him and somehow make sure that both my knucklehead CIA analyst, should-have-known-better brother and I don't wind up floating in the Potomac." She laughed. "Is that how you see that playing out at *my* job?"

"You never told Bryce where you worked?"

"No. All I ever said was that I took a new job practicing international law at a big firm headquartered in Washington. Boring stuff that would put you to sleep and much less exciting than driving race cars around the world."

They sat quietly for a time. And then Kyoto grabbed her phone and tapped away for a minute.

"What'd you do?" Jon asked.

"Two things. I ordered a pizza and then cancelled my flight to Montreal."

"Are you going to tell him you're not coming?"

"Not sure. First, I need to go throw up and get rid of the vodka. I need a clear head. Then we can talk while we eat. We can figure this out. I know we can."

Jon smiled. His sister always had known what to do in a pinch. "What can I do?" he asked.

"Clean up the plates – that's the least you can do for not telling me," she ordered.

He went about the chore while she took care of herself. When she returned to the kitchen, she had changed from her dark blue suit to white t-shirt and shorts, her long silky black hair pulled back with a tie.

"What do you think about me transferring to the CIA?" she asked, her tone serious. Jon did a double take at the thought. "That's funny," he said.

"I was just going to ask about a transfer to the work with you."

CHAPTER THIRTY-FIVE

SANDRA JENNINGS HAD never been to Montreal, but she'd flown there to meet with her counterparts at the CSIS, Canada's Security Intelligence Service. Their offices for Quebec province were located in an unremarkable walk-up in the lower city, a stone's throw from the St. Lawrence River. She wanted to kill two birds with one stone, meet up them and then spend a short time with Bryce to discuss a person of interest. He'd be racing in Germany in six weeks' time, and there was someone who needed to be dealt with there. She knew it would be a sensitive topic and was waiting for him in his suite at the Sheraton Centre downtown.

"How the hell did you get in here?" he asked, surprised to find anyone other than a maid tidying up his room.

She smiled and gave him a look that reminded him she was a spy with the CIA. Luckily, he'd discovered her sitting by the window in his room after he'd closed the door behind him. The F1 security team was in place now for the duration of the event. If they'd heard his declaration they'd have been in there behind him in seconds.

Jennings told Bryce she'd only be there for a short time to broach the subject of his next assignment and then be gone. When she noticed that his phone distracted him, she asked if everything was okay.

"Yeah, yeah – just can't reach someone. I have a friend coming up for the race, and she's not responding to my calls or texts."

"Kyoto Watanabe coming up?" she asked.

His shocked expression gave away surprise and anger. "Spying on me?"

"Just looking out for you Bryce. I told you when we met at the driving school that I wanted to work with you. You agreed to the new, friendlier, terms of our arrangement. We're not bugging your bedroom. Just making sure the people you are with are not there with sinister agendas. Wouldn't you want us to check up on the hot Russian models you date overseas to make sure there wasn't any possibility of compromise there?"

He got it. He shook his head and put his phone down. He walked to the window and stared up at St. Joseph's, a catholic basilica with one of the largest domes in the world, sitting high on Mount Royal overlooking the city. He wasn't Catholic, or a person of any faith for that matter, but could appreciate their architecture.

"I get it," he said. He wasn't sure how good his acting skills were on this day. He was concerned Kyoto hadn't shown up yet, the CIA had shown up in his room unannounced and uninvited, and he couldn't understand what Susan Lee had said in Paris. He remembered the words she'd written down for him in a much more extravagant hotel suite a few months earlier.

WHY DOES THE CIA HAVE A BUG ON YOUR PHONE?

Lee hadn't offered any proof at the time, but since then Bryce hadn't taken any chances. Anything he didn't want the CIA to know he didn't discuss, text, or email with his phone anywhere nearby. He began relying on burner phones, ones he could use and discard. As Jennings began to lay out the next assignment, Bryce found himself looking first at the lamps in the room, then the flat screen, then and the telephone on the nightstand. *Wonder if they've bugged the place?*

"Bryce, I can see you're distracted. Trust me – the background check on Kyoto was SOP, standard operating procedure, and she's as clean as a whistle, even though we bang heads with her employer from time to time."

Bryce focused. "Her employer? How so?"

"The State Department doesn't always agree on what we do or how we do it, but we get along, for the most part. Wouldn't that be funny if someday the two of you actually sat together at a briefing?"

State? She never said exactly who she worked for, and I never asked – what a dummy.

"Okay, tell me more about Germany." An hour later, after a discussion that seemed to hit on every emotion in Bryce's makeup, he agreed to the assignment. At least that was what he told Jennings.

"We think you are the only one who can get that close to him without setting off extra security, making him run, or leaving a suspicious trail. What we have planned will be humane. But I can assure you, if you don't execute this properly someone else will, and it will be in a much messier way."

"But he has a child," Bryce pushed back – the rule he swore he'd never break.

"Doing it this way, she'll at least be able to say good-bye. If someone else does, she won't. Think of it that way, Bryce," she suggested. "I know that matters to you." He nodded. Anything to get this meeting behind him; let him focus on where Kyoto might be. He'd process what he agreed to later.

Finally, a text came through that stopped him cold.

> NOT COMING. THAT PHOTO OF THE MAN ON FIRE I FOUND IN YOUR CONDO REMINDED ME OF HOW DANGEROUS YOUR LIFE IS. I DON'T WANT TO FALL IN LOVE WITH ANYONE TAKING RISKS LIKE THAT. WISH I HAD REALIZED THAT SOONER INSTEAD OF GETTING INTO THIS.
>
> PLEASE DON'T CALL OR PURSUE ME. I CAN'T DO THIS. GOOD-BYE.

CHAPTER THIRTY-SIX

Berchtesgaden is a small town in southeastern Germany near the Austrian border.

The German Alps, with lingering tufts of winter snow lasting late into the spring, surround the small city on the shoreline of tranquil Lake Konigsee. Max Werner's family had occupied a sprawling Alpine-style home here for decades.

A tourist destination located high on a mountaintop that was visited during World War II by Adolph Hitler, it continued to attract visitors from around the globe seventy-five years after the dictator's suicide in Berlin. Werner had never visited the top of the mountain, the so-called Eagle's Nest, and preferred like most Germans to put that embarrassing history far behind him and look only to the future.

Bryce spent a few minutes talking with the bodyguard who manned the front gate; they had known each other for years. As Bryce drove through the thin layer of gravel toward the Werner Estate, he had mixed emotions about the meeting that was about to take place. He expected to share a few laughs, shout a few times, take a little ride down memory lane, and then kill someone for the CIA.

Werner greeted Bryce at the front door with a smile and led his guest straight through the spacious living and dining rooms. Exposed wood beams formed the ceiling overhead, carrying all the way to the wall made of glass that revealed a magnificent view of the lake.

"It's spectacular, Max," Bryce said as he stood alongside his estranged friend and former boss. "Thank you for inviting me."

Werner muttered what Bryce believed was 'of course' and then followed his host through a doorway that matched the front entrance and led to a large and beautifully decorated home office. As Bryce took a seat at the front of Werner's desk he continued to admire the architecture and the space. The view of the lake was maintained across the entire back of the home.

"Mila's not here today?" Bryce asked of Werner's now nine-year-old daughter. He had met Werner's only child five years prior during a ski-weekend in Zermatt, and the two grew to regard their relationship as favorite uncle, only niece.

"No, she *never* comes here. Her mother would not allow it. I'm surprised you don't remember the story. This is where her mother found me with another woman. From that day on, this place was off limits."

Bryce *had* remembered that Mila wouldn't be there, but he intended to continue the charade.

"So, you asked to meet. What did you want to talk about?"

"I have a problem. One of the race engineers told me

the cat I gave Mila for her birthday died, so I brought her a gift. Damn it."

"That was very nice of you but not necessary. I fly to Munich in the morning. I can take it to her if you like."

Bryce gave him a thumbs up, got up from the burgundy leather chair and walked to the wall that Werner faced every day. Bryce admired the dozens of mounted photos of Werner's racing successes in NASCAR, Indy Car, and Formula One, noting the one thing they all had in common – Bryce's face was in each one of them.

"We did well together, didn't we?" Werner said. "But for the both of us, Canada and France were total disasters, wouldn't you say?"

The race in Montreal had indeed been a nightmare for them both; Bryce qualified poorly and then crashed out on the opening lap when he swerved to avoid a spinning car and hit two others. One of those cars belonged to Werner. Then, a week later, at the historic Circuit Paul Ricard in France the engine problems that plagued Bryce's team as the season began came back to haunt them and forced an early retirement. Werner's drivers, Bishop and the rookie sensation from Spain, Renaldo Patrice, had battled for the lead. With two laps to go, despite team orders to behave, they crashed out and allowed an up-and-coming Russian star, Nikita Pushkin, to take the win and move much higher in the points chase.

"Bryce, it's been a long time since we first met in New York. We've accomplished a lot together, a tremendous amount. But I have to say that you've changed and that concerns me," Werner said as he watched him examine the collection on the wall.

"I know I have, Max. I used to laugh all the time, tell jokes, party with the crew, but over time things have worn on me. They've torn the fun and laughter right out of me." Without turning to face his host, he related an incident that had taken place more than a year earlier in one city, and then another, and then another.

"You're telling me that your uncle killed those men, and you and Jack Madigan helped get rid of the bodies? Are you out of your mind?"

Bryce turned to face him. "No, Max, and what comes next will sound even crazier." He then related that the CIA had somehow discovered CCTV video recordings of Bryce and Madigan doing the cleanup work and how they approached them with an offer they couldn't refuse. "It was all too simple. They said that since we didn't seem to have a problem with getting a little blood on our hands, maybe we should help them out from time to time."

Werner got up from behind his desk and strode across the room to Bryce.

"Why didn't you tell me about this back when it happened? We could have put the lawyers to it and fixed it. You know how extensive my connections are around the world. We could have gotten you out of this mess."

Bryce looked at Werner and shook his head. He went on to tell him that the deal needed to be accepted then and there, on that yacht in Abu Dhabi. Any delay and the authorities in the U.S. and the three countries where Pete Winters had killed people and they would notify the authorities immediately.

"I had three things to focus on that night. Staying out of prison, keeping my ass in your race cars, and keeping the

Werner name out of a potential global scandal." He heard the air leave Werner's lungs as the man dropped into a chair beside him.

"I don't know what to say, Bryce. I just wish you had told me."

Bryce shrugged and looked away. "The arrangement was regarded as top-secret. Documents were signed, incriminating evidence held over our heads.

"Dear God," Werner groaned.

"What they didn't know, what I didn't tell them until after Pete died, was that *he* had been the killer. I wanted to protect him. He was my blood, my only blood relation left. I convinced Jack to take the deal, work with me, and ride this out. I put a million euros into his account to thank him and keep his mouth shut. The only out we had, was if I retired from driving. If I was no longer playing the part, doing the whole celebrity access thing, getting closer to power players than their operatives ever could, the deal was terminated and Jack and I were free to go. We had it in writing."

Werner sat quietly listening, staring across his desk to the lake and the mountain scenery on the far side.

"You're telling me that the CIA has turned you into a hit man? That's incredible. I can't believe it."

Bryce gave him a look that said 'believe it.'

Werner stood up and walked to the small but well-stocked bar in the corner of the office. He poured himself a Scotch and turned to Bryce, gesturing with the bottle. Bryce shook his head no and watched as Werner made his a double then went back to his desk chair. He spun it to face the water. The two men didn't say another word for what to Bryce seemed like five minutes. Then Werner spun back around, his glass empty, and his eyes red with emotion.

"That is why you didn't sign the new deal, isn't it," he exclaimed, shaking his head with what Bryce read as regret.

"Yes. It is. I couldn't tell you why I didn't want to extend the deal. I wanted to win the title, *I thought we were going to win the damn thing*, and I could have one up on Andretti and be done with the CIA." He stared at Werner. "And then you got your britches in a bunch and signed that asshole. Those two shit heads teamed up and cost me, cost us, the championship. All I could see was red. Something I've gotten used to now, I guess. I signed with ProForce."

"Fuck!" Werner shouted as he threw his glass across the room. He glared out the window. "I am a billionaire with contacts and contracts around the world. Some of these people and organizations may have questionable reputations, but their money is good, very good, and their connections in government have helped get me to where I am today. And funded your racing, Bryce. I could reach out to them, a few in particular, who might help. Since you are now operating in a dark world, perhaps we can use a few others that swim there to get the CIA off your back."

Bryce said, "That's the problem, Max. Your name came up last time I was with my handler. They told me that *you* were swimming in those dark waters and were now the focus of their attention." Bryce watched as Werner's expression changed abruptly. The German's eyes focused, relaxed, and refocused. He could see his breathing change. Werner was a cool character, but this had rattled him.

Finally, the billionaire's gaze focused back on his guest.

"What are you telling me? That you've been sent to kill

me? That's absurd. What would that accomplish for them? Nichts – nothing!"

Bryce gave his friend a sad smile. "No, Max, I've not been sent here to kill you. *That* truly would be absurd. I've come here to warn you. Someone else might be coming for you." Bryce walked closer to the expansive window overlooking the lake. "Maybe some night when you're in here working late, a shot from a boat will pierce this window and your head. That's the way they play this sort of thing. They'll use their technology and underworld connections to plant the seeds that Iran or China or the Russians – entities they wish you hadn't been working with – took you out for some reason. Perhaps a broken deal, a jacked-up price, an unfulfilled order. Whatever."

Werner looked panicky. He moved to one side of the window and pulled the heavy burgundy drapes across to close off the view and hide their target. Bryce suggested Werner pour another drink and consider flying off somewhere to a really tiny island where he'd be forgotten. Maybe.

"Screw that," Werner stated as he slammed his now empty glass down on his desk. "I don't run from anyone or anything, Bryce. You know that. I will develop an action plan and go to war if I need to. Two can play this damn game. Tell me your handler's real name, and we'll start with them, leave a head in a box for their boss."

Bryce shook his head. "Max, think of Mila. Better to see her when you can than to have her see nothing more of you than a gravestone. I can assure you they are going to take you out if you stay in business. I'm not, but they are."

"Fuck them," Werner stated bravely. "I cannot run. I will not run."

"It's over my friend. Please take my advice," Bryce said as he approached Werner. "What's it going to be?"

"Fuck them," he stated again.

Bryce saw the determination in Werner's eyes and words. He shook his head with regret and then checked his watch. "Walk me to the car. I want to give you Mila's gift. You can give it to her tomorrow as you said."

When the two men walked through the front door out onto the gravel they stopped and turned toward each other.

"Max, no matter what, I will never be able to thank you enough for all that you have done for me. You've given me an opportunity that I can never repay." They stood quietly and then embraced, tears forming in their eyes.

"This feels like goodbye," Werner said as he choked back the emotion and took a step away, forcing a smile.

"Only till next time, my friend. Now here," he said, opening the passenger side door of his rented dark blue BMW. He handed Werner a gift-wrapped box, purple paper and bow – Mila's favorite colors, he had remembered.

"Bryce, there are holes in the damn thing. You really did get her another cat?" Bryce smiled.

"Give her my love," he said and then walked to the driver's side, got in, buckled up and drove off, giving Werner a wave from inside the car as he approached the gate.

Bryce spent another few minutes talking again with the guard and then drove off, headed for the airport a half-hour's drive away in Salzburg. He would head back to relax in Monte Carlo for two days before the race in Spielberg at the Red Bull Ring. As he drove, he envisioned what was happening at the Werner estate. He knew the man well, very well. He pictured him taking the box into his office, opening it up to inspect the new arrival, and shortly thereafter dying quietly in his chair.

At first it had sounded like science fiction to him. The CIA had done a good job picking a particular kitten out of the lot, a black one that had quite a temper and clawed, clung to, and fought with any hand that came toward it. The toxin they painted on the kitten's nails would only remain active for three hours and then be rendered useless in the air. Once assured the method had been successful many times before, he reluctantly bought in.

Bryce pictured Werner cursing but carefully placing the cat back in the box or perhaps getting it a bowl of milk in the kitchen before returning to his office. He'd need to be making calls, a lot of calls, to deal with what Bryce had just told him. Within thirty minutes, though, the undetectable toxin would have taken advantage of the arrhythmia Werner had dealt with all of his life and killed him without pain or warning. His head would drop to his desk and someone would discover his body later that day.

At least that is what the CIA had told him. That was the deal he had made with them. No messy head shot from a stranger in a boat. No closed casket, as a result. Mila would at least have the chance to see his face one last time and say goodbye. The cat would find a home and Bryce would be alone. He turned his thoughts to Mila and pictured her tears. He considered calling Max but couldn't. Then his thoughts turned to Kyoto.

He imagined the tears she had shed when he broke her heart. He'd tried to explain how much safer racing was these days – that refueling during pit stops had been eliminated in F1 and that he didn't intend to race forever. But she'd never responded to his calls, texts, and emails so he finally let her go, too. Eventually, he turned his emotion over her loss from sadness to anger, his way of coping. *She didn't even give me the chance to talk it out, so screw her*, he thought as he drove into Salzburg.

Moments later, he forced thoughts of her to the back of his mind. He admired the impressive Hohensalzburg fortress, a castle-like structure built in 1085 that rested atop the highest point in the city. He loved the region and had pictured taking Kyoto there someday. But now those dreams were gone. As he pulled up to the rental car return he shut the car off and paused, waving off the attendant who had approached to offer assistance or request an autograph. Bryce just sat there and stared through the windshield, lost in his thoughts. He looked to the rearview mirror and stared into his own eyes. What had he just done? What had he become? After a minute he reached for his phone and brought up Max's contact listing. His stare returned to the mirror. When he was racing Bryce had ice in his veins, fearing nothing and determined to defeat his opponents. Here and now, he was just a sad man who loved his Uncle Pete and had been forced to become a killer to protect him. Now he had just put an end to the life of someone he had cared for. Then he thought of the crimes the CIA said Max had committed that put America in harm's way. *Fuck him*, he whispered as he wiped away a tear that had started the ride down his right cheek. He put the phone back inside his jacket pocket and minutes later, after taking care of a few autographs and putting on a smile for a dozen selfies he climbed aboard his jet for the short flight home to his oasis overlooking the Med.

CHAPTER THIRTY-SEVEN

The Red Bull Ring at Spielberg near Vienna was one of Bryce's favorite tracks. He loved the circuit, the mountain vistas that made up the horizon, and the Bavarian atmosphere he looked forward to each year. This time, things would be much different in the racing community.

Many there had taken the news of Max Werner's death with shock. He'd seemed fit and strong, and the news of a heart attack due to a congenital disease stunned many. The Werner team manager polled the engineers and support personnel headed for Austria and those operating out of home base in central England. To a man and woman, everyone agreed they should go on and race.

There was never a question with Bishop or Patrice – they were racing for a world championship. Whether or not they cared about their now deceased car owner, they both proclaimed on social media that they would dedicate the rest of the season to Werner's memory. Werner's Board of Directors had met in Munich the day after Werner died and agreed to continue to operate the racing team and fulfill the requirements and provide the entitlements of the very lucrative team sponsorships. How things might change for the New Year could wait until after the season-ending race in Abu Dhabi. So, they would all race at Spielberg and then assemble again in Munich on the Tuesday after the race to celebrate Werner's life and bury him in the town where he was born.

The weather cooperated and provided the perfect setting for the weekend-long duel between Bryce and Bishop. They had set a record in qualifying only to have it shattered on the next lap by a rival and then bettered that record, again and again. Starting on pole, Bryce sat in the car, the bright sun blocked slightly by the halo device above his head. He shook his head at the thought – a halo over the man who had just killed another. Bryce had said many good things about his late friend and former boss as he addressed the media on set-up day, but that was all behind him. Now it was time to race and race he did.

He fought off Bishop, who eventually fell out due to engine failure, and then held off his own teammate Dickie Jones to win the event. On the top spot of the podium as he held the trophy high, with tears in his eyes, Bryce dedicated the win to Max Werner.

From Vienna Bryce flew directly to Munich where he attempted to call on Mila and her mother to express his sympathies before the funeral, but they had gone to her father's home, in Luzerne Switzerland. Instructions had been left with her staff that they wanted total privacy. He respected the family's wishes and prepared for the agony of what was to come.

The dedication, camaraderie, and passion in the racing community make it a tightly knit group. The fact that people die doing what they love, what they are really good at, makes motorsport a brotherhood – a family – of men and women. When a loss does occur, the community responds and in Crailsheim, Germany – Max Werner's birthplace – *everyone* had come to pay their respects. Werner may have been a ruthless businessman, international law breaker, and a cheating husband, but this tight-knit community had seen none of that. To the people he touched at the races he was a good man who was liked and respected by nearly all.

The Johanneskirche - Saint John's Church, a classic German church built between 1398 and 1440, and the only structure in the inner city to have survived World War II unscathed, was filled to capacity. Bryce took his seat in the second pew from the front, acknowledging the other attendees while everyone waited for the service to begin. Then he sat quietly deep in thought. He stared up at the high arching roof and thought for a moment of his home back in America, the one in Park City with an arch much like this but not nearly as grand and not nearly as dark. His heart broke when he saw little Mila enter the church from the far side entrance, led by her mother and maternal grandparents. He caught himself, his jaw almost dropping, when he saw her carrying the present he had left in her father's care. A week ago the CIA had used the animal to eliminate a problem. Today it brought her comfort. She sat quietly while the minister read scripture and three family members addressed the assembly and spoke of happier times.

When Mila finally noticed Bryce sitting so far away, she called out to him at a very quiet moment, and her mother let her down to cross past her father's casket to sit with her favorite uncle – Uncle Bryce. It was a poignant moment not lost on anyone. Bryce was known to be cool under pressure, but it took everything in his being to hold it together as he held her there on his lap. The kitten seemed to remember him and purred. This was torture and he couldn't wait for it to end.

After the service, a much smaller group of invited guests, immediate family only, followed the procession to the outskirts of town where Werner would be laid to rest among his parents and blood that dated back as far as the town church itself.

As Bryce watched the black Mercedes hearse lead a procession of four black limousines from the church, he stood by himself. Never had he felt more alone than in that moment.

The local police had cordoned off the area and kept the media, race fans, and curious onlookers far from the site. Also missing was Jack Madigan. While he usually accompanied Bryce to events like this one, Madigan hadn't attended the funeral, continuing to nurse the ill will he'd developed toward Werner for the way he had replaced Bryce on the team. The skies overhead darkened in various shades of gray as Bryce turned to walk toward his car. Someone called out to him in an unmistakable Russian accent.

"It seems death follows you everywhere, Mr. Winters. An acquaintance of mine died at an event you attended last year in Sochi. Now, another dies right after you visited him at his home. I hope you don't carry bad luck, like the black cat you left behind." The man paused and stared at Bryce. Perhaps he was looking for something, anything from Bryce, to indicate that this was all much more than just a coincidence.

Putting his race face on, Bryce gave him nothing in return. Instead, he looked around to see how many people the man might have brought with him. But the crowd had continued to dwindle and Bryce decided that an approach in an open square might not be a threatening one.

"Not sure what you mean about Sochi. But yes, I was the last to see Max before his heart attack. He and I had much to talk about. I am very happy that I had the chance to spend time with him. I'd like to believe he felt the same." Bryce paused. "How did you know Max?"

The man stepped closer. The cigarette smoke on his breath took Bryce's mind back to Sochi and the police detective who smelled much like an ashtray. Bryce stepped back. He didn't assume a fighting stance, he didn't get that vibe, but he also didn't want to be close enough for a knife to find its way into him either.

"We all have covers, Bryce Winters. You are a race car driver among other things," the man said as he winked. "I am an international trader, based in St. Petersburg, as well as other things. I used to work with the FSB in Moscow, our country's intelligence service." The man paused, and Bryce watched as he now took his turn looking past Bryce to see who might be lingering. He coughed, a raspy cough, and then reached into his pocket and took a cough drop from its wrapper and tossed it in his mouth. He waited, studying Bryce.

"Listen, I have to get moving. Did you want to cut to the chase as we say back in America or are you going to keep dancing? Get to the point. I'm a big boy. I can take it." The two men locked eyes. Anyone watching would have thought it was time for someone to step in.

"Da," the man began. "Be careful in Sochi this year, Mr. Winters. I am no threat to you, but I can tell you that someone has spread the word through the dark circles many of us travel that you were somehow involved in Gregori Ivanova's murder there. Personally, I did not like the man. He was an animal, but he did have friends and business associates. They are not just pissed that he was killed. They were infuriated that he was left in a commode and then in a casket that had to be a closed one. I would watch yourself in Russia or bring some of your CIA friends for company. It could make for an interesting time."

Bryce smiled. "Sounds like you and the boys back in Russia have been watching too much television. I have no idea what you are talking about, Mr…?"

"Misha Chernyenko," the man said as he tilted his head and reached out to shake hands.

Bryce delayed his response but extended his hand just as the man decided to end the awkward moment and had begun to withdraw his. "Not really sure what just happened here, Misha, but thanks for the heads-up about Sochi."

Chernyenko smiled. "It is good to have friends, don't you think, Mr. Winters? Safe travels." With that the man turned and left.

The rain the clouds had warned would come was now beginning as Bryce stood alone in the square for a moment, replaying in his head what had just occurred. As the storm intensified he hustled off to his rental car and began the drive back towards Munich. He'd stay the night downtown, somewhere off Marienplatz, the city central square. He knew the people who ran the famous Hofbrauhaus just a few minutes' walk from there and would be assured of a beer mug that would never empty and an endless plate of Bavarian-style pot roast and potato pancakes. He had a lot to think about as he drove the 140 miles to his stop for the night but on the autobahn, the ride would be a very fast one.

"What the hell just happened there and what does it mean?" was the only thing on his mind. Should he inform Jennings? If what the man had just told him was true, Bryce had no idea who he could trust anymore.

CHAPTER THIRTY-EIGHT

Part of the international appeal to Formula One racing, off the track, is the variety of experiences one encounters throughout the year. The cities, the cultures, the languages, are all different and special in their own unique ways. The track configurations and consequently the car setups differ from race to race as well. The only constant is the team's garage.

From track to track, from Australia to Abu Dhabi and every venue in between, the team reconstructed the garage area and support cubicles and meeting rooms so they were familiar and easy to settle back into, especially when coping with the recurring jet lag they often endured. Much like a tool going back into the same spot in the same drawer every time.

The parties, the sponsor commitments, the media sessions and all the rest were a cost of doing business for a successful or upcoming driver and team. For Bryce, they were the last things he was interested in. He'd slid into a funk that those closest to him suspected was due to Werner's death.

At least that was the theory Jack Madigan had intimated to the team. "He might seem distracted or preoccupied," he told Burns and Kazaan. "He lost two people who were very close to him – the uncle who raised him and now his mentor Max. He'll be fine. Just give him some time."

Silverstone was the first stop after the funeral in Germany. Bryce cut back his time in front of fans and photographers as much as possible. He was happy the CIA didn't call on him because if he'd heard from Jennings around this time, he might have gone shopping for a kitten, or perhaps a mountain lion, for her, too. He'd finished third in the race and forced a smile from the lowest spot on the podium.

Hockenheim was the next stop on the circuit, the track located between Frankfurt and Munich and close enough to Crailsheim that Bryce was distracted the entire weekend in Germany. Then it was off to the race near Budapest in Hungary, where he got through the commitments, as best he could, and carried on.

There was a long summer holiday break that was traditional for F1 so with the time off he opted to head back to Africa where he could focus on doing something good – saving Rhinos and Elephants. He had a simmering rage inside that he needed to focus elsewhere, or it would eat him alive. He had killed people and was now heading out to protect animals from slaughter. *Who the hell am I to make these decisions – to decide who lives and who dies*? He'd asked himself this time and time again. He considered the career he had chosen and now finally agreed with Kyoto. It was unfair of him to invite someone into a relationship, knowing he could be burned up or knocked apart in a racing accident.

Luckily, when he took inventory of how he and the team had performed prior to the break, he'd done well. After spending a month chasing poachers in search of their own, illegal trophies, Bryce had come to peace with what he had done and what he wanted to do. It was time to get back into the car, back to what he did best. At the next race, at Spa in Belgium, he was like a new man. He embraced the media, spent longer than was required with them and with fans and his sponsors. He took the team, the entire trackside team, to dinner to thank them for their hard work and for putting up with his funk while he mourned his loss. It was *losses*, but only Madigan got that.

The F1 in Italy was next. After taking the pole and the win at Spa, he arrived at Monza with high hopes and expectations. He loved the area, loved the people there, and had even met up with a woman he knew– a model from nearby Milan, who he took to dinner on Sunday night after the race. She was as beautiful as the exotic Ferraris built in nearby Maranello. While she may have hoped for more than the matching kisses he placed on her left and right cheek, this had been a good night for Bryce. Kyoto was behind him now and so was Werner. He was done with mourning the past. It was time to move on.

CHAPTER THIRTY-NINE

The idea of driving across country might sound romantic or adventurous to some, but to a man who drove for a living it was much more. For Bryce, driving when he wasn't in a race was relaxing but also an opportunity to reconnect with ordinary people who weren't millionaires or movie stars. He'd never forgotten his roots and, despite fitting in quite well in those circles, he preferred jeans and blue collar folks any time. In his own mind, he was just a regular guy who loved to drive and put to full use the God-given talents he possessed.

When he woke up in his hotel on Monday morning he took in the aroma of the coffee room service had delivered, opened the curtains in his suite overlooking the mountains of Northern Italy. With ten days to kill and no commitments to fulfill between now and the Singapore race, he could head back to Monte Carlo and relax. Then he could drive north to Como and hang out with friends, or head to Zermatt and hike in the mountain air pierced by the magnificent Matterhorn. Instead, he made a few calls. Three hours later he was out over the Atlantic, headed for New England.

The race in Italy had gone well until a tire puncture with two laps to go handed the win to the young Russian who had been hot on his tail throughout the event. Rather than lick his wounds there was one last thing he needed to do back in Vermont and now was as good a time as any.

The black Subaru WRX car he kept in storage at the Burlington airport hadn't been out for a run in some time. It had been months since he'd last driven it. With Pete now gone there would be little reason to spend much time in Vermont. He could have just sold off the vehicle outright; the F1 champ's modified street car would bring a great price at auction. He could have donated the money to charity, serving two causes. Instead, he wanted to keep it. He knew the roads in the Mountain West were just begging to be taken by Bryce and his little black beast – a nickname he loved but couldn't remember who had come up with it.

Landing eight hours after takeoff from Milan and having followed the sun, he had a good bit of daylight ahead of him. Having slept most of the way he was ready to roll. Thirty minutes of yoga in the center of the jet cabin had stretched him well, especially his neck. The G-forces at Monza had been particularly hard on him this time around. He had flown with this crew before and invited the lone flight attendant to join him. To his surprise, she had.

He stocked up on water, diet soda, and a variety of snacks and then checked his phone. Just 220 miles south and then west, he'd target Syracuse, New York as the spot he'd stop for the night.

With his bags tossed in the trunk he jumped in behind the wheel, hooked his phone to the charger, closed the door and then it hit him. Her scent was still there – the slightest touch of the Obsession Kyoto wore when she rode around with him five months earlier still lingered. "F," is all he said, then clicked the ignition and heard the purr of the exhaust as he idled there for a minute.

Just two hours and fifty-three minutes later he pulled into the hotel parking lot. He'd sworn to do it in less than three hours, he was as competitive with himself as with anyone else, and with little-to-no troopers on patrol along the way he'd done it.

Having raced many times in the area, on dirt at Weedsport and Fulton and he knew it well. He preferred to remain incognito. He wasn't that vain to wear shades into a restaurant to hide his identity so he opted for the drive-thru window at a Wendy's.

"Leave me alone," he heard a girl yell.

He turned to see a guy she was near let go of her arm and jump into a white Ford pickup. He'd noticed the truck earlier, three big blue drums of racing fuel strapped into the bed of it. With the amount of racing that went on in the area, that wasn't unusual. He'd also noticed the name on the driver's door – Jenson's Auto.

As the truck pulled away, he heard the man yell something back at the woman. Bryce began to slowly roll forward from the pick-up window. The girl walked in front of his car and reached for the door to the restaurant. He could see she'd been crying. Worse, he could see she'd been hit.

"You okay?" he said softly as he clicked off the ignition and pulled the brake.

At first she ignored him but he asked again. "Did he do that?" He stared at her swollen right eye and the puffy lower lip.

She nodded.

"You guys going to kiss and make up later? Is that your thing – or is he just an abusive asshole you never want to see again?"

"The only thing he loves more than slapping girls around is his piece-of-shit race car. No. He's dead to me. And my dad's a cop so he'll leave me alone, or else."

"Cool. Well get some ice on that and take care," Bryce said as he clicked the ignition again and rolled toward the parking lot exit.

When he reached the first traffic light he considered his options. Head back to the hotel and crash for the night or go for a ride and see if he could do some good.

He entered Jenson's Auto into his phone. The location popped up within seconds. - just five miles from his location. He could be there just as he finished his food. He looked into the mirror at himself. *You sure you want to do this?*

Minutes later, he arrived at his destination. The pickup was backed up to an open garage door on the side of the building. It was a small shop located on a quiet wooded road, a mile off the state highway. It was dark now, and Bryce sat at the edge of the driveway feeling the wear and tear of the overseas flight beginning to pull at him. The watch on his wrist read nine pm, but his body clock, still on Italian time, made it feel more like three am.

He looked in the mirror again. *What are you doing?* he asked. *He could have a gun. Probably has a few, maybe even a dog? Go back to the hotel and get some sleep. Let the girl's father handle this. But what if he can't? Maybe his hands are tied.* Then he remembered the girl's face and pulled forward down the drive.

"We're closed!" the man yelled.

But as Bryce walked from the darkness into the garage lights the next expression didn't surprise him.

"You're Bryce Winters!" the man said, stunned to see the American race car champion standing in his shop. He extended his oil-covered hand but pulled it back when he realized it was dirty. That was fine. Bryce didn't want to shake it – he wanted to break it.

"Got any kids?" Bryce just had to know. When Jenson shook his head no, he'd sealed his own fate. They carried on a conversation about racing. Johnny Jenson showed him the shop, showed him his dirt-modified race car, and then reached for his phone to call a few friends.

"They aren't going to believe you're here. They'd kill me if I didn't call them to come over!"

Before Jenson could hit the call button, Bryce shouted "Hey!" Jenson turned and his face met Bryce's fist. The phone hit the floor.

For the next ten minutes the two punched, wrestled, kicked, threw, and punched some more. They were pretty much the same size, and apparently condition. Bryce had thought *he* was fit and could fight, thanks to his training, but this guy could, too. As the battle waged on, neither man seemed interested in running out the door or calling for help. This was one man against another, possibly to the end. Nearing exhaustion, Jenson reached back to the top of his toolbox and turned toward Bryce, who was bleeding from the nose and lip.

"Now, *that's* a knife!" Bryce said in his best Aussie accent, channeling Crocodile Dundee.

Jenson swung up at Bryce's torso with it. Bryce employed a painful but effective move he'd learned long ago. He sucked his stomach back to avoid being stabbed and at the same time brought his right hand down hard, behind the knife, smashing his wrist against Jenson's. As bones smashed together, both grimaced.

The knife fell from Jenson's grasp as he groaned in pain. Bryce threw a left hook that spun the man around and then down to the ground. Operating on instinct and in survival mode now, Bryce reacted. It was time to end this. He jumped into the air, tucked his knees in tight and landed cannonball style with his full weight on Jenson's chest. Bryce felt and heard the man's ribs crack. He rolled off and looked at his victim, Jenson's eyes were panicked. The only thing moving was the blood flowing from his mouth. These two had been in a fight to the death, and this fight was now over.

"You'll never hit another girl again, you piece of shit," Bryce stated, just in case Jenson had any chance of understanding his point. Bryce stood up and looked around. There wasn't a sound except for the noises of night bugs and critters.

Okay, you could argue this was self-defense, Bryce, he said to himself as he stared at the body lying at his feet. *But you talked to his girlfriend, followed him here, and then crushed the life out of him. You might beat this. Maybe.*

Then it dawned on him. He could use something he'd done plenty of times years before to cover his tracks. He kicked the knife across the shop floor and watched it slide under a toolbox. Then he grabbed Jenson by the ankles and spun him to the angle he wanted him. He peeked out of the garage door at the road to make sure no cars were coming. He looked in the man's truck and smiled as he spotted the keys still in the ignition.

Back in the shop, he grabbed a greasy red rag, then another, jumped into the driver's seat and started it up, shocked by the volume blaring Guns n' Roses. He turned it down as he backed the truck into the shop just far enough to make this work. He stopped once, got out to check – not far enough – and then headed for the cab again. He noticed Jenson's phone lying there on the floor and used his foot to slide it under the driver's side rear tire. He backed up another foot and left the door open and the engine running. He was almost set for the big finale.

There was an old truck tire in the bed between the tailgate and the drums of race fuel. Bryce dropped the gate, threw the tire down so that it landed beside the body, and then went to work. Drums of race fuel weigh between 350-400 pounds. Without a forklift they aren't easy to load or unload. Someone had shown Bryce a trick years before saying, "Let gravity do the work." So, Bryce did.

He grasped the top of the drum using the red rag and tilted the drum back on end so he could roll it to the gate. There, he laid it down on its side, hopped down onto the ground, and placing a hand on opposite ends of the now horizontal drum, pulled it so that it fell. Normally racers would use an old tire to catch the drum and guide it with their hands to make it vertical again on the rebound. Without the tire, the drum landed hard on Jenson. *Shop accidents happen all the time.* Bryce looked around again. Something told him to check the office.

He'd been in there as part of Jenson's tour, showing off photographs of race cars he'd worked on. All quiet. No shop cameras. No recording devices. He'd leave the engine running in the truck to make it look like Jenson had intended to unload the drums and pull the truck back out but had this unfortunate freak accident.

Not long afterward, Bryce was back in his hotel room, washing his hands and trying to figure out how he'd explain the marks on his face if anyone asked. With a ball cap and shades in place the next morning he'd move on without leaving anything behind but a woman who might be a bit safer.

As he drove back onto I-90 and headed west, he picked up the slight scent again and stared into the mirror once more. *Best not make a habit out of that Bryce,* he whispered. *Last night, you were lucky.* He sat staring at his reflection longer. With 2,000 miles of interstate ahead of him, he hoped that would be enough of a ride to finally get Kyoto out of his system. That, and come to terms with what he'd just done.

At first, he was bent on getting home to Park City and figured if he averaged 80 miles per hour all the way and kept the coffee flowing it could be done in twenty-four hours. But hours later he looked again into the rear view mirror and asked, *why*? He played with the MapQuest app on his phone and smiled when he saw two stops he could make to break up the marathon.

Dayton, Ohio—home of the National Air Force Museum—gave him a break where no one seemed to recognize him. He'd always loved planes, and where else could he climb aboard three former Air Force Ones, check out the evolution of America's warplane development, and stand alongside the famous Memphis Belle.

After crashing for the night at a Hilton where the desk clerk didn't know the significance of the Bryce Winters name, he was headed to his next stop and looking forward to it more than anything. An hour into his drive, he pulled up in front of the Indianapolis Motor Speedway Museum and bought a ticket to take the self-guided tour of another special building he'd never entered before. He made his way to what he was really there to see – the Mario Andretti display. He knew a great deal about this American hero and had matched his win record in the 500's at Daytona and Indy. But there was so much more to the man.

He read about how his hero had raced a dirt track event near there years before and then flew overnight to Italy to compete in the F1 at Monza, only to be turned away by race officials for an arbitrary reason. He still marveled at how different the cars of Andretti's day were to today's technological race cars. The drivers were so much more vulnerable to injury back then from fire, open cockpits and on and on.

Bryce was halfway through the exhibit before anyone spotted him. After an hour of posing for photos and signing autographs he was back in the Subaru, hammer down, westbound. The swelling in his right wrist had gone down within twelve hours of the brutal assault it had endured back in New York, but it still ached. He shook his head, thinking back to the event that could have derailed his career and life. *What were you thinking?* he asked as he peered into the mirror again.

It was at that moment that Bryce decided to push hard and keep driving. All he wanted was to get home and get some sleep in a familiar bed.

He watched the sun set ahead of him. With not much ride left, Bryce was just starting another audible book, James Patterson's *The President is Missing*, when a text lit up the car. It was from Jennings at the CIA.

> YOU CALLED THE WHITE HOUSE ON US?
>
> I THOUGHT YOU LIKED NEW ARRANGEMENT

CHAPTER FORTY

In Washington, Kyoto's day had been a short one. Having worked twelve-hour days for the past week to get a report ready for a presentation she was exhausted. Her boss had sent her home with direct orders to relax, sleep, and sleep some more.

She lay there on the sofa, a light throw pulled over her to fend off the air conditioning she'd forgotten to adjust. She stared at the ceiling, the flat screen she had turned on, and then a stack of books and magazines she'd left on the coffee table and hadn't touched in months. She'd focused on her work, completely, to keep her mind off the breakup with Bryce.

As she looked at one stack in particular she saw something she'd forgotten she'd brought home. It was Pete Winters' journal. She reached for it, sliding it from mid-stack. As items fell off the pile she sat up with the intention of putting the last vestige of Bryce Winters in its place –the trash—but curiosity got the best of her. She lay back and began to page through the man's most personal thoughts and recollections from his life. Three hours later she was stunned by what she'd discovered and she texted Jon.

COME VISIT. NEED MY BROTHER. NOW.

Over the next few hours Kyoto and Jon read through the entire diary. As an attorney, she began to treat the book as evidence to be presented in a case she wasn't sure how to try. Tuesday morning, while Bryce was miles away driving somewhere across the Midwest, Kyoto walked into her boss's office at the U.S. State Department and closed the door behind her. An hour after that, Deputy Secretary of State Jessica Sorenson, her boss, was headed to the White House.

Sorenson had been able to get on Chief of Staff David James' schedule – fifteen minutes only – and was anxious to present Kyoto's findings. As the information she presented to James carried a good bit of weight, the fifteen minutes spread into twenty-five before the COS excused himself to check in with the president before he left the Oval Office for a cabinet meeting. When James walked back into his office and closed the door behind him, Sorenson sat forward to hear what had happened. She handed copies of the relevant pages from Pete Winters' journal to James and left, satisfied the meeting that the Director of the CIA was being called to later that day would sort this out. It was in the White House's hands now, as far as she was concerned.

I-80, Wyoming-Utah State Line

"No idea what you're talking about," Bryce assured Jennings after he called her from his car.

She wasn't buying it. "You and I made a deal, that you would serve your country as a contract operator for the CIA. You proved that when you took out Max Werner for us, but then you sent someone your uncle's journal? You've just stabbed the agency in the back, Bryce. Heads are rolling here. You're going to have to watch your *own* back going forward. The three musketeers got the axe, too, and they stormed out of my office hours ago. No doubt looking for your head on a platter."

Bryce continued to drive, slowing to 70 mph – slower than a pace car's speed during caution laps in F1.

"I still have no idea what you are talking about or how anyone could have gotten hold of Pete's journal. I can't believe he would have written that stuff down anyway. This is bullshit. Something else is going on here."

Both remained silent for a moment.

"You're off to Singapore soon. I think we need to meet up there, if not sooner," Jennings stated. "How long's the flight from Monte Carlo?"

Bryce paused. If they were indeed tracking him through his phone she knew exactly where he was.

"Too long," he replied. "Listen, I've been up for some time. Let me get my head around what you've just charged me with. I will call you back in the morning. It's late here."

Jennings ended the call without another word.

Bryce pressed hard on the accelerator. Park City, a shower, and some space to process what he'd just been told were now less than an hour away. He set a goal and swore he'd be under some hot water, and hopefully not in it, in record time.

The miles clicked past as he thought back to the late-night, grueling rides he'd had in competition at Le Mans and Daytona where he and two other drivers had taken turns in their 24-hour endurance races. He was really on his own now, alone in more ways than one it seemed.

After driving another ten minutes he reached into the bag of goods he'd picked up at a rest-stop convenience store a few hours earlier. He popped the tab on a large, sugar-free Red Bull and chugged it down. He needed to come up with a proactive plan. Then he realized he needed to alert Jack Madigan that he could be at risk, too.

Bryce grabbed his phone and texted Jack: 911. He wasn't sure where in the world Madigan was at this time of the night, but if he got the message he'd know to call. He'd also know to raise his awareness immediately. Then Bryce thought back to the last time he'd seen his uncle's journal. He remembered it dangling in his hand over the fireplace, how he'd just about let it go when he decided he couldn't – not then, not yet. *What had become of it? Had someone broken into Pete's cabin and stolen it?*

Shit – what else could be in there?

As he drove up the final stretch of winding road that led to his property on the mountainside, red and blue flashes from the light bars atop Park City's police vehicles were lighting up the trees. His heart sank. It was too late to turn around. He'd undoubtedly been seen.

They're *on to me,* he thought. *I don't know how, but someone must have seen something back in New York.* He slowed as he pulled up to the front gate of his property. A policewoman standing guard recognized him as he put his window down.

Okay, she's smiling, he thought. *Can't be all bad.* Then, coming toward him were two other officers and a man he thought he recognized. He was in cuffs. It was Russo, formerly of the CIA. Bryce didn't let on that he knew the man. He thought it smarter to let the police tell him what had brought them there.

"Bastard climbed your fence," the Chief of Police said as he shook Bryce's hand and escorted him into the house. "Whoever he is he's sharp. He overrode the silent arm system but must not have known about the motion sensors that lead up to the house. Soon as the cruisers arrived they got over the fence, saw this guy walking around inside the house, and drew on him. Dipshit left the front door ajar."

"Do you know if he broke or tried to take anything?" Bryce asked hoping to hear good news. The trophies and mementos from his driving career meant the world to him. Replicas could replace them, but no amount of money could replace their sentimental value.

"Looks like he intended to torch the place. We found two road flares on him and a compact automatic tucked in his front pocket."

"Any idea who he is?" Bryce asked as he stared back at the police cruiser where they'd placed the intruder.

"No, but we will. Once we book him and run his prints we'll know pretty quickly – if he's in the system that is."

Bryce walked into his trophy room and looked around. Nothing seemed to have been disturbed.

"And you've checked the place? You're sure there's nobody hiding in here," he said. The chief nodded 'yes.' Bryce let out a sigh of relief. He was worn to the bone.

"You okay?" the chief asked. "You look like hell, if you don't mind me saying so."

Bryce rubbed his face. "I'm just beat. I'm pushing myself on long night-drives to get ready for a race. I might enter an endurance event in Asia while I'm over there for Singapore."

The Chief suggested Bryce get some much needed sleep and a shower. If they came up with anything he wouldn't disturb him until at least after ten the next morning. "We'll also leave a cruiser here at the front gate just in case, if that's okay with you."

Bryce thanked him for being so good at what they do and escorted the chief out the front door and then waved as he watched two of the three patrol cars drive away into the darkness. Minutes later, alarm reset, and one of his Sig pistols tucked under a throw pillow on his sofa, Bryce began to nod off… but then reached for his phone to send a text to the CIA.

RUSSO ARRESTED AT MY HOME IN PARK CITY

With still no response from Madigan, Bryce's mind began to race. The Red Bull hadn't let go of him yet. With all that had occurred in the last few hours he now had a second wind and he needed to act before he crashed hard. He sat up on the sofa and began to think it all through.

First, he needed to be safe. Russo was one of three that he knew of. In many cases CIA agents had friends and associates, very well-trained ones, straight out of Special Forces, like SEALS and Rangers. Many of them retired to Park City or Jackson Hole. A few might be willing to go after Bryce at the CIA's request. Clandestine behavior is just that and black ops, like taking out someone who betrayed the agency, happened all the time.

Bryce thought back to that day in Werner's office when he warned Max that a shot could come from a boat in the lake. He turned his attention to the expansive panes of glass that would reveal the mountain beauty once the sun rose in a few hours. For all he knew, a sniper could be setting his sights on Bryce at this very moment.

"Well, you might be out there but that doesn't mean I have to sit here and wait for it," he said as if talking to someone looking at him through a riflescope. "Time for Plan B."

He went into the kitchen and made a pot of coffee, checked his phone again, spent ten minutes on his laptop, and then jumped into the marbled shower with room for two. He booked a charter flight from Park City to San Francisco and from there he'd board a Singapore Airlines A380 double decker jet for the 17-hour non-stop to his destination. *Better to get the hell out of here*, he decided. *Put some ground between us and regroup.*

Bryce knew that if you wanted to get lost in a crowd somewhere Singapore was one city that could facilitate his needs. He didn't know who had been involved in outing him. But he'd find out. As soon as he arrived in Singapore his life outside the cockpit of a race car would really begin to race.

CHAPTER FORTY-ONE

THE MARINA BAY Sands is one of the top hotels in all of Singapore. Its location on the water provided views from Bryce's Harbour Suite that were spectacular. He'd checked in after an uneventful flight from San Francisco and slept nearly ten hours straight, to the surprise of the flight attendants who had flown with him on other journeys across Asia. No coffee or food or movies until he took the Do Not Disturb off the sliding door to his suite.

After the first three cups of caffeine and a liter of water got him moving, he was back to the happy-go-lucky, friendly and approachable person they'd flown with in the past. If a bullet was coming, there wasn't much he could do to stop it. The only thing he could do was find out what had happened back at the CIA and hope the personal security that he'd hired for the race would be enough to hold trouble at bay.

As long as they don't have a Pete Winters on their payroll, willing to shoot an American driver out to win a championship for his country I should be safe – for now. He laughed as he replayed that thought in his mind. *Who am I kidding?*

CHAPTER FORTY-TWO

Friday's qualifying session went well with Bryce winning the pole at a record pace, Tony Bishop taking second alongside him on the grid, and Dickie Jones in third right behind. The weather in Singapore had been dry, but the humidity was crushing. The heavy weight of the air and the heat made a July night in New York City or Philly seem more like a spring day.

Jack Madigan finally turned up, explaining to Bryce that he'd hooked up with a lovely lady and turned his phone off to focus on her, the beach bars and the parties of Ibiza. He and Bryce huddled at his hotel the night Madigan arrived. They were both looking forward to confronting Jennings when she would arrive on Saturday morning for a breakfast meeting in Bryce's Harbour Suite.

Before then, a text came in from someone he hadn't heard from in months, leaving Bryce dazed and confused.

LANDING IN SINGAPORE SATURDAY AM

CRITICAL WE MEET

WHAT TIME - WHICH HOTEL?

KYOTO

"Shit," Bryce said after reading it aloud. He stared out the window at the water and palm trees just below. "Think they're flying in on the same damn plane?"

Madigan looked at his friend and shook his head. "Who the hell's Kyoto?"

Bryce had never been involved in a serious relationship since he and Madigan had first connected back in their NASCAR days. The thought of a woman in Bryce's life threw Madigan. After Bryce laid it all out for him, from their first encounter in the air to their time in Monte Carlo where he introduced his new girl to a very inebriated Madigan, and then the no-show in Montreal. Madigan took it all in and Bryce watched as Madigan's expression showed more and more concern.

"*That* was Kyoto – the girl in Monaco?" Bryce nodded. "And she works in DC?" He nodded again. "What if they're working together?"

The two men sat quietly for at least ten minutes, Bryce thinking through every element of the situation. He looked to Madigan, deep in thought as he made another pot of coffee, and realized just how tight a spot he was now in.

Bryce couldn't envision trying to have an emotional reunion with the woman in the midst of race fans clamoring for attention. They agreed that Madigan would go to the lobby to greet Kyoto and escort her to Bryce's suite. She was an Asian beauty, but even in a hotel full of the exquisite creatures he knew his friend would spot her.

Bryce texted Kyoto, instructing her to wait at the hotel bar's entrance when she arrived and that Madigan would greet her there.

As soon as she texted that she'd was there, Madigan headed out the door but turned to ask the question both had forgotten.

"What if she *and* Jennings are there together?"

Bryce thought for a second and then smiled. "We'll double date." He paused. "Bring them both. Who knows what the night holds."

Looking for a beauty in a sea of beauties, Madigan thought as he walked out of the elevator and began to navigate the crowded lobby and headed for the bar. He scanned faces looking for anyone familiar. But he'd never met Jennings and wouldn't have known her if he tripped over her.

There – there she is, he thought as he spotted Kyoto. Despite having just flown for 24 hours to the other side of the world she cleaned up nice. *The guy has great taste, I'll give him that*. Silky black hair tied back, black t-shirt, black tights, white sneakers, and a tentative expression. They'd only met once before, very briefly, in Monaco, and Madigan assumed she might not remember him.

As he got closer he saw someone else approach her. At first, Kyoto smiled. But then he saw fear in her eyes as she looked down at something.

"Shit," Madigan uttered, finally recognizing the man standing in front of Kyoto. It was Chadwick from the CIA, one of the three musketeers who had just lost their jobs. "How the fu—" Madigan continued to approach.

His mind raced. *What do I do? Where's the other one? Where's Jennings?*

Was this all a set up and Kyoto was the bait?

He got to within two feet of the couple and Madigan decided it was time to act. He reached out to grab Chadwick's left arm, but the agent must have seen Kyoto's eyes focus on someone approaching. He turned ever so slightly to display the compact pistol he was holding under a jacket he'd thrown over his arm.

"What the hell are you doing here?" Madigan demanded, ignoring the gun.

Chadwick grinned. "Plan C – yeah, I think we're working on Plan C at this point, buddy boy. Russo's in jail back in Utah. Jennings – well, Jennings will be a no-show today. And Brownell, he's babysitting back in Washington." He paused. "Where's Bryce?"

Madigan looked to Kyoto and tried to sound confident. "Good to see you again, young lady," he began. "I've heard so much about you." She forced a smile. "Don't you worry one little bit about this dipshit. We'll sort this out, and then he'll be on his way."

Chadwick stepped closer to Kyoto, pressing the gun against her. "Don't get cocky, Jack. This bitch has ruined my career. My life. I don't have much to live for now, except revenge. Killing her right here in this crowded lobby doesn't faze me in the least."

"I was thinking more about *you* dying here and now. I can arrange that since you have nothing to live for." Madigan turned to Kyoto. "You know this prick?"

She shook her head energetically, eyes wide, terrified.

"He's part of a CIA goon squad. The shit heads who

aren't smart enough to do covert well, so they just keep them in a cage until they need someone to show up and scare people. This idiot came to Charlotte a few months ago and tried to talk me into killing Bryce. He said if I did, I would get a full pardon for everything these assholes have forced us to do."

Kyoto stared at Madigan.

"I can see it in your eyes," he continued, "that this is a world you're not accustomed to. What are you—a CIA lawyer or something?"

"I-I, yes, I work at the State Department," she stammered. "And yes, this is all very new to me."

Madigan turned to Chadwick. "Let's go upstairs and talk this thing out."

But before Chadwick had the chance to respond, three men came out of the hotel bar and recognized Madigan. Drunk as they appeared, they recognized him, greeted him loudly and fussed over the man they knew from racing. One stepped between Kyoto and Madigan, suggesting he come inside so they could buy him a drink.

Before Madigan could use the interruption to his advantage, Chadwick took Kyoto by the arm and pulled her from them and toward a hallway bustling with hotel guests and race fans. By the time Madigan was able to separate himself from the boisterous threesome without making a scene, Kyoto and Chadwick had disappeared into the crowd.

STILL COMING? WE'RE WAITING FOR YOU

Bryce texted Jennings as soon as Madigan explained why he'd returned to the suite without Kyoto. After several minutes and no response from her, Bryce called her number only to get a voicemail response. They went over the conversation in the lobby, word for word, trying to figure out what was going on.

Madigan finally said, "Who the hell is Brownell supposed to be babysitting?"

Bryce thought for a moment. "Jon – Kyoto's brother. That must be who they have. Double insurance. I can't think of anyone else. There's nobody in my life left for them to hold hostage."

Madigan nodded. "Me neither."

Bryce considered and looked to his friend. Their expressions the same, he found it sad. There was nobody else.

"This is crazy," Bryce muttered. He sat down and tried again to call Jennings. In the middle of his call a text arrived. It was from Kyoto's phone.

> THROW THE RACE ON SUNDAY AND WE
> LET THEM GO

Bryce ended the call to Jennings and tossed his phone across the room to Madigan. This was an impossible demand. Bryce couldn't do this to his team, or to his country for that matter. He was racing for the U.S. in an international series that had seen only one other world champion since 1978. He had never quit anything and had never thrown anything ever, not even to let someone win a simple footrace to make them feel better. It wasn't in his DNA.

"We have to call someone, but I don't know who," Bryce said as he caught the phone pitch back from Madigan. "Everyone I know at the CIA is gone or—" He stopped suddenly. There couldn't have been a worse time to remind Madigan that he'd had their handler and the man's former lover killed.

Madigan smiled. "I'm good, Bryce. We've made our peace."

Bryce shook his head and nodded. "Chadwick and Brownell are the only others I know of there."

Madigan's eyes brightened.

Bryce shouted, "Who?"

"Call the frikkin' president. You know the guy. Get him on the phone and ask him for help."

Bryce laughed, processed the idea for a moment, and then threw it out.

"Jack, I don't know who we can trust. I could call some friends back in PC or even people we have down in Coronado, but we're talking about real spy shit here. I don't know what orders or what allegiances might compromise us if we did."

"Bryce, even if you did throw the race, there's no guarantee that asshole would cut Kyoto loose. He could say he changed his mind and tell you to do it again and again. You'd get kicked out of racing so fast the only thing you'd be driving would be a taxi."

Bryce laughed at the thought but soon gave it a little more thought. Madigan was right. He picked up the phone and texted Chadwick.

DEAL

YOU HAVE TO SIT IN THIS SUITE WITH MADIGAN FOR THE START.

WHEN I CLIMB OUT OF THE CAR,

YOU LEAVE THE SUITE AND LEAVE HER BEHIND.

HE'LL BE ARMED SO NO GAMES

Madigan watched over Bryce's shoulder as he texted and then waited for a response.

NO DEAL. YOU QUIT, SHE WALKS OUT OF WHERE WE ARE NOW

As If they'd rehearsed their response, both men muttered *bullshit.*

Minutes later, another text came from Kyoto's phone. It was a video of her tied in a chair, her mouth was gagged, and her t-shirt torn at the neck. She was sobbing, her head down. Then her chair was kicked onto its side, crushing her left arm under it as it landed. Her muffled scream enraged Bryce.

He turned to Madigan, who nodded in agreement. They'd take the deal. This prick held the high ground, and the cards they'd been dealt were worthless.

Neither man spoke for some time, but then, Madigan looked across the room at him with something like hope in his eyes.

"What?" Bryce said.

"I know how to do this and you can save face. I will sabotage the electronics on the car so that when you use the clutch paddle at the start the car shuts off."

Bryce thought about the idea and then agreed to it in principle.

"And I know who I can call. She owes me, sort of," Bryce said. "She'll be our Hail Mary."

Madigan looked at him and then watched as Bryce began to text someone.

HAD A GREAT TIME IN PARIS

I NEED A BIG FAVOR. BW

"And who's that?" Madigan asked.

"Nobody special, just a Chinese spy."

CHAPTER FORTY-THREE

Two days later, Bryce had moved from the Marina Bay Sands to the official F1 hotel for the event. This would add an extra layer of security to the ring he'd already placed around himself. On Friday, as Bryce jumped into the chauffeured SUV for the short ride to the Singapore circuit, he texted Kyoto's phone once more. Again, there was no response.

He'd given up on Jennings. He and Madigan had developed a plan of attack that *might* work. It was sketchy at best and could leave Bryce in a bad way with his car owner, sponsors, fans, and countrymen. It could also leave Kyoto in a dumpster much like the ones Bryce and Madigan had used from time to time.

The practice sessions under the night lights went well, with the Werner and Kazaan teams each bettering the other's lap times again and again, giving fans something to look forward to as the four drivers would forget the rest of the pack and fight for the pole on Saturday. Uncharacteristically, Bryce opted out of the usual meet-

and-greets, blaming it on a cold he didn't want to pass along to anyone else.

During Saturday's ride to the track, he and Madigan huddled one last time before putting their plan into action.

"If they find out you'll be fired, fined, and banned from racing," Bryce reminded Madigan. "You don't need to do this. I can just pull off the track and take the heat."

"No, my plan works better, Bryce. The engine will blow during Q1, and you'll have to start dead last for the race. That way, when the lights go out and you stall the car, there won't be nineteen more cars rocketing around you or crashing into you. Less chance of anyone getting hurt. If anyone finds the bug I'll say I did it because I'm being blackmailed and throw myself on everyone's mercy."

"All right. Fine. That's how we'll roll." It seemed to Bryce the best they could do.

"Of course, you'll have to buy everyone dinner a dozen times to make up for the engine change. I just hope your friend Lee finds Kyoto before time runs out." Bryce peered out the window at the Singapore skyline. Nothing more was said until they arrived. He hurried to his mobile quarters to change into his driving gear and get ready to go.

He purposely continued to distance himself from his crew chief and engineers, keep up the act of not wanting to give them whatever bug he'd picked up. As far and he and Madigan could tell, nobody was the wiser.

An hour later, Bryce was walking back to the pits from where he'd left his race car – the engine steaming hot fluids of all sorts as it sat lifeless in the first engine failure they'd suffered in months. Rival Bishop took the pole and the next day, Bryce would start the race at the opposite end of the field. Early the next morning, Bryce sent a text one last time to Kyoto's phone.

NEED PROOF OF LIFE OR NO DEAL

Without a response, Bryce's hopes sank. He was preparing to wave goodbye to his dream and the team's dream of winning a second world championship. He cursed himself for having fallen for Kyoto. Then he cursed himself for even thinking like that. She was the first woman he'd had feelings for in a decade. In the hope of saving her life he'd willingly sacrificed his racing dreams. And now it appeared, the effort was for nothing. She might already be dead.

He hadn't lost sight of Kyoto's brother's dilemma either. He'd tried to find him using the internet, on Facebook, and all the other social media a Jon Watanabe might be on. Bryce kicked himself for not getting to know more about the guy, back when he and Kyoto were still together – *where he worked* would have been normal dinner conversation if Bryce had been able to keep his eyes off his sister that night.

With no news from anyone, anywhere, Bryce tried his best to focus on the race to come. Lyn Whitehouse, his newest personal trackside aide, just in from her home base in Sydney, handed him his energy drink for one last swig before pulling the fire-resistant balaclava over his head and then strapping on his trademark yellow helmet with red and black striping.

"G-day mate," he said as he patted her on the arm, something he'd done to every aide he'd worked with since his debut in Formula One. It wasn't part of a pre-race routine or to fend off superstitions. For Bryce, he knew there was a chance – although a remote one – that he might die that day during the race. It was just his way, a last touch of human contact before go-time. Some drivers had a wife or girlfriend to embrace. For Bryce, that simple touch would have to suffice as it always had.

As the last crewman in charge of checking the driver's safety gear and that communications were properly in place and ready for action, Madigan approached the cockpit from the opposite side and peered into Bryce's helmet-covered eyes. The engine sounds all around them were deafening. Bryce noticed Madigan wasn't wearing his headset and assumed that what he had to say was best kept between them. Bryce wasn't the best at lip reading, but he understood enough of Madigan's message.

LEE FOUND HER. SHE'S OKAY. NOW GO WIN THIS DAMN THING!

CHAPTER FORTY-FOUR

❧

THE FLIGHT BACK to Washington was intolerable for Kyoto. She thought back to the first time she'd flown over the Pacific alongside Bryce, the man now sleeping beside her. With eighteen hours left and a change of planes in San Francisco to come, she needed to keep her mind busy, numb it, or else cry the entire way.

The doctors in the hospital had reset her broken arm and given her pain pills, but she was trying her best to not take them unless absolutely necessary. Instead, she searched her bag for the sleep aids she had relied on during her years of red-eye and overseas flights. While she waited for the concoction of vodka and two pills to kick in, she couldn't help reliving all that had happened to her in Singapore.

Chadwick had been an animal. He seemed to enjoy her every painful moment.

She remembered the beast forcing her down the hall and out through an emergency exit to a van that was waiting nearby the hotel's deserted delivery dock. It was a faded red minivan of some kind, without windows. The driver was Asian but avoided eye contact with her as Chadwick shoved her through the side door and climbed in behind her. He pushed her down, making it impossible for her to see anything. She felt the stops, starts, lefts, and rights of Singapore traffic.

The van eventually pulled into a garage, and the door closed behind them. Then Chadwick helped her out of the van and led her to an office where she was tied to a chair, gagged, and left to watch Singapore television for hours until he came back with food and water. Once the TV was turned off, she lost all sense of time.

Later, Chadwick made the video, knocking her to the ground, breaking her arm. He'd left her there sobbing in pain for some time before righting the chair and shoving painkillers in her mouth, with water. She didn't know if he was being sympathetic to her plight or was just tired of hearing her groan. Every six hours or so he untied her and let her use the dirty bathroom off the office. But he insisted the door remain open while she was in there.

She remembered the incredible pain she'd felt when he forced her arm into a makeshift sling, but once he realized it was of no use to her, he simply tied her good arm to a water pipe that rose up out of the floor. Hours became days, and as the sun set through the high windows of the office, too high for anyone to peer in or for her to reach and climb out, finally someone came.

Violence was something Kyoto had only seen on the news or in films. But she got a close and personal view when two people dressed in black from head to toe suddenly appeared. Chadwick seemed taken by surprise, and she thought that must be a good sign. He raised his gun. The two intruders returned fire, killing him on the spot.

She'd never forget the confident smile of one of her rescuers when they removed their black hoods and told her she was safe now.

"My name is Lee," the Asian woman had said in a British accent. "I'm a friend of Bryce's. We're getting you out of here straight away."

Hours later, while many of the patients waiting in the emergency ward watched the Formula One race on television, Kyoto's arm was x-rayed and set and she was discharged. Lee and her partner drove Kyoto to Bryce's hotel where a key card had been left for them at the front desk. Later that evening, she remembered waking up when she heard Bryce's voice. The pills had made her groggy but there was much to say, much to explain including how she'd taken Pete's journal. But her focus was on Jon.

She made calls to her contacts at the State Department, who in turn contacted the CIA and made them aware of what Russo and Chadwick had been up to. An immediate alert went out for Brownell and Jon Watanabe. Bryce made reservations for the next, fastest flight back to DC for both of them and then raised the covers back over her and sat near her until she fell asleep.

For him, the race in Singapore would go down in history as one of the greatest ever. Millions around the world watched as Winters charged from the rear of the grid to battle with Pushkin, Bishop, Patrice and Dickie Jones. On the very last lap, on the final turn, in what officials would rule as racing accident, Bryce's and the Russian's cars bumped and spun into the gravel handing the win to Patrice – his first.

*

Lee and Madigan had been sitting near the bar in the second suite Bryce had occupied while in town, and he joined them to toast an unbelievable job well done.

"You owe me, Mr. Winters," Lee reminded him, and then she kissed his left cheek and left, passing the two F1 security staffers posted outside the suite door.

"Did she say what she did with Chadwick?" Bryce asked

Madigan who simply smiled, raised a glass, and replied, "Here's to dumpsters!"

Miles away in a roadside hotel near Colorado Springs, Colorado, now former CIA Agent Bill Brownell was cleaning the handful of weapons he'd brought along for the ride. He'd paid cash for the hotels, for everything along the way and switched to burner phones so he couldn't be tracked.

He looked to Jon Watanabe who was sitting on the floor below the coat rack in the back of the clean but worn room, and then to the man sitting in one of the two chairs separated by a table and lamp at the window. The curtains had remained closed throughout the day, and the Do Not Disturb sign dangled in the slight breeze on the outside doorknob.

They would wait until dark before loading up and moving on.

"You sure this plan is going to work?" Myers asked as

he reached for the remote and changed channels to the evening news.

Brownell kept his focus on his hardware but laughed. "Sure will. We're going big game hunting. You can hang his damn head in his trophy room when we're done."

Watanabe's eyes widened as he listened.

"What about Madigan?" the cheated-on widower asked. Brownell kept his focus and waited before responding.

"Bryce Winters first. Now that I'm out of a job, he's going to fund my retirement. And I like nice things, really nice things. Then I'll help you find the guy who was screwing your wife. The rest is on you."

Jon sat quietly and continued to listen from his spot on the floor.

"What about him?" Myers asked looking to their captive. Brownell turned and stared for a moment before refocusing on the maintenance at hand.

"He's our insurance. Russo's done, Chadwick hasn't checked in, so I have to assume he's done, too. As long as Johnny boy keeps his mouth shut and I don't have to beat the shit out of him again to keep him quiet, we'll go with the plan. Russo was allowed only one phone call from jail and now that we know there's a secondary detection system in use at Winters' place I have an idea how we can beat it."

"What if he doesn't come back to Park City? We can't wait out there forever," Myers pushed.

"He will," Brownell replied. "They always do."

CHAPTER FORTY-FIVE

At the White House, Chief of Staff James read through the file sent by the FBI. Special Agents had interviewed Kyoto and Bryce at her condo in the Watergate after she had been taken to George Washington Hospital in downtown DC to have her arm checked and a full physical given.

An agent who specialized in helping survivors of kidnappings and assaults cope had remained behind once the interviews concluded. She had assessed Kyoto Watanabe was one tough cookie who was doing very well. The chance of post-traumatic stress syndrome, PTSD, taking hold of her was slim, in her professional opinion.

The FBI had deemed both individuals should be regarded as targets, based on the events in Park City and Singapore. The agency was confident that Brownell had been the person who grabbed Kyoto's brother, either in retaliation, as a bargaining chip or insurance—or all three. State, CIA, and the FBI agreed the entire matter needed to be treated as confidential. Word from the White House was that the president had been briefed and his response would be forthcoming. For now, the FBI had two directives – find Brownell, Jon Watanabe, and keep Bryce Winters and Kyoto safe.

"We think it best that you do not compete in Russia," an agent suggested to Bryce who laughed at the idea. Then he saw Kyoto's expression, her shock that he'd even consider leaving her there in the state she was in to go racing"

"If Brownell's the guy you're after he won't be in Sochi unless he left the country already, which you say he hasn't, since *none* of his passports have been used."

The agent nodded.

"Unless he flew out private or some of his rogue CIA buddies helped him get out of the country some other way, he should still be in the U.S. Yes?"

The agent nodded again.

"I'll have my security on me the entire time and be back here in no time," Bryce reasoned.

The expression on Kyoto's face turned from surprise to disappointment to anger in the time it took to speak his peace. Kyoto told the agent how much she appreciated all that the FBI was doing. Then she asked if they could wait outside so she could speak with Bryce privately.

"How can you leave?" she cried as soon as the door closed behind the agents. "How can you even think about racing, with me lying here beat to crap and my brother still missing, possibly in worse shape?"

Bryce considered her words and then walked to the window overlooking the Potomac. "Kyoto, this is what I do. This is what racers do. I can't be of any help right now trying to find Jon. The professionals are on it and you're safe." He turned to look at her. The anger he had seen in her face had softened again to disappointment. She didn't get it.

"Listen, we have a lot to talk about and we'll have time to do that once Jon is back home and safe. You and I can process everything that's happened. Since the moment he told you I was a hit man for the CIA, and you broke off all contact without giving me the chance to explain, I put my walls back up. The day you were supposed to be in Montreal I stood over a grave and said a final goodbye so I could fully open my heart to you. But then Jon broke the law, you shut me out, and I threw my walls back up with the intention of never letting them down again."

"If you were *so* into me why didn't you fly down on one of your private jets and knock at my door?"

Bryce tensed, anger creeping back. "Because I wasn't in a good place, emotionally. You had shut me out, told me you never wanted to see me again. I figured the last thing I needed to do was risking you outing me if I came here to explain and asked you to let me in. You might have been scared of me, for Christ's sake. How was I to know how you'd react?" He sighed and shook his head in frustration. "I had decided to finish the season and then, after you had some time to calm down a bit, I would reach out to you. But after you read Pete's journal, and I have no idea why you brought it here from the cabin, you let me know you wanted nothing to do with me."

She opened her mouth to speak but he held up a hand to signal he wasn't yet done. "Let's get one thing straight here, Kyoto. None of us would be where we are today if Jon hadn't opened his mouth. You already know that I was forced into this life. Plenty of people kill for their country

– only most of them wear uniforms when engaging our enemies. What was going on at CIA was way over Jon's pay grade, but you didn't consider that either. There is more to this than the shit he told you about me."

Neither of them said another word for a time. Bryce went back to the window while Kyoto just stared into space.

"The reality is, we had a really good thing going. I think we still could – now that you know the most important stuff. But only if you can live with the fact that I do what I do for the United States—whether it's race or playing the grim reaper when I'm called to do my duty. You mentioned back in June that the cover on that book scared you. That it reminded you of how dangerous my world is. Well, your brother works for the CIA, and he's been kidnapped. You could have been killed in Singapore. *None of this is my fault!"*

Bryce's emotions were getting the better of him and he didn't like the way it felt. He walked over to her and took a knee in front of her.

"Racing is the life I've chosen. Yes, it can be a lonely and dangerous one. If you want to talk about this after Jon's found and I'm done for the season, let me know." He stood up, leaned over and kissed her cheek, just missing the tears running down her face, and then left without looking back.

CHAPTER FORTY-SIX

SOCHI, RUSSIA LOOKED and felt the same to Bryce as it had twelve months before. Some racing series are referred to as traveling circuses, and F1 was that indeed. But it was an upscale version with the most expensive budgets, latest technology, and extraordinary venues. Bryce flew directly from Washington to Moscow and then down to Sochi on the Black Sea, where he reconnected with Jack Madigan. Jack had traveled with the team from a very humid Singapore to the north and west of it to the cooler breezes of early fall in Russia.

After everything that had happened in the last few weeks, Bryce declined an invitation to the VIP event he and Madigan had attended the year before. He blamed the lingering cold that had been with him for a week now. But, in reality, he just wanted to get into the race car and never get out. There, on the track, he was in his element, doing what he did best, without distractions. He was fully engrossed while in the cockpit just like a booklover locked into a novel or a movie buff captivated by the tale playing out on the big screen. Before qualifying on Saturday, as he rested in his little hideaway above the team's hospitality area, his aide Lynn Whitehouse interrupted with a soft knock.

"Hate to bother, but there's a representative from the U.S. Embassy here. A Jason Ryan, asking to see you."

Bryce remembered him. They had first met during the pre-season testing in Barcelona and then again with Sandra Jennings at the driving school where he got to play with armored SUVs. This was the first contact from anyone at CIA since Jennings texted that she was en route to Singapore – the last he'd heard from her.

"Sure, I remember him. Send him in." Bryce sat up and reached for the bottle of water he'd been nursing. "Would you bring up some coffees and something sweet like chocolate and caramel, please. Need to get the juices flowing for qualifying!"

Whitehouse held the door open for Ryan to enter and closed it behind him. The two shook hands, Ryan took a seat, and then began to speak. Bryce quickly placed his right index finger to his lips for silence, but Ryan shook his head.

"No need for the little black box, Bryce, not this time," he told him. Then, over the next five minutes he brought Bryce up to speed on what had happened to Jennings and what was going on back at the agency.

Jennings' body had been found two days after the race, floating under a dock where fishing boats tied up at night. She'd been shot in the back of the head. Dental records were necessary to identify her as creatures of the sea had nibbled away at anything edible, including her fingerprints.

Her body was flown back to DC where she was later interred in a private ceremony at Arlington. She was entitled, Ryan said, because of her years of service in the U.S. Air Force before continuing to serve her country at CIA.

Bryce hadn't known much about the woman but had liked her and felt sorry that she'd been killed. After Whitehouse delivered a tray of drinks and sweets, she left the men to it. She'd learned his signals well, Bryce thought. She gave him the look he required, and because he didn't wink in return she didn't suggest he had to get ready to race. Not this time.

"So, what happens next – to Madigan and me, that is," he asked.

"Right now, absolutely nothing. Things are up in the air back in Washington. Your girl and our guy got things really stirred up. Even POTUS is involved now. Nobody is sure how many heads, if any, are going to roll over this mess."

Both men prepared their coffees and said little, other than to comment on the weather. A moment later, Bryce noticed Ryan's expression had changed to a very grave one.

"I do have to tell you this though," he began but waited until he'd set up the little black box to jam bugs or communications. "After Max Werner died, we picked up a lot of communication from the bad actors he'd been working with. Everyone seems sure it was a hit."

"Everyone?" Bryce asked for an explanation.

"Werner had accounts and formal and informal ties here in Russia, the Ukraine, Iran, Saudi Arabia, and China. His death threw his business into a state of chaos. Some board members were already in on his activities but others seemed honestly shocked to hear of them. Several resigned and tried to make deals to avoid any chance of prosecution. I expect at least a few fear for their lives. It's good to be in the bodyguard business in Munich these days – there's plenty of work, from what I am told."

"And who owns the business now – shareholders?" Bryce asked.

"Werner left his shares, 51% of the company, to his daughter Mila. The girl's mother will be in charge until Mila reaches the age of twenty-one."

"Let me guess. That puts her in a sticky spot. The people her husband had dealt with, illegally, will want to continue profiting from the business relationship with his company. And that puts her – and Mila – at risk in a variety of ways."

"Yep."

"Shit."

A knock at the door from Whitehouse let Bryce know it was indeed time to suit up and head over to the pits for qualifying. He gave her the thumbs up and then finished his conversation with Ryan.

"She has ample security on them both?"

"As far as we can tell. But where this all goes from here, who knows."

Bryce shook his head, thanked Ryan for the update, and then sent him on his way.

Soon after, Bryce set a track record in winning the pole for the race. A day later, he battled with his adversaries for 53 laps until he captured the win and took back the points lead for the championship. With just five races to go, he was back in front. And with ten days off before the next race in Japan he found himself back in front again, in first class, high over the Atlantic headed home to Park City instead of Monte Carlo.

His life was still in a state of flux. Kyoto and he hadn't spoken since he left her. Neither Jon nor Brownell had been found. Most of all, he was exhausted. He needed the healing warmth of his mountain home and its surroundings far more than the cool Santorini décor of his condo on the hillside. Time spent hiking the hills, capturing moose with his camera, drinking real beer, not the zero alcohol kind, and laying low was what he most longed for.

By the time he drove through the gate and pulled up to the front door, saying hello to the grizzly bear staring back at him on the door, he was spent. The cold mountain air that greeted him when he climbed out of the car was just what he'd been missing. He turned on lights, turned up the heat, and drank down a glass of water as if he was being timed on a pit stop. His paid caretakers, a retired couple that lived down in the village, had kept things clean and in order. They had done a great job as always, but when he looked across the room at the wall of trophies on the far wall something looked out of place.

Too tired to worry about that now, he thought. He lit the fireplace and turned on the flat screen in the living room, then headed back to the master bedroom. He smiled at the familiar comfort of his own bed and turned on the electric blanket, just high enough to take the chill off. Following his routine, he then headed to the safe behind a fake wall in his walk-in closet. As he entered the combination, pulled the lever down, and opened the door he heard something behind him.

"Looking for this?"

CHAPTER FORTY-SEVEN

Brownell, he thought. *It's must be.* The man had nothing to lose. And for the first time in a very long time, Bryce thought he might die.

"You know the drill, Winters. Lift up those hands so I can see them and turn slowly – very slowly – toward me."

As Bryce did, he saw Brownell was holding one of the many Sig Sauer weapons Bryce kept in the safe when he was on the road.

"I see you took the guns as well as my money," Bryce said in a calm voice. In addition to the weaponry, he'd always kept $250,000 in U.S. dollars locked away for emergencies.

"A pittance compared to what I'm going to take." Brownell ordered Bryce to slowly walk toward him and out into the master bedroom. He gestured for Bryce to stop and then removed another gun from inside the black North Face jacket he was wearing. This one had a silencer.

"No need for a muzzle flash to light up the place and attract attention," he said as he threw Bryce's Sig on the bed, well out of reach.

Brownell motioned for Bryce to head into the great

room and he did, his mind racing, imagining a half dozen maneuvers he might try. He could wait for the opportune moment to make a grab at the gun. Or attempt to bribe his way out of this. Appealing to the man on a variety of emotional levels – seemed pretty useless. Brownell clearly had no conscience.

Bryce's plotting came to an abrupt end when the man pushed him down onto the massive sofa and then leaned against the wall facing him. Bryce could see his precious trophies and awards in the room behind the intruder, the moon lighting them and the room through the slivers of skylights that stretched between the wooden beams in the cathedral ceiling.

"And all I ever wanted to do was race," he muttered.

Brownell laughed. "Those days are done."

"So, how'd you get in?" Bryce asked. "Past the security and alarms."

This seemed to feed Brownell's ego. He proudly explained, in detail.

Once he'd learned of the secondary alarm system that Russo had been unaware of, Brownell applied good old American computer technology to override the exterior motion detector and silent alarm. Discovering the key code was simple, he said, then all he had to do was figure out the routine of the couple that looked after the place. He found out where they lived, took their keys and made sure they wouldn't show up at an inopportune time and ruin his surprise.

"Made sure, how?" Bryce asked, fearing the worst. "You're comfortable with killing so should I assume the Colemans are dead?"

Brownell nodded.

Bryce worked hard to maintain the appearance of calm—while, inside, he was on fire. He ached to lunge across the room and beat the bastard to death. For now, the gun pointed at him kept him in check.

"But how did you know I was coming here? Or when? That kind of information isn't something I broadcast."

Brownell smiled again. "Simple. We stayed at a hotel near here. When we intercepted your call to the old folks, telling them you were arriving late tonight and not to show up in the morning because you intended to sleep in, we were set. Spent the night waiting in the dark downstairs. You didn't notice the motion was off when you hit the keypad – you wouldn't have – I only reset the door and window alert once we were in."

"We?" Bryce asked, and turned quickly to his right when he heard something crash onto the floor. It was Jon Watanabe, dazed, bound, gagged, and now lying on the hardwood floor bleeding from a cut on his forehead. Bryce's eyes moved quickly to another figure that now stepped into the room. The man was carrying a silenced handgun just like Brownell's and it was pointed straight at Bryce.

"Billy Myers – you're caught up in this shit?" Bryce asked in amazement.

"Why isn't he tied up?" Myers shouted nervously.

Apparently, this was not the sort of scene Myers was comfortable with. The heartbroken, jilted widower had lashed out before, but was now in the middle of a violent crime scene.

"Because I can put lead in his head in the blink of an eye. He tries anything and he's dead, that's why." Myers looked down at Jon on the floor. The blow he'd taken to the head from the butt of Myers' gun was wearing off and the look Bryce saw in the young man's eyes was pure fear.

Bryce refocused on the man in charge. "What's your grand plan? Let's get to it."

Brownell grinned. "This is going to be easy. I don't even have to kill you, although that might be the end-result anyway." He seemed immensely pleased with himself. "Tonight, you're going to fire up your laptop and transfer twenty-million dollars to an account number I give you. Then we'll tie you up and leave you and Johnny boy here to sit until someone comes to find you or you set yourself loose…or no one frees you and your bodies shut down eventually and you die."

"You're bluffing. There's no way you're leaving witnesses. We're both dead the minute you no longer need us. Plus, if you're so damn smart you know I don't have that sort of money sitting in a bank. It's all invested."

Brownell shrugged. "Okay, I at least tried. Give me credit for that." Brownell walked to the laptop bag Bryce had put down when he entered the residence. He unzipped it and removed what he needed. With one hand holding the gun and the other the computer, he kicked a stool out of the way and placed the computer on the kitchen island.

"Hey!" Myers called out and Bryce realized why. That was the stool Joan Myers had sat on the last time she was there, the one Bryce had pointed out to her husband months earlier when he'd shown up broken and alone.

Hmmm, Bryce thought.

"Billy, this isn't the way you should go out. I can tell you right now this prick has partnered with you for one reason alone. He doesn't care about Joan. He needed help to pull this off. Once any money is wired to his account he's going to kill you just like he did that poor couple. He's just using you the way the CIA used me. You're a dead man walking. He knows it. I know it. So should you."

"Don't listen to him, Billy," Brownell growled. "He had your Joanie killed, and you deserve to get compensated for your loss. You may never forget or forgive her for cheating on you, but the money will put you on a beach in Tahiti where some beauties in bikinis will help you cope with the pain."

Hmmm, Bryce thought again.

"Billy," Bryce said and then looked directly at Myers, "did he tell you he was fucking your wife, too?" It was a lie, but he had nothing better to work with.

Bryce watched as Myers' eyes widened with rage. Now the anger he'd held inside for his wife and Jack Madigan had a closer target. Without blinking, Myers raised his gun and fired at Brownell. A second muffled shot was heard, and Myers fell to the ground, blood pouring from the bullet wound in his forehead.

"Told ya," Bryce said softly and then turned his attention back to the CIA-trained killer.

"You're smart, I'll give you that," Brownell said. "You knew his days were numbered. Now get up and log into that laptop!"

Bryce didn't move. Brownell fired a round into the sofa, punching a hole in the cushion six inches to the left of Bryce's elbow. Bryce waited another moment until he saw Brownell's expression intensify and the suppressed gun barrel move slightly, now aimed at his chest.

"You can't knock a guy for trying," Bryce joked, maintaining his calm as he got up from the sofa and walked to the island.

Brownell followed him there. As Bryce logged in he felt the barrel press against the back of his head. It took some time for the entire process. The sign-in required retina verification, fingerprint verification, and then an access code texted to Bryce's phone. When he was finally logged into his RBC bank account Brownell peered over his shoulder and laughed.

"Only three million – that's all you have access to?"

Bryce turned his head slowly to face him. "Told ya."

Brownell stared into Bryce's eyes, looking for the lie. But all Bryce was gave in return was a look of contempt and fury. "So, what's your exit strategy, big guy? I'll be dead before you leave, I'm sure of that. Might as well tell me the plan."

Brownell gave him a smug look and stepped a few feet back. "Okay. Why not? First, I'll use some of the cash from your safe to have a third party bail Russo out of jail. They never tied him to the CIA, thanks to friends I still have back at Langley. Then he and I will drive north to Canada. Most people will assume we're headed to an island somewhere, but we can disappear into western Canada pretty easy. Passports we used in the CIA, with our aliases, will do just fine. Eventually I'll access the cash you're going to transfer and then lay low. If the money ever runs out, we can do some contract-work overseas."

"You've got it all figured out but—" Bryce began. But a sudden movement on the floor startled both men.

Bullets began to fly toward Brownell. Bryce jumped

away as Jon continued to fire from his spot on the floor. He'd managed to grasp the gun Myers had dropped and was unloading the fifteen-shot clip. Brownell took a bullet to the shoulder and flung himself behind the island. Jon's shots flew wild, tearing up pots and pans that were hanging from the wall over the kitchen stove. When Bryce saw Brownell extend his arm around the corner of the island, gun aimed toward Jon, Bryce went for the gun. In the ensuing struggle, the weapon went off and a bullet tore through Bryce's right hand before striking something in the next room. He fought against the pain, maintaining his grip on the gun with his left hand. Brownell shoved him away as Jon resumed his fire. The man dropped to his knees and then sat back on his ankles but remained upright. A bullet to his neck and two in his chest left him stunned and gasping for air. He dropped the gun. Bryce kicked it away and called out to Jon to stop firing.

"You okay?" Bryce called out as he grabbed for a kitchen towel to wrap around his injured hand. Jon appeared to be in shock. "Jon, are you hit?" he called out but didn't get a response. The man who had just saved his life was spent. He lay the gun and then his head down on the floor. "Jon, can you hear me?"

Bryce walked the few feet to him and removed the gag from the hero who was still lying on his side on the floor.

"Don't think so," Jon finally replied. Bryce drew a breath of relief then turned his attention back to the intruder. From the look in his eyes, the man was aware of his circumstance. He was dying.

In the excitement and with all the adrenaline flowing, Bryce hadn't felt much pain in his right hand, just the loss of control in it. But now, the pain was coming, his hand felt like it was on fire, and he focused on the three things he had to do, *now*.

He picked up his phone with his left hand and dialed 911 – that would get the police and an EMT on the way quickly. Then he grabbed a knife from a kitchen drawer and cut the plastic zip ties that had held Jon's hands together. Bryce peered into his trophy room and saw where the noise had come from. If Bryce hadn't been pissed off before he most certainly was now. He turned and went down on one knee, picked up the gun Jon had dropped, and aimed it.

"Hey, shit head," he called out to Brownell, "you shot my favorite trophy!"

He watched the confusion in the man's eye as he raised the gun and shot him in the head, a red mess blasting the wall behind him like spaghetti. The body fell over. Bryce turned to look at Jon whose expression reflected the lingering terror of a young analyst who had been kidnapped, beaten, threatened, nearly killed, and had just watched a second execution carried out just a few feet from him.

"It's okay, Jon, " Bryce said. "That needed to happen. The world will be a better place without a piece of shit like that walking the planet." He looked down at Jon as the room began to flash from red and blue light bars on the vehicles bringing help.

"Hey, Jon," he said softly, helping the young man sit up, "what do you say we call your sister and tell her you're okay."

CHAPTER FORTY-EIGHT

The last event of the Formula One season was nearing completion during the night race at the Abu Dhabi circuit. The championship had long been decided and, with one lap to go, Bryce could be heard over the radio congratulating the team on having done such a phenomenal job preparing a car that had started from the pole and would, in a matter of moments, take the checkered flag for yet another win.

"Well done, ladies and gentlemen," he said. As the young Russian, Nikita Pushkin climbed out of the car to begin celebrating the victory, Bryce was the first man he ran to and embraced. Minutes later, his right hand still protected by an array of black Velcro and material his physical therapist insisted he wear, Bryce listened as Pushkin shared the love from atop the winner's podium.

"Bryce Winters is someone I have looked up to in racing from the very beginning of my career. I can't thank him enough for picking me to drive his car and for the coaching and encouragement he's given me since his accident."

While the winning team watched the podium festivities and shared in the champagne celebration, others began the task of tearing down the garage setups and taking care of the cars and their equipment, preparing to head home after the grueling season they'd all endured. The holidays were coming. But before long they'd all assemble in Spain to start racing around the world again. As Bryce sat down to take questions during the post-race press conference, he smiled as everyone kept asking if his driving career was over.

"I think he's done," one reporter whispered to another, "nobody recovers from a hand injury like his – nobody."

"Then you don't know Bryce Winters," Jack Madigan offered through a smile from his spot standing between them.

"So, what is it, Bryce? Is this your curtain call?" another called out.

Millions around the world had been shocked and disappointed when the news of the home invasion broke a few months earlier and they'd learned he'd been shot in the robbery attempt. Now everyone wanted to know – had his dream of winning a second F1 championship been destroyed by that nightmare?

Bryce scanned the audience and smiled when his eyes met Kyoto's.

"This has been a very exciting and rewarding career," he began but as he formed his words he scanned back to where he'd spotted Kyoto. There had been a familiar face standing behind her and to the right. Then he realized who it was – it was Ryan from the CIA and he wasn't smiling. Distracted, he continued, "and I can tell you that my rehabilitation is going well and is way ahead of schedule. I *will* be back in the car next season in pursuit of another championship." He smiled.

"See you all down under!"

THE END

Printed in Great Britain
by Amazon

78427692R00190